C000272041

Praise for the
DETECTIVE INSPECTOR MAHONEY SERIES

HIGH BEAM is 'a seriously welcome addition to the Australian thriller genre. It's tight and gripping from the start.'
— Quintin Jardine

'I love reading novels set in Tasmania; *HIGH BEAM* didn't disappoint. Can't wait to get my hands on the sequel.'
— *Examiner*, Launceston

'*HIGH BEAM* is clever, relevant, well-written and has momentum. Brown has developed a tough, uncompromising central character.'
— *Mercury*, Hobart

DEAD WOOD's 'combination of racy thriller, local context and relentless crime fighter prove a winner with its sophisticated context of power politics, big business and issues that influence the future development of the state.'
— *Mercury*, Hobart

THE DETECTIVE INSPECTOR MAHONEY SERIES

High Beam
Dead Wood
Big Stake
The Square Up

ABOUT THE AUTHOR

Stephen Brown resides in Hobart where the DI Mahoney series is set. When not writing he walks his Border collie, makes plans to play more golf, and endeavours to contribute to family life.

The intention of his fiction is to enable readers to explore Tasmania in its various guises and to investigate the harsher realities of modern life.

Readers of his work are invited to contact him at:
sjbrownauthor@gmail.com

A **DI Mahoney** mystery

THE SQUARE UP

sj brown

Cover design Kent Whitmore
Cover image Alamy Stock Photo

Published by
Forty South Publishing Pty Ltd
Hobart, Tasmania
fortysouth.com.au

Printed by IngramSpark

Now I have his full attention. No choice but to focus on me. Can't glance away and pretend I'm not there. Nor can he feign indifference. He has to mark my words.

So far he's done better than I thought he would. Hasn't fainted or soiled himself. Not bad ... under the circumstances. When he came round there was confusion in his eyes. At some time over the weekend he'd expected to be trussed up, but not like this, I bet. The Rohypnol worked a treat. He'd been out cold for three hours: longer than I needed, but to have him coming out of it early would have thrown my plan.

It was all pretty easy, really. Element of surprise helped. I knocked on the door of his holiday home early evening. When he answered there was no recognition. Why would there be? I'm just an ordinary guy. Run of the mill. Not an achiever like him. Spun him a line about having just bought a block of land along the road. Said I'd seen his great place and did he have any design tips? He reckoned he could spare a few minutes. Only too happy to show off his schmick layout. I'd brought a couple of stubbies of his favourite beer. Whipped the top from one I'd 'prepared earlier', as the TV chefs say. He wasn't going to refuse. As was his habit, the first swig drained half the contents. After that it was just a bit more chat before he got the wobbles and collapsed on the couch.

I waited a little while to be sure he was knocked out. Then took his mobile phone off the kitchen bench and sent a text to his bit on the side. Made up a credible excuse to make sure she didn't turn up for their planned rendezvous. No fun and games for her. But there would be for him—Scott 'Hotshot' Hellyer. Just not quite the way he expected.

Then it was a quick duck out to the car to grab the gear I needed. He was a solid lump to manoeuvre, but I'd been training and I managed to truss him up just right.

And then he was coming round, struggling to comprehend what was happening. He shook his head to clear the fogginess. Lifted his gaze and saw me standing a couple of metres away.

There's a sex toy gag strapped in his mouth. He snorts. Twists his neck to see why his arms aren't moving. They're both extended out from his side in a crucifix pose. Tethered with climbing rope to the oak beams on the ceiling. Gives a tug as best he can but they're not moving. His spread-eagled feet are tied to the bases of the posts. No give there either.

He's naked: his manhood and sculpted frame on full display. He scans the room. Curtains are drawn; nobody can see in. Tacked up behind him is a heavy grey blanket. As he leans his head back, his hair brushes it. There's a faint rustle. Then another struggle with the ropes. All he does is tighten the knots.

I lean down and press play on the iPod I've brought. The sublime notes of Liszt fill the room. I'm a practical person but this touch of theatre pleases me. It's the music that plays in 'Schindler's List' as the German troops enact their violent rampage through the ghetto. Its significance is lost on a philistine like Hellyer, but I like it.

Stepping forward, I brandish the tennis racquet in my right hand and hold up the basket of balls in my left. His eyes are angry now.

There's another snort. I bet he's dying to let rip with a volley of abuse. But the gag has to stay in place. Hotshot must suffer in silence.

The one thing I was good at in my teenage sporting days was serving a tennis ball. Hard. Along with the weight training, I've been on the court brushing up on my serve. I step back a few feet. The gallery design is perfect for my game. I can wind up and smash the tennis balls into him. Any that miss him will be cushioned by the hanging blanket. Minimal noise. The first few hit the target at three-quarter pace. I'm warming up. Number five hits him square in the package. The jolt of pain races up his nerves and shows in his face. Panic replaces the anger. He's beginning to register that he's not in a good place.

The first dozen or so serves are aimed at his midriff. He's really beginning to hurt now. For the next one I angle the racquet slightly and the ball lands flush on his eye socket. Now that must really hurt—that is the intention after all. I pummel him for a while. After fifteen minutes I'm perspiring and he's beaten. A couple of the red marks are starting to bruise. I'm serving at about sixty per cent. Good strike rate. I try to get one in the other eye socket but it's a tough ask. Still, the original one did some nice damage. He's too arrogant to cry but his nose is running. He senses he can't sniffle or he won't be able to breathe. Him choking on his own snot is not in my plan.

I've had enough of the pummelling. So, stage two. I take a knife out of my satchel. Wiltshire stainless steel. Razor sharp. He's still conscious. I hold the knife up to his good eye. The alarm bells must be a cacophony now. I wink at him. It's almost as good as I imagined it would be. I nick his scrotum with the tip of the knife. His good eye nearly pops out.

Enough fun for now. Time is of the essence. Time for the coup de grâce. I move the tip to his groin. His torso trembles and the bastard finally pisses. For a moment his body is still. I drive the shaft into the flesh. The artery ruptures and I jerk the blade out. Red liquid gushes forth in a series of strong spurts. If he lives, he'll need to get some cleaners in. But he won't. Nobody can survive the loss of this much blood.

I walk into the kitchen and rinse the knife under the tap. Then back into the living area where I jam the blade into one of the tennis balls. He's already expired. No more Hotshot. I leave the punctured ball and blade resting in the pool of blood. You've got to love it when everything goes to plan.

CHAPTER ONE

'Holy smoke.' Detective Inspector John Mahoney was trying to take in the tableau before him, and it was a struggle. Twenty-five or so years as a police investigator meant he'd seen his fair share of corpses. Even here in southern Tasmania—a placid tourist destination—there was violence and grisly death. But rarely like this.

Newly-promoted Detective Sergeant Kate Kendall stood a few feet to his side. She couldn't verbalise anything. It wasn't so much shock as dismay that such a gruesome act could occur. In the face of this macabre scene she breathed slowly and waited for her superior to make a move. In her peripheral vision she noted his head adjusting slightly; he was taking in the dimensions of the large room and the activity of the forensic officers.

Waiting for Mahoney to initiate something, she focused her gaze on the male hoisted between the upright posts in front of a suspended blanket. His head was bowed on his chest, face obscured. Thick dark hair covered the scalp, but the torso was smooth. Reasonably hairy legs and arms suggested the victim must have waxed his chest. She noticed the pubic hair looked trimmed.

All four limbs were tethered to the oak beams spread-eagling the body. An ugly gash at the groin appeared to be the decisive incision that accounted for the volume of blood on the floor. Aside from that, the striking impression was the number of welts splattered across much of the skin. Collected around the man's feet was a host of yellowy-green tennis balls.

A foot or two to the side of the body was a middle-aged balding man wearing silver spectacles. He reached in to touch the groin wound, looked down at the pool of congealed blood, then up at the Inspector. Doctor Sam Johnson stood and took a few steps toward the police officers.

'That's the cause, right there. Ruptured the artery leading to sustained haemorrhaging of blood and heart failure. Quick and decisive. It's not a clinical incision. It was a forceful thrust and tear.'

'And the other marks?' asked Mahoney.

The police pathologist pointed to the tennis balls in reply.

'Caused by those. I'm no expert on velocity but I'd guess a succession of those were belted at him. In some cases bruises were formed but the quick onset of death meant the majority remain as red welts. One actually hit the eye. If he'd lived, the eyeball would probably have been lost … but of course he didn't.'

'No hope.' Mahoney rubbed his brow and exhaled. 'Time of death? Approximately.'

'Very hard to say.' The doctor held up a palm as if to deflect criticism. 'In situ is never easy and this one has some particular difficulties.'

'Such as the lividity,' Kendall said as she pointed to the small lake of blood.

'Absolutely, Kate. Good point.'

Johnson took a laser pointer from his pocket. A green dot waggled across the legs of the victim.

'Hypostasis has occurred in the lower limbs, but it is limited owing to the massive blood loss. That variable and the low body fat means lividity is not a lot of help.' The speck of light now played across the victim's chest and shoulders. 'The musculature is almost fully relaxed indicating rigor mortis has passed.'

'So more than twenty-fours?'

'Yes, John. I could safely say that. Supporting that is the body temperature. It's cooled to room temperature. Assuming a relatively constant temperature in here, that indicates a significant lapse of time.' The dot now speared at the midriff. 'Stomach contents will help, but you'll have to wait for the post-mortem for that.'

Mahoney nodded. 'Of course. This looks bad enough as it is. Does the blood on the floor help?'

'Yes, but Kitchener's forensic experts will be the ones to assist you there.' Johnson turned to the open-plan kitchen where a tall rangy figure stood with a digital camera in his hand. 'Looks like Jim McLeod is ready. Are you?'

Mahoney waved the scene-of-crime photographer in.

'Jim, Doc Johnson will guide you to start with. I'm very interested in full scene shots for this one, okay?'

McLeod nodded. 'Sure, no problem. Nasty business.'

'That it is. Kate and I will be over there by the balcony door for a bit.'

McLeod and Johnson advanced towards the dead man as the detectives retreated.

'You all right?' Mahoney asked.

'Fair to middling. Don't think I've witnessed worse.'

'It is bad. Very bad if you consider the totality of it.'

'As in the mindset of whoever did it?'

'Exactly. Your thoughts?'

Kendall looked again at the scene. 'Very methodical. The blanket, the ropes, the weapon, the method. It had to be *this* victim in *this* way. Revenge, maybe.' She let out a slow breath. 'Punishment of some particular sort must come before death. Who knows, but there's a dark symbolism playing right through it all. And a shrewd practicality. I think the identity of the victim will help explain the why and lead to the who.'

'Agreed. That man's identity is vital: what he did in life and how he did it. Either the perpetrator is a total nutjob or someone who hated the victim to a compelling degree.'

'Or hated what the victim represented.'

Mahoney looked around the interior: clean lines, a simple design masterfully crafted. 'Quite feasibly.'

A flash of ginger hair to his right caught Mahoney's attention.

'David, anything?'

DC Gibson stepped tentatively to the edge of the main living area. 'Yep, I've run it down. This house has a registered owner in the company name of Newcrest Nominees Pty Ltd. Car outside is a fleet vehicle for the same business. The principal of that company is Mr Scott Hellyer.' He looked up from his notebook. 'Is that him?'

'I honestly don't know, David. As you can see, we've got bodies scouring the house looking for material, but zero personal effects found thus far.'

Gibson was still relatively new to the Serious Crimes Squad. His question was hesitant. 'How do we find out?'

Mahoney led Kendall through to where the constable stood. 'As tactfully as possible. God forbid we alarm a Mrs Hellyer and later find out we've made a colossal cock-up. Your data suggests it's likely to be that guy, but we can't be blundering in with bad news.' He looked at the kitchen bench. 'It would be a bonus if a wallet or something was handy nearby.'

The trio moved outside. Mahoney and Kendall had seen enough to form an initial assessment, and there were plenty of forensic personnel in the dwelling. Mike Kitchener's team could be trusted to comb the interior for any evidence that might help solve the crime.

They stood near the centre of a gravel turning circle. A metallic red BMW sat with its nose to the boundary fence. Aside from a patina of dust on the underside, it gleamed in the late morning sun. The storm clouds gathering over the ridge of the Wellington Range could soon put paid to that.

Members of the FSST—Forensic Science Service Tasmania—were combing the ground around the house. To the rear of the block were several uniformed officers searching for relevant material. Mahoney's hunch was that they wouldn't find a whole lot.

Kendall ran her foot over the crushed gravel. 'Not so good for tyre impressions, is it?'

'Bugger all use,' answered Mahoney. 'Although if we do get a suspect, there's bound to be pebbles in the tread.'

'If.'

'Yeah, I know. Bog standard gravel by the looks of it.'

Mahoney looked across at Gibson. 'David, I hope you're not texting your mates. We are kind of busy.'

The constable turned abruptly and strode towards them. 'So am I, Sir.'

He held up his phone horizontally and placed it in the DI's hand.

'This may help.'

On the screen was a photo of a tall dark-haired male. Tanned, chiselled face. Had what advertising people call a *winning smile*. When the photo was taken, the subject had been standing almost exactly where Mahoney was now. The detective tapped the screen and the image disappeared.

'What have I done? Sorry, David.'

'No worries, Sir.' He took the phone, swished across the screen and held the picture at eye level for his boss. With his index finger and thumb he zoomed into a headshot of the male, then adjusted the image back to the original showing the male standing nonchalantly by the red Beemer.

Kendall was peering in from the side.

'Where's this from?'

'It's the Facebook profile pic of a man called Scott Hellyer. He looks like our guy, doesn't he?'

Mahoney and Kendall nodded in unison.

'He looks like that really handsome guy who doles out investment advice in the media. You know the one? Used to have his own mortgage company,' Kendall said.

Mahoney did know but couldn't find a name.

'Mark Vasouris,' said Gibson.

Twice, in quick succession, the blood nut had surprised his boss, although Mahoney tried not to let it show.

'Right, David, that's good. Yeah, you'd think that he was our victim. Anyway, anything else about this Scott Hellyer?'

Gibson scrolled down the page. 'Director of Marketing for the Tiger Brewing Group. Lists golf, quality beer and people as his interests. Lives at Kingston Beach. Married to Sophie and has two children at high school. Looks like the kids enjoy a private education, judging by the uniforms. And the whole family knows how to smile.' He held the phone up for his colleagues to see.

'Kate, I think that gives us enough to justify visiting his wife. Be sympathetic but clinical. I think what happened in there is way beyond a marital rift. It indicates there was something badly wrong in the guy's life, and the wife is our first lens into the kaleidoscope. Bring David up to speed on the manner of death and take him with you to their house.'

Kendall was all business. 'Yes, Sir. What about the wife identifying the body?'

'I'll check with Doctor J and McLeod. Early this evening I'd say, with an autopsy first thing tomorrow. Ask her to be available later on today. And contact Family Support to have an officer on standby.' He looked from one face to the other. 'Anything else?'

'Initial briefing?' asked Gibson.

'Eight o'clock tomorrow morning. There's still a lot to be extracted here … well, at least I hope there is.'

CHAPTER TWO

Kendall and Gibson walked to her vehicle, a new Ford Focus purchased as a gift to herself to celebrate her promotion. She beeped the doors unlocked and they got in. Gibson ran a hand over the upholstery and breathed deeply.

'Got to love that new car smell. And it's in my colour as well.'

Kate shot him a quick look as she pressed the ignition button. He looked very comfortable sitting there. 'Yeah, it's called techno-orange. Suits you.'

'Thanks, Sarge. Nice little motor …'

She hoped he wouldn't finish the sentence with 'for a female' and, thankfully, he didn't. She loathed those smug assumptions that skirted misogyny. Now her work partner, Tim Munro, had transferred she would have to spend more time with Gibson. The young man was surprisingly sharp. He looked to the world like a jovial lad, but Kate suspected there was more going on upstairs than he let on.

Munro would be missed, no doubt about it. The flagged reorganisation of Tasmania Police had fallen over. A cash-strapped public sector couldn't countenance another shuffling of resources. Her boss's rise to rank of Commander was on indefinite hold. If Munro was to advance, it would have to be in another section of the force. So he'd taken an Acting Inspector role in the Drugs Squad operating out of the Clarence station. The hotshot in the passenger seat was now confirmed in the vacant position of Detective Constable, and he was champing at the bit. Kate was charged with directly supervising his progress. As long as he kept a hold on the jokes, it shouldn't be that onerous.

She eased the car down the hill and turned left onto Spitfarm Road, the only route in and out of Opossum Bay holiday retreat. Gibson pointed across the dashboard to the row of beach houses fronting onto the lower reaches of the River Derwent.

'A few spanking places there.'

No argument there. Only forty minutes by road to Hobart but, thanks to geography, a totally separate space.

'I'd imagine it would be a pocket of hot property these days,' Kate commented.

'Too right. Silly money just for an old fibro shack as long as it's on the beachfront. Even the block where we've just been would have cost a packet. Wonder why he built there.'

'The view, bit more privacy, wanted to have their own place from scratch …'

'I get all that. But his family residence is at Osborne Esplanade. By the looks of it they're in one of those beaut weatherboard bungalows just across the street from the beach. It's a getaway in itself. Why does he need another one?'

'Maybe he's got a jet-ski and commutes on it sometimes.'

It was hardly a feasible suggestion, seeing as the BMW was in the man's drive, and she chided herself momentarily. There was no need to manufacture ideas to impress her new sidekick. He'd come up with plenty of his own and she should be filtering them. It wasn't a competition.

If he thought she was being flippant, he didn't reveal it.

'If I got on one now, I'd be there in ten minutes. Dead quick. As it is we get to do a gigantic loop. Oh well, it is what it is. Got any decent music?'

□

It turned out that the radio was superfluous as Gibson chatted the whole way. He talked about growing up in Launceston ('great time') and his first couple of years in uniform ('fair bit of drudgery, to be honest'). Given Kate didn't like talking that much when driving, it was a reasonable diversion—a welcome distraction from the apprehension she was experiencing. This would be her first time doing 'the knock': part of the job that even the seasoned officers dreaded. Fronting up to a stranger's house to deliver the very worst news.

Kate angled the car into a parking bay opposite number twenty-three. The house was as Gibson had predicted, except grander. On top of the original ground level a second storey had been constructed, with large windows at both ends: a vista south to Storm Bay and north to Mount Wellington. From street level it appeared to be one open-plan space. They could see a woman sitting in a lounge chair through the front glass pane as they approached the picket gate.

'He must trust you, Sarge. Break a leg.'

Whatever Gibson's intentions were, it was not a remark that quelled her nerves.

They headed up a flagstone path bordered by trimmed rose bushes. The woman must have seen them because the front door was answered moments after Gibson pressed the bell. The female who opened the door had subtly tinted blonde hair combed back from a tanned face, deep blue eyes and a clearly distinguishable jaw line. About five and a half foot in the old scale, she was dressed in a summer frock and barefoot on the pine floorboards.

'Mrs Hellyer?'

'Yes, I'm Sophie Hellyer.' Calm and not lacking in confidence.

'I'm DS Kendall and this is DC Gibson.' Both officers flashed their ID cards. 'May we speak to you please?'

Something in the carefully modulated tone alerted the woman.

'You'll need to come in, won't you? Is one of the children in trouble?'

'Not that we know of. It's another matter.' Kendall glanced around. 'Is there somewhere we could sit?'

'Yes, of course. Come in.'

Sophie Hellyer led them down a hallway as Gibson closed the door. He caught up just as they entered the kitchen which overlooked the backyard. It was a stunning space: appliances along the left wall and a polished concrete-topped island facing the dining area. Aside from the sharp grey of the fridge and stove top, the dominant colour was white. It made the space seem that much larger. From the oak dining table the eye was led out to a manicured garden with raised vegetable beds and luxuriant settings of flowers.

'I'm the green thumb. That's my testing space. I've a business designing sustainable gardens and it all starts here.'

Sophie clicked the kettle on as Kate hovered nearby and Gibson sauntered over to the glass sliding door.

'I'm sorry. Automatic reflex to get some coffee going.' She placed her hands flat on the smooth bench. 'It looks like you need to tell me something.'

Kate swallowed. 'Mrs Hellyer, do you have a property at Marsh Lane in Opossum Bay?'

'Yes. It's Scott's project. That's my husband. Has it been burgled?'

'No.' *But you won't be wanting to go there in a hurry.* 'Was your husband intending to be there this weekend?'

'Not that I know of. He told me he was off to Bridport to host a corporate golf weekend.'

Did he? Softly, softly.

'I'm sorry to tell you that was probably not the case. A body we have strong reason to believe is your husband was discovered this morning at your property.' *How to put this?* 'I'm afraid he looks to have been the victim of a violent attack.'

'He's dead?'

'Yes. I'm sorry.'

Kate moved round the end of the kitchen island in case the wife collapsed. Sophie Hellyer remained upright, but her fingers clawed at the sparkling surface.

'I think I'll skip coffee. Can you help me to a seat at the table?' She looked at Gibson. 'There's a decanter of brandy and glasses upstairs. Would you bring them down please?'

He nodded and started off. The two women sat at the head of the dining table.

'I'm sorry. How do you mean violent? What happened?'

'I'll get to that. Perhaps if you have a drink first.'

Gibson returned with the glassware and alcohol. He placed them on the table before retreating to take up the coffee preparation.

'I don't suppose you can join me? On duty and everything.'

Kate smiled as Sophie poured a large measure into a crystal tumbler.

'Best not. But I think you could do with one.'

Sophie took a small sip and then pushed the glass away.

'Actually, I think I would prefer coffee after all. Strong.'

Gibson nodded, holding up a cafetiere and spooning in the ground coffee.

He's not bad, thought Kendall. Instinctively knows his role. Now time to play hers.

'You mentioned the children. Are they away somewhere?'

'Hardly children now. Tilly is twenty and studying in Queensland. Simon's eighteen and on a gap year in Scotland. He's working as a green keeper somewhere near St Andrews. Sounded like he was having a ball last time we chatted.'

'Right. Well, as I said, it's your husband that we need to talk about.'

A bolt of realisation finally hit her.

'He's been murdered, hasn't he? How?'

You don't want to know.

'It was a violent attack. I'm unable to divulge all the details, but we don't think it was a robbery gone wrong. He was stabbed and died from the loss of blood. The manner of it suggests it was premeditated.'

Gibson brought the coffee, sugar, milk and mugs over, and sat down to Kendall's left. Sophie Hellyer turned a mug in her fingers for a while. She looked up at Kendall.

'I don't know what I'm meant to feel. We've separated. After we dropped the children at the airport, January long weekend, he moved out. He went to an apartment in Salamanca Square. It hadn't been very good for some time, but we stayed together until Simon finished school. That done, there was no reason for Scott to stay. We've been living separate lives for about a year.'

'But he still let you know what he was up to? Like his movements at the weekends.'

'Not really. I have no interest in Opossum Bay so I don't visit there. Last week I bumped into him at Barcelona wine bar. He was drinking with Kevin Cheung. I said hello and he mentioned he was away up north this weekend. Strange. I must have got the days wrong.'

Although Sophie Hellyer appeared strangely composed, it probably didn't amount to anything untoward. The death certainly seemed news to her, and the symptoms of shock would come later. For now, the simple processing of facts was keeping her together. The phone calls to her children would be stressful.

'I appreciate this is hard. Did your husband have any enemies? Anyone who might want to harm him?'

'The phone book is in the third drawer down,' she replied. She ran a hand through her hair. 'Sorry. That's not fair. He was well liked in plenty of circles. But the zip on his pants wasn't just for using the toilet. There might be a husband or two who wouldn't be that keen on him.'

So, the way he had lived may indeed account for how he died.

CHAPTER THREE

The start of the working week. Various members of the Serious Crimes Squad were at their desks with takeaway coffees; rare was the person who came in without one. The old tearoom was going the way of the photocopy annexe: obsolete. Technology was transforming police work. Gibson had demonstrated that fact yesterday with a few taps on his mobile phone, but Kendall had also underscored the perennial value of speaking to people face-to-face. Some things change, some stay the same.

Mahoney clicked the electronic smartboard on and checked the cable connection to his laptop. All good to go. As he called the team together, he noticed anew the absence of Tim Munro, and wondered how he would fare without his favourite hard nut. He was going to miss him, but he would never have prevented Munro's transfer to the Clarence Station; it was a good move for the officer and for the force. DS Kendall brought different strengths—more cerebral— and he couldn't overlook Gibson's sheer enthusiasm. He was like a young football recruit who, having marked time in the reserves, immediately shone when promoted. One to watch, in a good way. Change and continuity.

A few officers carried chairs to the front of the room; those with desks near the smartboard stayed in place. All appeared alert and ready for the race, which had to be a sprint—the weekend's discovery of the execution dictated that. That was the catch 22 of detective work, especially a homicide. You had to be methodical or clues could be missed. The chain of evidence had to be secured, all the bases covered. But this had to be done at a blistering pace. During the 'hot phase' chances had to be grasped. The chilling reality in this case was that the perpetrator may have further plans.

Mahoney was familiar with the paradox of calm urgency. It was always asking a lot, but the investigators had to assume the mindset of a Formula One driver: to win a turbo-charged contest going as slowly as possible, to stay grounded amid the mayhem.

Mahoney tapped the arrow key on the smartboard and an image of the Opossum Bay house appeared. He addressed the officers

'I shan't say 'good morning' because it isn't one. It's a hell of a morning because at this location yesterday a foul murder was discovered. We've had some doozies over the past few years but this one is particularly ugly. We must be on our game. If you haven't already, cancel your normal life for the rest of the week.' He cocked a thumb at the screen. 'What happened in that dwelling is horrific, and the onus is on us to sort this out as soon as possible.'

A variety of acknowledgements came from the floor: nods, verbal assents, a 'righto'. They were all here because they wanted a job that was way beyond ordinary. Coppers that ran on adrenalin in order to get a result. It beat pushing a pen.

'Good. Sergeant Geason is taking the notes so, for the moment, you need to sit and listen. Any questions, jump in. I don't want any flashes of insight disappearing.' He tapped the arrow again to show Hellyer's smiling profile picture. 'Our victim. Scott Hellyer, forty-seven years of age. Employed as Director of Marketing at Tiger Brewing. Quite a high level job with a healthy salary package. Bit of a go-getter with his own business on the side: Newcrest Nominees, which is the development company behind the proposed golf links at South Arm. That probably explains why the property on the previous slide was built at Opossum Bay. Ten minutes by car, tops. This is a successful man with a high profile in our local business community. He'll have supporters but also, perhaps, a few enemies. Certainly one.'

Mahoney fixed his gaze on a burly officer by the window.

'DC Dunstan, you do the background checks on the finances of the golf course development. Usual thing: irregularities, who else is in on the deal … right?'

Dunstan nodded.

'OK, good. Mr Hellyer had been separated from his wife for a couple of months. She stayed in the family home at Kingston. The two children are grown up, both out of the state. Hellyer had moved into a rented apartment in Salamanca Square. The property at Opossum Bay is in the company structure. According to his wife, she's never even visited it. DS Kendall's initial impression is that she's probably not a suspect. Is that a fair reading?'

'Yes, I think so. Unless she's a sublime actress. She wasn't distraught by the news initially but, after it sunk in, she had a tough time of it. I spoke to the Family Liason Officer who stayed at her Kingston property last night. After we left her, she had a difficult night and breaking the news to her offspring really shook her up. She's moved on from the marriage but it's still going to be a rough period for the family. I didn't get much sense of hostility towards her ex, and it looks like she had nothing to gain from his death. No life insurance policy and no transfer of assets now he's gone. He ceded the Kingston property, mortgage-free, back in January. Anything else he has is locked into Newcrest Nominees. She wasn't indifferent to his fate. She appears to have nothing to gain from his death. The worst thing for her is that the children have lost their father.'

Mahoney's finger hovered by the board. 'Now, she also told Kendall that her spouse was not one to let the chance of extra-marital activity pass him by. Not to speak ill of the dead but he was, apparently, something of a womaniser. Given what I'm about to show you, I would suggest there's definitely an element of revenge in the manner of his death.'

Mahoney pressed the black arrow and a few eyes went out on stalks as the next shot of Hellyer appeared.

'DS Geason, the forensic findings should come to you this morning. Do your usual stuff.' The DS nodded his understanding. 'A savage thrust with a sharp blade to the left groin severed the artery. From there, death was very quick. The weapon was sitting in the pool of blood by his left leg. No transference, alas. What is obviously catching your attention is what happened prior to that action, and I share your amazement. It is a carefully orchestrated attack. Tennis balls were pelted at Hellyer pre-mortem. Done with such force that his right eyeball was wrecked.'

'Boris Becker is back.'

'Thank you for the black humour, Constable Herrick. Doc Johnson confirmed that to cause tissue damage like that, the balls were propelled at great speed, much faster than a throw. We're looking for someone with a powerful serve. Unfortunately, no racquet or any implement was found at the site.' Mahoney pointed to the space behind the battered torso. 'The killer gave himself time. The blanket suspended from the rafter effectively caught the balls and stopped them ricocheting noisily around the room. All carefully planned and executed.'

Gibson held up his hand and received a nod from his boss.

'That planning must have involved some form of site inspection. Were there sightings of any strangers in the area? Somebody may have noticed something.'

'Yes, good point. There's a keen intelligence revealed by all this. Whoever did this prepared diligently and gave himself sufficient time. Toxicology should confirm what you've already assumed. Hellyer must have been drugged. This is way beyond some adaptation of a bondage ritual. No matter what sort of sex the victim preferred, he'd hardly sign up for this.'

A call from the back. 'Autopsy?'

'Starting right about now. DS Kendall and I are attending once we've wrapped this. She is also task co-ordinator. But remember, I can always call Tim Munro back in if anybody misses a beat.' Smiles all round. 'Until Forensics give us more, we're concentrating on the victim as a way to find the murderer. There has to be a specific reason why this happened.'

CHAPTER FOUR

As Gibson and Herrick travelled across the isthmus separating Ralphs Bay and Storm Bay, their conversation turned to conditions in the force.

'Good on you and all that, getting into the Squad. Suits you,' Herrick affirmed.

'Cheers. Yeah, it does.'

Gibson feathered the brake pedal in response to the speed limit sign marking the approach to South Arm.

'Not for me though, mate. Need to keep on the regular shifts for me footy.'

Gibson hadn't realised the option of leaving uniform secondment to the squad for full-time work as a detective was one available to Herrick. He doubted it.

'That is one downside. But not a dilemma for me as it turns out.'

'Pity. Heard you were pretty handy up north. Underage state rep, wasn't it?'

They passed the small primary school and went back up to normal speed.

'Yep.'

'Didn't kick on?'

He'd missed out on the AFL draft; all those hours of training in vain. He could have kept knocking, but by the end of his teens he'd fallen out of love with Aussie Rules football. He was still active—golf, cycling and cross-training—but now just for health and recreation.

'Nah. Needed a break from it and haven't felt like going back.'

'If you do, give us a shout. You'll still have the goods. Come down the Huon. Great money, plenty of beers and good blokes.'

Wild horses couldn't drag him down there.

'I'll keep it in mind.'

Braking again, they entered Opossum Bay.

'Now, what are we looking for? To make it worth a trip down here.'

'Suspicious behaviour,' Herrick replied.

Gibson glanced sideways; his passenger was deadpan. That was obviously his complete answer.

As Gibson indicated and turned into a parking space outside the village shop, he continued talking. 'Actually, we're looking for indications of normal behaviour. We don't want to scare the horses, and the perpetrator wouldn't have done either. So to start I'll ask a few questions about Scott Hellyer. How often he came down, that sort of thing. Then we'll doorknock the residences along the next stretch of Spitfarm Road. If it's right with you, just be the strong silent type. The uniform helps people focus.'

'No worries. Your call.'

They entered the store, brushing through the rainbow of vertical plastic strips hanging from the door frame. Inside the layout was slightly schizophrenic, reflecting the area's transition from a sleepy beachside collection of shacks to a more upmarket locale. Cheek by jowl with the old staples like Weetbix breakfast cereal, were trendy offerings like organic pasta and dukkha. A plumpish balding man with a flushed complexion stood by the cash register fitting a new till roll.

'Good morning, gents. Won't be a sec.'

With his task completed, he looked up at them with a perceptible double-take.

'Sorry. Good morning, *officers*. I'm Frank Barta. You'll be following up from yesterday then?'

'Yes, that's right. I'm Detective Constable Gibson and this is Constable Herrick. You're aware of an incident in this vicinity, I presume?'

'Awful lot of activity going on yesterday.' He pointed to the radio on the shelf behind him. 'And it was just on the local news bulletin. So, yes, I'm au fait with an *incident* as you put it.'

Gibson gave himself a mental uppercut. *Don't try to be clever. Be yourself.*

'Of course. Missed it. What's been released?'

'You mean you lot don't know?'

Had they got off on the wrong foot, or what?

'Well, yes and no. We know a fair bit already. But we don't control what an ABC radio journalist puts in the bulletin. We were on our way here as the media release was being distributed.'

The man nodded. 'S'pose so. Just said police are investigating the suspicious death of Scott Hellyer sometime over the weekend at his Opossum Bay property. Mentioned the golf course development. That's about it really. Asked for public co-operation, as they do.'

Let's hope we get some from you, Gibson thought. 'You weren't open yesterday?'

'No. Nor last week. First chance for me and my wife to get away in eighteen months. Put a sign up the week before giving notice that we'd be closed for refurbishment purposes.' He gave a knowing smile.

'But you simply wanted some downtime for a change?' Gibson returned the smile. 'Can't blame you. Hours here must be pretty horrendous.'

'Too right. Not complaining, mind you. Don't tell the Tax Office but it's a cash cow. Financed it with my Telstra redundancy. Plenty of money down here these days. We've been here six years. One more and we'll cash in and hop it to Bali. Won't have to lift a finger again … except to raise a beer to my lips.' The smile grew wider.

'Half your luck,' Herrick chipped in.

Gibson took up the running. 'So you returned here yesterday?'

'Am I a suspect?' Barta asked indignantly.

'I hope not. I just wanted to gauge what you'd heard on the local grapevine. This is as close to a central point as there is round here.'

'Right, yeah. Sorry about that. This fella makes me feel like I've done something wrong. Does he have to stare like that?'

Maybe Herrick wasn't such a big help after all. Before Gibson had to say anything, Herrick had the sense to suggest he check all was good back at the Station. Once he'd shuffled out to the car radio, Gibson got the conversation back on track. 'So you were back around what time?'

'The plane landed right on schedule, ten past one. Back here by two thirty. At two forty Jeremy Boxhall knocked on the door, full of his news.'

So, it was Hellyer's neighbour who first made the call.

'He was all abuzz. Full of himself too. Thought he was some brilliant pathologist because he'd noticed a few more blowflies than usual hovering around Hellyer's place when he went up.'

'A few more? By the time we got there it was practically a festival.'

Frank Barta chuckled. 'Very good. You've read your Clive James then?'

'Too right. The dunny man. Classic.' Gibson straightened his tie: a little reminder to get back to business. 'And what did he tell you? That there was plenty of action at Hellyer's?'

'Yep. No-one knew for sure because you guys weren't saying much. But we added two and two. Blowies zero in on blood and guts, or maybe a dead body. And you don't get half the Hobart force down for a broken sewerage pipe, do you?'

'We can confirm that Scott Hellyer was killed in his own dwelling, but we're trying to ascertain more accurately when that was. Mr Boxhall told my colleagues that he'd seen the deceased arrive late on Friday afternoon. He didn't notice him after that, but that's not surprising given they're not exactly on top of each other.'

'Yeah, good sized blocks that side of the road.'

'The only other thing he noticed was an electrician's van arriving later that evening.'

'That figures.'

'How so?'

'Been a sparky van pop down a few times over the summer. Just assumed he was getting some work done up there.'

The van that Boxhall had seen was gone by morning. This was getting interesting, but the detective kept that nugget close. No need to publicise the targets.

'Yeah, bit of wiring. Not the type of thing you'd want to fiddle with yourself. So, how often would you see Mr Hellyer down here? In recent months, say.'

'The odd weekday and almost every weekend. He'd get down around six of a Friday, pop in to get a coffee and the paper, then up to his place to get it ready for Madame Butterfly.'

'And he or she is …?'

'A very beautiful Asian lady. In looks at least. Chinese would be my guess. Stunning figure. Regular as clockwork. Same order each time: punnet of strawberries and thickened cream.' His eyebrows went up appreciatively.

'Did she ever introduce herself? And how did you know her connection to Hellyer?'

'The third or fourth time she said her name was Alice, but never said much else. My wife, for all her charming characteristics, could stickybeak for Australia. She just happened, by sheer coincidence, to be strolling in Marsh Lane one Saturday as Alice drove by.'

'Did she notice the car Alice was driving?'

'Audi Quattro, silver, late model.'

'Wow, she's good. Rego number too much to ask?'

'Yeah, she's not quite that good. But they were consular plates. Not sure for where though.'

'And this was the pattern for several Saturdays?'

'Yep. She'd head back late afternoon.' Frank cocked his head to the rear of the building. 'According to Janey Eagle-eye, that is.'

'Wonder what they got up to?'

'Well, I don't think they were playing Mah Jong.'

☐

When Gibson left the shop and looked over at the car there was no sign of Herrick. Brilliant. Where had he gone? A call from behind him provided the answer.

'Just been talking to a few people over there in the park. All daytrippers on their first visit. Not much help.'

Gibson gave Herrick the gist of the fresh information. 'I'll head up to check this stuff out with the Boxhall guy. If you go door-to-door along this stretch and enquire about the electrician's van and a silver Audi, that would be good. Be non-committal. We're just asking a few general questions if anybody presses you for more info, okay?'

'Meeting up again when?'

'I'll take the car and text you when I'm done. About half an hour I'd say.'

Herrick was already at the first dwelling when Gibson drove past. About two hundred metres along he turned into Marsh Lane, then pulled over outside Boxhall's address. It was a further fifty metres up the rise to Hellyer's shack where a marked car was parked, maintaining a presence to stop snoopers. One of the FSST vans was next to it—leaving no stone unturned.

Gibson got out and headed to the alfresco area where a shortish man with sinewy limbs was scrubbing his barbecue plate. 'Mr Boxhall?'

The man turned. He was wearing thongs, footy shorts, a blue singlet and a terry-towelling floppy hat. His skin was tanned to a deep hue, and he looked like a character from a 1980's beer advert. He wiped a hand on his shorts and held it out.

'Yeah, but Jezza will do.'

'Sure. I'm Detective Constable Gibson.'

'No, you're not,' his gravelly voice joked. 'Not on my turf. First names only, son.'

'OK, it's David.' Whatever it takes. 'Giving her a good clean?'

Gibson nodded to the sheet of metal.

'They've sent a sharp one then.'

Everyone's a joker. Suck it up and keep him talking. 'It's just that this place looks so well done out. Kept spotless. Surprises me you've left it.'

'Oh, right. Yeah, no, had a monster day yesterday. Feeding of the five hundred.'

Surely not. 'But the lane was cordoned off yesterday. No-one was allowed in. Who came?'

'Your lot. I'd got in a stack of meat for a family do. Found out pretty quickly that I had to cancel that, so what was I to do?'

'So you ran an all-day cafeteria for the boys and girls in blue? Nice one.'

'Yep. Hungry buggers. Had to get extra down from Woollies at Howrah.'

'I hope you've been compensated. Bloody good of you.'

'Just doing my bit. Already sorted on the money front. Some bloke called Mahoney gave me a number to call with my bank details. It's going in tomorrow.'

This was taking the responsibility of Senior Investigating Officer to a new level. 'John Mahoney. He's my boss. It's at his request I'm here actually. Bit of a follow up.'

'No worries. Beer?' Boxhall reached into an esky by the barbecue.

'Love to, but I can't really. I'll be fine.' Over the sound of the swooshing twist top and the initial glug Gibson asked, 'Have you seen a silver Audi round here of late?'

'Alice in Wonderland. Of course. I live down here full time so I don't miss much. Most weekends she's been down. Scotty boy reckoned it was the one thing he'd miss golf for.'

'Did he tell you anything else about this lady?'

Boxhall squinted in the effort to trawl his memory bank. 'Nup. Just her first name and that Saturday afternoons were now the highlight of his week.'

Gibson nodded. The beer looked very enticing. 'Was she here Saturday just gone?'

'Nah, not this week. No sign of her.'

'Okay, just to tick the boxes. So, Mr Hellyer arrived early Friday evening as per his normal pattern?'

'Yup.' Another glug. Nearly done.

'Then you said that an electrician's van went up a bit later. One that's been here a couple of times perhaps?'

'Yeah.' The stubby was gone and out came another; cleaning a barbecue must be thirsty work.

'Did you hear the van depart?'

The second stubby was raised to his lips. 'Mate, I sleep like the proverbial log. No idea when it left. It wasn't there on Saturday morning is all I know.'

'Righto. Anything else you noticed on the Saturday?'

'Alice didn't come and the curtains on the big picture window stayed drawn all day. I assumed Scott had left early. When she didn't turn up, I guessed there'd been a change of plan.'

'But you popped up on Sunday?'

'He parks around the back so it's hard to tell if he's there sometimes. I wanted to invite him down for a feed. Had a sticky note to leave on the door.'

'And something alarmed you.'

'Too right. It's March, so fly season and all, but mate, they were queuing up to get into his place. I couldn't smell anything, but those little buggers can sniff a sausage at a hundred paces. Everything was locked up but the car was there. No response when I knocked on the back door and called out. Didn't sit right so I called Jimmy at South Arm.'

Constable Jim Richardson: the sole police presence on the peninsula. He'd alerted HQ which is when the investigation started.

'Good that you did.'

'When did the dirty deed happen?'

'It's hard to say. Honestly, it's not like on the TV. There a several ways for determining time of death but none are that much help here. They're doing the autopsy in town this morning, so that should help. From mid Friday evening to sometime late on Saturday. Just between us, tracing that van will help.'

'Good luck with that. I had no joy.'

Gibson hadn't realised that Boxhall had joined the team. 'How do you mean?'

He took another quick slug and pointed to his roofline. 'I'm thinking of getting a fan in the bathroom ceiling. Need a sparky to do that one. Thought I might try the guy who went up to Scott's place. Couldn't trace him.'

'How did you try to contact him?'

'Googled the name on the side of the van. Electric Eric was all I'd seen, but nothing came up in the local business directory or the phone book either. Rang Jackson and Cooper in the end, but they'd never heard of him either. Bit strange, eh?'

Gibson asked if any other details had registered. Any stickers or details? No, just a white van with black lettering was all Boxhall could recall. Still, it was a good lead. Alice and Electric Eric ... what did they know? Perhaps Herrick had elicited some similar sightings.

Now it was time to get his skates on. Mahoney and Kendall should be pleased with the morning's work. Gibson thanked Boxhall—Jezza—and got out his phone.

CHAPTER FIVE

Inside the autopsy suite, in the bowels of the Royal Hobart Hospital, the atmosphere was clear and cool—akin to the manner of the new pathologist in town. Madeleine Pitney, recently of Launceston, had been promoted to the position formerly held by Bede Harcourt. The venerable surgeon was now spending the first months of retirement working as a volunteer medical officer in Nepal. Their gain was Hobart's loss, but not a loss too keenly felt. Pitney was all class: an exemplary physician and a professional who always presented well. Mahoney imagined a few of his officers were still gobsmacked by the startling presentation she'd given eighteen months before. His new Sergeant had confided that Pitney was a model she wished to emulate.

Personally, the DI was relieved about this particular change of personnel. Six months prior, it was the deputy pathologist conducting the autopsies. Michelle Timms was now gone—back to Queensland, he'd heard. There had been personal involvement that sparked a professional imbroglio. Mahoney was wholly innocent of the accusation she'd levelled at him, and it was quickly found to be baseless. Still, it had been an unsavoury episode. Timms's greater blunder was the cack-handed attempt to hide her own forensic incompetence. For whatever reason, there had been crucial oversights in her procedural analysis and, in endeavouring to cover this up, she had fabricated material. It was determined that she had to go, and by Christmas she had.

Pitney had just concluded her examination when they arrived in the room. Still in her white body suit she directed them over the metal table on which rested the body of Scott Hellyer. Mahoney looked at the mortal remains and wondered anew at the euphemisms people relied upon to assuage the grim reality of death. Hellyer was at rest, his soul departed to eternal life, he was now at peace …

In fact, he'd been tortured—ceremoniously, from what the investigators could gather. What had occurred was barbarity. Not for the first time that day, Mahoney considered the psychology of this crime. The person who had dispatched of the man on display was functioning at a different level to your average criminal.

One of Mahoney's first homicide arrests was a man who'd slammed an axe into his live-in partner's skull, an extreme example of domestic violence. That was the background to so many of the injuries and deaths the police dealt with: family members battering each other. Or violence fuelled by drug and alcohol abuse.

This death was unusual. The treatment meted out was particularly sadistic and punctiliously enacted. The sort of 'sick shit'—as Munro would have called it—that could entail bringing in a profiler. Pitney's clear voice brought him back from the reverie.

'The numerous welts on the body were inflicted prior to the fatal wound in the groin. In all, there are thirty such marks. With twenty of them there was a transference of minute particles from the projectile to the skin.'

'Tiny green fibres.'

'Correct, Sergeant. The initial on-site forensic report catalogued forty-eight tennis balls laying around the body. You don't need to be Sherlock Holmes to correlate the link. I'm not putting my hand up to be the guinea pig, but I would assume the balls were hit towards the human target at great speed.'

'That is a quirky test that Graves at the New Town laboratory will sort out,' said Mahoney. 'I spoke to him a short while ago. He was nutting out what to use as the flesh component. We should hear something later today.'

Pitney placed a latexed hand by the corpse's temple. 'By fluke or design, one ball hit the eye and caused major damage, damage beyond repair. The perpetrator really had it in for this victim. Did Hellyer support Collingwood?'

The detectives smiled. 'I doubt it. All indications are he was quite bright. And he had all his own teeth,' Mahoney quipped.

The pathologist moved her hand down the body. 'His scrotum is bruised. One of a few bruises. So we can presume an early shot struck there. Also at that spot is a small nick. No coagulation so that was probably inflicted immediately before the iliac artery was savaged.'

'Savaged?' Kendall's query seemed to be in relation to the term.

'I use the word advisedly. The blade was inserted with some force and then twisted. The artery, and it's a major one, would have ruptured.'

'Causing significant spurting?'

'Yes, John. Considerable blood loss was obviously the intention. The initial loss would have been a river of blood. Strong virulent bursts. It would have cascaded over at least the arm of the person wielding the blade, possibly more. For the first number of heartbeats it would have pulsed from the wound in an arc, and then subsided as the heart weakened.'

'And left an unholy mess on the floor,' Kendall said. 'From the way you describe it, the attacker must have been partially covered. So did he have protective clothing on or did he sluice himself down right there and then? The blade was rinsed before being shoved into one of the balls, wasn't it?'

'Yes, to the latter,' replied her boss. 'As to the former, we await the findings of Kitchener and the Forensics squad.'

The pathologist pointed to an exhibits bench by the side wall. 'The knife is over there. Certainly the murder weapon. The blade configures exactly with the dimensions and shape of the wound. It was rinsed pretty thoroughly, but a smidgen of skin was still connected at the point where the blade meets the handle. Jones is comparing the sample to tissue from the body now.'

Mahoney nodded. 'That pretty much covers the physiological how. What about the when?'

'The body was initially examined by Doctor Johnson at quarter to twelve on Sunday morning. His first action, as per good practice, was to measure the temperature of the body and the room. He recorded an ambient temperature of twenty degrees Celsius, so we can assume that Hellyer had been dead around eighteen hours, give or take.'

Kate pointed at the body. 'Relatively low body fat level and no clothing, so perhaps it could have been quicker.'

Mahoney added, 'The room temperature was probably fairly constant. It's a well-designed property from a thermal point of view. And the curtains were drawn. All helping to keep the ambient temperature within a limited range.'

Pitney smiled. 'I should get you two down here. I got Jones earlier to put the relevant data in a nomogram and that also suggests the death was at least eighteen hours prior to Johnson's reading.'

'Saturday afternoon,' said Mahoney. 'Rigor mortis?'

'Pushes the timeframe out to earlier. Relaxation of the rigor had progressed to approximately halfway down the torso according to Doctor Johnson. A ballpark figure is approximately thirty-six to forty-eight hours prior to that initial examination.' Her eyes narrowed. 'Only ballpark, mind you.'

'That's still pretty good. The team at New Town lab are testing samples of the blood left on the floor. That should help too.' Mahoney pointed to the midriff. 'Stomach contents?'

'With Jones. I'll go in there presently to help with the analysis. From what I can gauge, it's not more than forty-eight, based on what I observed in that area of the body. No signs of putrefaction had a chance to begin. If it had been left another day, the chemical breakdown would well and truly have started. No marbling on the skin and no bloating. All the internal organs intact.'

Mahoney found himself gazing at the corpse's chest. The large Y-shaped incision was startling. Inordinately large stitches were needed to close up the wound. It looked like a strange version of a lace-up football guernsey from a bygone era. It had to be done of course—the body literally sawn open to reveal the inner workings.

'Any anomalies with the organs or anything else on the body?'

Pitney held her hands open to indicate that it was a bit premature for a considered answer. 'To the naked eye the internal organs were fine. Regular size and colour. No lung discolouration so not a smoker. The sample testing is still to be done but I'd say this man would have continued to live a healthy life.'

'Okay, so we know the method and the brutality of the death. The tests here and at New Town will tell us more. Without prejudicing your findings, we're thinking some form of drug was used.'

Pitney pointed to the skull and nodded. 'Apart from the aforementioned eyeball there was no damage to the head. He wasn't knocked out that way. So, yes, you're safe to assume drugging.'

'Have you seen the pics from the scene?' Kendall asked.

'Of course. The blanket is crucial to your thinking.'

'And the gag,' added Kendall.

The pathologist moved to the foot of the bench. 'You may need a profiler. No, ignore that. You *will* need a profiler. This is serious.'

The detectives were struck by the weight of her tone. 'Any suggestions? Given our size we don't have a dedicated shrink within the force.'

'The reason I feel sufficiently confident suggesting this is that I've been studying some forensic psychology over the past year. It's an online course run by Monash University, but it's involved three residential study weekends in Melbourne where I met the course convenor, a gentleman called Adriano Cortese. Smooth but absolutely brilliant. Get him down.'

She was so emphatic that Mahoney nearly got out his phone on the spot. 'What's your reading of this?'

'A perpetrator who outwardly is quite controlled, but internally is a seething volcano of supressed emotions, principally anger. This isn't rage. It's so methodical in its way. This is a climax of a long period of bitterness, culminating in revenge.'

'Revenge on Hellyer in particular?' Kate interrupted.

'I'd say not necessarily, but bear in mind that my knowledge is incomplete. Cortese, if you consult him, will elaborate. I'm thinking your guy is a complex mechanism. Firstly, the planning involved. That's your area so you'll know it's hardly a random effort.'

'Agreed. Kate and I are meeting later to more fully consider that aspect.'

'Understood. I'll move on. Second, the enactment. Restraining from the killer blow so the torrent of balls could be launched. It's very controlled.' She pointed to the lower reaches of the body. 'The knife to the groin is both functional and, perhaps, metaphorical.'

'As in severing a principal artery and the old saying "a blow to the groin"?'

'I think so. A low blow.'

'Is there a sexual element involved there?' Kate asked.

'Again, I'm hypothesising as an amateur, but I don't think so. Not for the murderer or the victim. There's a nick to the scrotum but that's more to get the victim's attention. Gets his imagination fearing the worst. The penis is untouched.' She gestured to the far table. 'I think the sex toy was used simply because it's such an effective gag. No more than that.'

'Hellyer's not being punished for sexual proclivities then?' Mahoney asked.

'I doubt it. But that's just my educated guess. It could be the opposite. The human mind is a fiendishly complex thing.'

Don't I know it, thought Mahoney. He spent a disproportionate amount of time wishing he could switch his own off.

'Would the perpetrator have got a thrill?'

'Perhaps. The linking of violence to sexual ecstasy, in various ways, is well established. No seminal fluid was found at the site as far as I know. Was the murderer aroused? It's hard to say.'

CHAPTER SIX

As the detectives exited the mortuary building onto Argyle Street, Mahoney's mobile started buzzing.

'Yes, David. Where are you?'

'On the way back. I've got you on speakerphone.'

'No problem. Go ahead.' Mahoney gestured to Kendall to pause for a bit.

Gibson's summary of findings at Opossum Bay was succinct and promising. Mahoney was fast realising that the loss of Munro was quickly being covered by this fresh Detective Constable.

'Have you got all that, Sir?' asked Gibson.

'Yes, good work. As soon as you return, work with Dunstan on finding anything you can on that white van. From what we've been informed at the autopsy, whoever was driving it is very much a person of interest.'

'Righto, Sir. No worries.' Gibson's enthusiasm was evident even against the background noise of the car. 'I'll get straight onto it. Constable Herrick did another doorknock. A couple of people remembered seeing the van but thought nothing of it. No further identifiers on it. No-one else recalls seeing the Audi.'

'Alright. I think I can track the lady down. You have the thankless task of the van. Kate and I will be back at headquarters sometime this afternoon. We'll go over things again then.'

'Righto, Sir.'

Mahoney ended the call and turned to his sergeant. 'Kate, can you get your car and pick me up at the Bathurst Street exit?'

'Of course. Progress?'

'In a fashion. It might be a lot more in an hour or so.'

Kendall jogged across the street to the reception area of the station while Mahoney scrolled his contacts list. Tapped on the screen to dial.

'Clinton, it's John Mahoney. How's tricks?'

'Hiya. Not bad. Bedding down the new automated program is a bugbear, but could be worse.' The Motor Registration Board always seemed to be struggling with systems. 'Need a favour?'

'Yep, quick one. That okay?'

'Shoot.'

'Vehicles with consular plates. You got a list of registered users?'

'Sure. You got a number?'

'Afraid not.'

'A country?'

'No, sorry. Just the first name of a driver. I can hazard a guess as to the region.'

'I might be able to find something. This is one database that works. What's the name?'

'Alice. Probably an Asian-sounding surname.'

Mahoney could hear the tapping of keys.

'Right. Not all the consular representatives provide the full list that they should. As far as I can see the only match is for a Mrs Alice Cheung. She's listed as the consular representative for Taiwan. Her husband's name is …'

'Kevin.'

'Yeah. Know him?'

'Just heard of him in passing. Any chance of a contact number or an address?'

'Sure. I can text them both to you.'

'Perfect. Clinton, you're a lifesaver. Cheers, cobber.'

'No hassle at all. Big case?'

'Looking that way. This lady is secondary, but she could help.'

'Don't worry, John. We haven't had this conversation. In fact, I'm not even here. See you at The Ocean Child one day.'

'No worries. I owe you a few schooners. Thanks again.'

Right on cue Kendall steered the Ford Focus out of the under-ground car park. Mahoney got in the passenger side.

'Where to, Sir?'

Mahoney heard a ping and checked his screen. 'West Hobart. Fielding Drive. It's off Knocklofty Terrace.'

'I know it. Great views. I go walking up there sometimes.'

'Perfect. Let's go.'

□

In the driveway of number seventeen Fielding Drive was a silver Audi saloon sporting consular plates for Taiwan. Bingo. As they got out a figure emerged: a woman with sleek dark hair cut to shoulder length. She was wearing a peach-coloured halter top and grey knee-length shorts. She had sandshoes on her feet and gardening gloves in her hand. She waited for them by the front steps.

'My word, you're prompt.'

Mahoney presumed she'd called the station.

'Mrs Alice Cheung?'

'Yes, that's me. I heard the dreadful news on the radio earlier. Thought it best to call immediately. I knew you'd track me down sooner or later, Inspector …?'

'Mahoney. And this is Detective Sergeant Kendall. If I show you our ID inside, it's less of a spectacle.'

A small smile. 'Thank you. Please come in. I've been gardening to still my thoughts.'

She stepped up the concrete stairway as the detectives followed. The front door led into an imposing reception room. The walls that weren't plate glass were bookshelves from floor to ceiling. She gestured to some leather chairs and the trio took a seat. She gently placed the gloves on the polished oak floor, then stood abruptly.

'My apologies. Would you care for some refreshment?'

'No, thank you. My sergeant and I will be fine. Unless you would like something.'

She sat with her knees pressed together and her clasped hands resting on her thighs. 'I shall be fine. Your professional courtesy is appreciated. May I request your discretion? Mine is a delicate position. As the Honorary Consul, undue publicity would be harmful in ways beyond my personal status.'

Mahoney noticed she spoke English more clearly than most inhabitants of his hometown.

'All I can assure you is that if you are not directly connected to the death of Mr Hellyer, then any other connection you had with him will not be shared beyond this room. You are possibly part of our investigation, but that doesn't need to be made public. That is the best guarantee I can offer.'

'That is sufficient. I'll trust you, and I hope I can assist you.'

As Kendall opened her notebook and clicked a pen, Mahoney considered his first question.

'How well did you know Mr Hellyer?'

'Intimately but not in any great depth. We met at a cocktail fundraiser for the Tasmanian Art Gallery in December. We chatted for a time and I warmed to his confident manner. My husband owns three restaurants in this region and he had done some business with Scott before. He'd been for a drink with him occasionally. So, I had heard mentions of his name, but I never actually met Scott before that evening. It wasn't very long before I wished to see much more of him.'

Her long eyelashes were noticeable as she blinked. 'You can imagine how it went. One moment we were sharing a convivial chat in a room full of prominent people, and seemingly the next we were lovers.'

'How often did you meet up?'

'Each Saturday afternoon at his holiday home at Opossum Bay.'

'Any other occasions?'

'No. We had a harmonious schedule which suited us both.'

'Did anybody else, your husband perhaps, know anything of this liaison?'

Mahoney thought about the proprietors of the local store.

'I don't think so. Scott could be brash, but he was very discreet. A rare quality in an Australian male.'

Mahoney didn't take offence. 'Did you rendezvous on Saturday just gone?'

'No, he cancelled. I don't know the precise reason. Around eight o'clock on Friday evening I received a text message saying he had been called away to a meeting about the proposed golf course at South Arm. Apparently, it required him to be in Melbourne all day Saturday and we would have to, in his words, "raincheck" our meeting.'

'Were you able to speak to him?'

'No. I texted a reply to say I understood. We kept our communication to a minimum so I did not call him.' Her fingers clenched just a little tighter. 'If I had visited regardless, what might I have witnessed?'

You don't want to know, thought Mahoney. 'We can't be sure. At this stage we know the homicide occurred sometime on or after Friday evening. If it was committed by Saturday afternoon, we'll know once our forensics officers have tallied their findings. I can't be more precise than that.'

She nodded. 'Thank you.' A tear glistened at the edge of her eye, which she delicately brushed away. Otherwise, she was relatively composed.

'Have you noticed anything suspicious on your trips to the deceased's dwelling over the past few weeks?' Kendall asked.

Alice Cheung shook her head slightly. 'Nothing at all. We had established a very agreeable pattern. I am not aware of any strange occurrences, nor do I truly believe anyone else was aware of our meetings. I'm sorry but that is all I can tell you.'

There was still one box to tick.

'Are you able to account for your movements from Friday evening till Sunday morning?' Mahoney asked.

If she was flummoxed, it didn't show. 'I attended an exhibition opening at the Colville Gallery on Friday evening and on Saturday, having found myself to be free, I spent the day on Bruny Island. Maria Amos was at the art opening on Friday and she asked me down to her property for the weekend. I accepted. My husband, Kevin, was away in the north of the state so it was a welcome invitation. I was on the nine o'clock ferry across the channel on Saturday morning and returned late yesterday afternoon.'

Mahoney nodded. It was an alibi easily checked: a quick job for Dunstan back at the office.

The detectives thanked her and left. Once seated in the car, Kendall said, 'Somebody else must have known about the affair.'

'I'd say so. Somebody knew only too well, but didn't want her potentially interrupting proceedings or discovering the body.'

'Perhaps a murderer with a touch of sensitivity. How bizarre.'

'Agreed. I think we will need the help of the Cortese chap.'

CHAPTER SEVEN

'What are we thinking?' Mahoney asked as he stood by a large Perspex board with a marker pen in his hand.

Kendall and Gibson stood facing the orderly collage of photos stuck to the surface. Gibson spoke first. 'From what Alice Cheung told you and the siting of the van, the perpetrator was at work on Friday evening.'

The sergeant nodded. 'The initial conclusions from the autopsy and the crime scene support that. Our killer did his homework on Hellyer: knew the pattern of his weekend sojourns at Opossum Bay—when Hellyer was going to arrive, who he was expecting the next day, the layout of the house.'

'Agreed,' said Mahoney as he pointed to the head shot of the victim. 'Hellyer was having an affair with Alice Cheung. To the best of her knowledge, it's unbeknown to others.'

'Apart from the proprietors of the shop knew about it, and Hellyer told Boxhall. Not completely discreet after all.'

'Exactly, David. If they're aware of it, other people could be too—including somebody targeting Hellyer. The van was seen a few times over summer, wasn't it?'

'Yes, Sir.'

'We'll go with the van person being the killer for now. Alice Cheung's alibi holds water according to our checks. Local witnesses recall only one person in the van, although there could have been an accomplice in the back. Remember, Hellyer is not a small figure to be manhandled. Even drugged, it would take a fair degree of strength to string him up. So one, perhaps two, involved. The forensics report should help there. Mrs Cheung has agreed to be fingerprinted so we can eliminate her traces at the house.'

'She is not likely to have done it?' asked Gibson.

Kendall shook her head. 'No motive. And beyond her means, I think. But what about her husband, Sir?'

'Dunstan's covered that as well.' Mahoney raised his eyebrows: the chunky constable was evolving into a fail-safe intelligence researcher. 'Kevin Cheung is an investor in the golf course scheme, so it's unlikely he'd wish to dispatch the prime mover in the development. And he was in Devonport from Thursday to Sunday. Dunstan pulled up some photos from the online version of The Advocate. Cheung was at a tourism function on Friday evening and a food fair on the Saturday, both in and around Devonport which is about four hours away from the scene.'

'As both Mrs Hellyer and Alice Cheung said, Kevin Cheung and Hellyer were drinking buddies too. Seems a stretch for Cheung to know what was going on behind his back.'

'I think you're right, Kate. Having met Alice Cheung, I'm inclined to believe her version that her husband was oblivious to the affair. I don't wish to alert Mr Cheung of it if I don't have to. Her calling the station could be a bluff, but that seems a bit far-fetched. Her husband may have known and wanted Hellyer punished, but it's hugely hypothetical at this stage.'

Gibson pointed to the image of Hellyer's desecrated body. 'The manner of the execution seems extreme for that too.'

Mahoney stared at the wounds as if seeing them afresh. 'It's barbaric, yet so methodical.' He breathed deeply. 'I'll have to call

Cheung under the guise of getting some background on Hellyer. I can't let the chance of letting the cat out of the bag override our need to know as much as possible. David, keep working on the van and get hold of whatever Dunstan's got on Newcrest Nominees. The business side could be an angle. Kate, go up to the offices of Tiger Brewing. Find out what you can about Hellyer from his colleagues. I'll meet with Cheung but it's my guess we have to spread the net wider.' Mahoney looked at his watch. 'See you back here at five o'clock.'

Gibson was straight off to sit with Dunstan at the computer.

'The profiler, Cortese?' Kendall asked before moving.

'Yeah.' He rubbed his brow. 'I'll sound him out too. I think he'll be needed.'

□

Having left a voicemail message for Cortese, Mahoney exited the building to meet Cheung. Half of him wished he could do it over the phone; it would be a lot quicker and he could perhaps avoid the delicate issue of his wife's infidelity. Alice Cheung had seemed so decent. Yet, Mahoney's professional half dictated that he must go face-to-face. He couldn't put a ring around the sensibilities of certain people. The squad was dealing with a grievous homicide so pussyfooting about simply wasn't on.

Halfway up Liverpool Street the vehicle traffic was crawling. As Mahoney walked past the construction site causing the stoppages, he wondered when the development would be completed. The city heart needed it. In an economy this size any investment by a major company was welcome. Just why the government had flatly rejected a proposal by a consortium to create a new hospital precinct was anybody's guess. The state was hanging on by its nails and the politicians wanted to use the clippers.

He crossed Harrington Street and, halfway up the block, arrived at a plain double storey brick building, cream paint with green trim for the window frames. It was impossible to decipher what sort of aesthetic statement was being made. The top floor of number 207 contained the offices of the Southern Spice Trading Company. Kevin Cheung, the owner, had asked to meet there.

Mahoney ascended the stairs to a space that was utilitarian, at best: bare wooden floors with cartons stacked in one corner, and a forlorn cheap-looking desk with a kettle perched on it. Through a doorway was another space that was carpeted and looked brighter. He coughed to indicate his presence.

'Inspector?' A man appeared in the door frame. His jet black hair was given shape by a touch of product. He was wearing polished black shoes, navy trousers and a shirt so white it belonged in a Persil ad.

'Yes, DI John Mahoney.' He opened up his ID card.

A dismissive wave with a wide smile. 'Of course it is. Who would say that which they are not? Come in please.'

He followed Cheung into the corner office and took the offered seat. 'Thank you for agreeing to see me at such short notice. I imagine you're a very busy man.'

'That is true but I must make time for you. My sincere apologies. I have nothing to offer you but water.' His hand pointed to a stack of plastic water bottles on the floor.

'No, thank you. I'd rather get straight on to things.'

'Of course. You are very busy.' He had a slight accent but it was the stilted diction that revealed he was an outsider. Hobart was hardly a melting pot, but it was improving on earlier days. How monochrome the country would be without immigration.

Mahoney decided to risk a few curly questions; perhaps Cheung would miss the nuances.

'When did you find out about Hellyer's death?'

'My wife called me late this morning. She had heard the sad news on the radio and wished to tell me.'

Mahoney wondered what she'd said.

'She told me what I already knew.'

'Which was?' It seemed Cheung was controlling the nuances.

'She and Scott were lovers.'

Mahoney stayed silent in case the husband was bluffing, looking for a confirmation of his own suspicions. Cheung sat straighter.

'My wife called me before she rang your station. She told me of their liaisons and asked me what to do.'

'And you advised her to contact us and be candid.'

'Correct, Inspector. I have not told her I already knew of their weekend liaisons at Scott's house. It would confuse her.'

'How?'

'She would wonder why I had let it go on.'

'And why did you?'

'Because I, too, also enjoy this type of liaison. With Mrs Hellyer.'

Mahoney tried very hard to keep a straight face. Bob and Carol, Ted and Alice. Now this was unusual.

'Last week at Barcelona. You were having a drink with Mr Hellyer and you saw Mrs Hellyer there?'

Cheung let a small smile slip. 'I had not meant to see Sophie that evening. It was pure chance that she visited the wine bar where I was meeting Scott. She was very composed and was with us for just a few moments.'

'So Hellyer didn't twig to that side of things?'

'Twig?'

'Cotton on ... umm ... realise.'

'No. He was prompted to claim he would be away in the north of the state for the weekend. Perhaps for my benefit or for that of his former wife. I do not know.'

Mahoney decided he could do with a bottle of water after all; he helped himself and sat back down. 'Let me get this right. You and Mrs Hellyer have been conducting an affair. For how long?'

'Approximately one year.'

'And neither your wife nor Mr Hellyer knew of it?'

'No. If my wife knew, she would have mentioned it today. Would she not?'

'So you and Sophie Hellyer get away with it. But he and Alice don't. Who else knew about them? Sophie?'

'Not at all. I certainly did not tell her. In such matters, the fewer the people who knew, the better. She suspected her husband of being unfaithful but she would not have thought of Alice.'

'Why not?'

'Because Alice is Asian. Sophie is an Anglo woman. I do not think she can imagine anyone apart from a pretty blonde being sexually attractive. She is a nice woman, but blinkered.'

'What was the attraction for Alice?'

'Of Scott?'

'Yes.'

'He was an assertive man. Confident. That and the thrill of an extra-marital affair. Much of the excitement with these matters is in the mind.'

That, or a cry for attention. Mahoney really didn't want to divulge his musings on relationships and their pitfalls. He had to press on.

'I'm thinking this state of affairs doesn't give you sufficient motivation to wish harm upon Mr Hellyer?'

Cheung burst into laughter.

'My apologies. That was inappropriate. I can assure you that Scott's death is perhaps the last thing I would desire. The affairs were a small matter. It was his role as a frontman that was important. His death has suddenly given me a very large problem.'

'In what way?'

'Have you heard of the proposed tourism development at South Arm?'

'Yes. Golf course, conference centre. All the bells and whistles. So far we've established Mr Hellyer's holding company was behind it.'

Cheung nodded. 'That is correct. Newcrest Nominees is holding the purse strings of bags of foreign money.' He frowned as if carefully considering his words. 'This is a marvellous country, Inspector. But there continues to be a prejudice against the so-called Yellow Peril.

I, along with some other gentlemen from Taiwan, saw the potential for just such a development. The airport is being improved. The atmosphere here is clear and the attractions are easy to reach. It's a perfect location for Asian travellers.' He looked Mahoney levelly in the eye. 'A boon for the economy. But we must tread carefully. Foreign investment is crucial for this country, but it scares some people.'

The same people who enjoy a good standard of living thanks to China buying our iron ore, Mahoney thought.

'So you'd established Scott Hellyer as the driving force behind the proposal? An acceptable face for public consumption.' He paused slightly. 'You would hardly get rid of him.'

'Precisely, Inspector. To be blunt, Scott Hellyer was immensely valuable to our consortium while alive. His death, unfortunate as that is, gives us a great obstacle to overcome. There is no personal or professional reason for me to have wished Scott any harm.'

And that was that, concluded Mahoney. An intriguing, but ultimately fruitless, dead end. They chatted further about the development and Cheungs's impressions of the deceased, but nothing of help was forthcoming. He thanked the businessman and left.

Out on the street he realised he was two blocks from Tiger Brewing and decided to catch Kendall there.

CHAPTER EIGHT

Mahoney cut through Centrepoint Shopping Centre to get to Collins Street. As he hit the open air, he saw his sergeant on the opposite pavement tapping on her phone. He jaywalked across.

'Ah, Sir. Just texting you. There's a visitor for us at headquarters.'

'Tell me on the way.'

The sun was well over the central blocks leaving them in the shade. The cooler air also heralded the turning of the seasons; autumn was here.

'So, Kate, how did you go?'

'The woman in charge of the advertising accounts, Jennifer Jones, is away on leave. The admin assistant for her and Hellyer was there but she couldn't really tell me a whole lot. Her name is Lizzie Norwood.'

'Bit reticent? Shocked?'

'Neither. She never met him.'

'You're kidding?'

'No, truly. It's her first day. Just came down from Melbourne. She was interviewed by the Jones woman about two weeks ago and instructed to start today.'

The DI's brow furrowed. 'Bit strange.'

'Not how she tells it. She had a formal handover day on Friday with the girl she's replacing. All went fine. Jones is due back tomorrow.'

'Where was Hellyer on Friday then?'

'Tourism seminar at Freycinet. Most of his work was out of the office apparently.' They sidestepped a jogger. 'Young Lizzie brought up his work diary for the last month on the computer. He was a pretty busy guy.'

'Anything unusual?'

'Not that I could see. I saved a copy of the file to my memory stick so you can check.'

They turned into Argyle Street for the final stretch. 'I don't suppose you got a look at his colleague's diary.'

'Norwood was accommodating but not naïve. I decided it best not to push our luck at Tiger just yet. We hardly want the Jones woman offside before we meet her.'

'Yes, you're right. So bugger all at his workplace so far, and not much more from Cheung.'

He gave her a precis of their meeting, finishing the tale as they crossed the foyer at HQ.

'That's pretty freaky, Sir. This can be one hell of a small town, can't it? Who'd have imagined. No wonder Sophie Hellyer wasn't too fussed about the end of her marriage.'

'Strange days indeed.' Mahoney opened the door to the incident room for her. 'Now, who's this visitor we're meant to see?'

Kendall pointed to the far corner where Gibson was standing by the Perspex board with a stranger. From behind, all Mahoney could see was a slim man with a smoothly shaven head. The jacket looked expensive. Armani? Gibson caught his boss's questioning look.

'Sir, good timing. I was just showing Mr Cortese a few of our findings.'

'Were you now? Good for you, David.'

Mahoney ignored the newcomer. 'And we know this is the profiler because ...?'

'Doctor Pitney brought him up and introduced him.'

Mahoney's sails slackened; he had to stop assuming Gibson was wet behind the ears.

'Of course. And where is she now?'

'She has returned to her cavern of macabre delights, Inspector. May I introduce myself, as DC Gibson hasn't had the opportunity. I'm Adriano Cortese.'

Mahoney turned and met a pair of green eyes twinkling with amusement. He resisted the urge to poke them out, and held out his hand instead.

'DI John Mahoney and this is DS Kate Kendall. I'm sorry, Mr Cortese, you've caught me unprepared. I didn't realise you'd be here quite so soon. I trust you didn't drop everything in Melbourne to fly straight in for us.'

'I thought you knew. I was already in Hobart visiting my parents. They retired to this quaint little place a few years ago.'

It hadn't been mentioned; cunning little bugger. But he was here now and they might as well use him.

'What do you know of our case?'

'I've inspected the corpse and looked at the scene-of-crime photos.'

That was an interesting idea of protocol; Pitney may need to be reminded how procedures functioned in criminal investigations.

'Would you share your initial thoughts with us?'

'Certainly. You're looking for a skilled mechanic, first-generation child of Slavic immigrants, lapsed Catholic, unmarried, tidy in appearance, and quite possibly paranoid.'

Gibson's excitement got the better of him. 'That's brilliant. All that from this?' He waved his arm at the board.

Cortese smiled broadly and bowed theatrically. Mahoney slapped him on the shoulder.

'Nice one, Signor Cortez. I was a tad concerned but I think we'll get along fine. Come into my office. We need to formalise your involvement.'

Gibson turned to Kate with a bewildered look. 'What was that all about? Am I missing something?'

Kate smiled. 'Just a bit of experience. The portrait Cortese gave us wasn't for our perp. It's a textbook one developed years ago by one of the first profilers to be taken seriously. Chap called Brussel who made startling observations about who the New York Bomber was in the 1950s. They eventually caught the guy through methodical policing and it turned out Brussel's portrait was close to the mark. Once people realised it was logic and not magic, profiling was seen to be of help. Not voodoo.'

'I've got a bit to learn,' Gibson conceded.

□

Once inside the compact office, Mahoney offered his visitor a seat and took his own on the other side of the desk. Cortese reached into the inside pocket of his linen jacket, extracted a business card and placed it on the desk.

'My credentials, Inspector. As you can see I've studied the science here and abroad, most notably in the US. Presently, I am acting as a consultant for Victoria Police. My main line of work is in the academia, training officers as to the value of forensic psychology.'

Mahoney studied the embossed card—not quite as many acronyms as a government directory but up there.

'Ever considered private practice?'

Cortese rolled his eyes. 'Several years ago I did such work for a short time. The search for happiness is a quest that can wear one down. It seemed to me that many of my patients relished being unhappy. It gave them an excuse to harbour grudges and bemoan their perceived lack of success. Many actively worked against my proposals for them.'

'Which were?'

'Very generally, to be connected, to be open to love, and to have a project which fires your imagination.'

No wonder I'm up the creek, thought Mahoney. Unless he labelled his investigations as projects.

'Sounds like it's easier said than done.'

'No, it's easily done. The trouble is, so many people don't want to do it. You can simply have what you want by wanting what you have. Precious few people accept that increased lifespans already give them the greatest gift they could desire. And it's free. We have universal education and healthcare, albeit not perfect models.'

'I take it you're referring to developed economies.'

'Of course. There isn't much call for psychologists in Eritrea. So many people there purely focus on staying alive.' Cortese patted his pocket and took out a slim plastic cylinder. 'Do you mind?'

'Probably not. What is it?'

'An electronic cigarette. Fulfils my chemical addiction without befouling the atmosphere. Not the ultimate solution, but we all have our little quirks.' Cortese sucked lightly on one end and the other end of the six-inch tube glowed briefly. He then blew a small cloud towards the extractor fan in the ceiling.

'I'll take your word for it. As I will for any insights you can give me on this case.' A small jerk of his head toward the door. 'Your party trick was well done. My constable was all set to kiss your feet.'

'Oh that. It was done more to test you.'

'Me?'

'A quick way to gauge your attitude to my branch of detective work.'

'And?'

'You passed with aplomb. Madeleine told me of your record as an investigator. It is also heartening to know your knowledge of my area is sound. It leads me to believe you will afford my work its due credit, and such a thing is important.'

'Agreed. I've got the odd dunderhead, but the vast majority out there recognise that expert help is needed. The more I collect from the crime scene, the more I appreciate how chilling the act was.'

'Precisely. A most apposite word: chilling. That was also my impression from regarding the photos. It was a cold, calculated act of violence, not opportunistic rage. This, in itself, narrows the field.'

'Good. That is what we were thinking already and Doctor Pitney nudged us further. I hope you can advance things again.'

He took another puff and tilted his head to exhale upwards. 'Will you be taking notes?' Cortese glanced pointedly at the notepad on the desk. 'It's just that Madeleine led me to expect ...'

'... that I'm a pedantic pen-pusher who writes to help him comprehend information.'

'Well, yes.'

Cortese noticed the inspector's smile.

'Our man ... I'm assuming you're considering a male owing to the physicality of the act.'

'Yes. Or a pair.'

'No,' Cortese's voice was particularly decisive. 'This is a solo act. I'll get to that later. The killer is intelligent and well-educated, possibly tertiary level. By the way, Gibson told me about the electrician's van. I trust you don't mind his enthusiasm.'

Mahoney did mind a bit—actually, quite a bit. His new man must become more aware of demarcations. A lot of the formal procedure had a point, but he'd have to let it ride for now.

'Not at all.'

'One obvious point is that you will have little problem formulating a murder charge. Given the high degree of planning involved, it seems impossible not to accept pre-meditation. That level of planning reveals intelligence and an ordered mind.'

'Mind? I'd hardly have thought his mental state to be orderly.'

'On the contrary. His mind is extraordinarily so. The scheme was thoroughly researched and meticulously enacted. A clear level head. In his mind he is enforcing a sense of order upon the world. He believes he is fixing a problem. But let me get back to my progression.

I don't want to be overbearing, but if I lay it out first, any queries you have can come later.'

Mahoney nodded; just be a scribe and allow the expert's train of thought to choof along.

'The surveillance of the property, the knowledge of the affair with Alice Cheung, awareness of Hellyer's routine … all indicate a patient and painstaking approach. Above average intelligence. With regard to education, what is one characteristic that all university graduates must share?'

'Capacity for hard work? Not sure.'

'Deferred gratification. They appreciate that by making sacrifices of time, and by not seeking income immediately, they will prosper in the future.'

'Less jam now, more jam tomorrow.' A fleeting picture of Mahoney's old Economics teacher came to him. Where did those former mentors end up?

'Indubitably. They invest their efforts to be better off down the track. Some need to be very bright—psychologists for example—but not all.'

If he hadn't already, Mahoney was genuinely warming to the man opposite. Cortese was likeable. 'Nice point. But plenty of crims plan, don't they? Bank robbers are a prime example.'

'Certainly. It isn't just the intricacy of the short-term planning that alarms me though. The mis en scène at Opossum Bay is very disturbing. In the bludgeoning of the body, a revenge play is being acted out. A desire for revenge that has been controlled for years, decades even.' Cortese pocketed his nicotine dart. 'To explain clearly, I shall have to actually draft a report. The theory underscoring my hypothesis should be clearly argued. And, to be honest, I need more information about the victim.'

'As do we all.'

'Indeed. Now we may discover that the victim was thoroughly deserving of his fate. However, I am thinking that Mr Hellyer was chosen because he represented something more general. And that is a serious concern.'

Mahoney sat back in his chair. 'He might not be the only victim? You think there have been others, or there are more to come?'

'No to the former. He wants the victim to be found in situ. It's a further confirmation of his power. What I'm afraid of is that this could well be the first in a series. The only compensation being that the killings would not be random.'

'That isn't so reassuring to be honest.'

'I'm not seeking to reassure you. The brutal truth is that the signals suggest the killer won't stop here. He has a mindset that's been fostered over an extended period. Some event has sparked the transition from meditation to action. This deed was rewarding for him, but the yearning to correct the world continues. It does mean you will catch him, because he wants to be discovered. Then he can explain the rationale for doing what he strongly feels must be done.'

'Some solace then.'

'Yes, Inspector.' Cortese stood. 'I shall bend my will to the task. My report will be delivered personally in the morning. Till then.'

□

For a few minutes Mahoney stared at the notes on his pad, trying to get his head around what they were dealing with. He worried for a moment that this crime might be beyond them, but dismissed the thought just as readily. Cortese would assemble a 'portrait' to help them. That was one way in.

Mahoney told himself to remember that it was careful fact-checking that often facilitated breakthroughs. The case mentioned in Cortese's play-acting earlier was just like that. Brussel, the profiler, had initiated a call for public assistance that opened a line of communication with the Mad Bomber. A reply from the bomber led an office clerk to check through old employment records and letters of grievance. The repetition of a telling phrase from that correspondence and the recent reply narrowed the search to the bomber.

Perspiration versus inspiration. In fact, it was perspiration *with* inspiration.

Mahoney walked out to where Dunstan was toiling away on the computer next to Gibson. He called his new detective over.

'Yes, Sir.'

Mahoney spoke softly and kept his shoulders relaxed; he didn't want this to be a telling off, and he tried to show that.

'Great work at Opossum Bay this morning. I appreciated you getting the information to me promptly. It made interviewing the Cheungs much easier.'

'No worries.' Gibson's eyes were bright and his head up.

'There is always room for initiative, no doubt about that. Your go-ahead attitude on this one is already being mentioned. DS Kendall liked your work at Kingston.'

Gibson looked to be fighting a swell of pride, and his boss knew the next comment would be a sucker punch.

'But I think she'd agree with me that the Cortese episode was a bit of a stuff-up.'

'Yeah, it was. I just don't know much about the history stuff yet.'

'That's not what I meant.' Mahoney's tone was a bit gruffer, but his posture was still relaxed. 'I'm referring to the guy being here in this room.'

'But Doctor Pitney brought him in.'

'So?'

'She's on the case, and that.' There was doubt creeping into his voice.

'No, she's not.'

'But ...'

'But me no buts, DC Gibson.' The reversion to title was a verbal slap. 'She is the pathologist contracted to the Police Department. She is not a member of the investigative team. Therefore, whatever her level of excellence, she is not entitled to waltz in here without my express permission. We may invite her in, but that's it. She and us are interdependent but theoretically independent. Get it?'

'Got it.'

'Good. As for her bringing Cortese in, I can't begin to bore you with the issues of protocol there. Don't get me wrong, he's good. But he is an outsider. Just because Pitney likes him, it doesn't mean we have to lay out the red carpet.'

'She's keen on him?'

It was time to take the chat into his office.

'Put it this way, I doubt her effusiveness vis-a-vis the good Signor is purely professional. Call me cynical, but there's enough to be sceptical about.'

'Sorry, I didn't see that.'

'That's alright. Sometimes we don't.'

'Thanks, boss.'

'Now, to Cortese. I have the authority to bring him in as a consultant. You don't. Therefore, I have to make the decision before he has all the intel he saw on the board. What if he wasn't brought in by me and he took off with all that stuff in his head? He could talk to anybody, including the media.'

'But he wouldn't do that.'

'Why not? Because he's one of us? Like I said, he isn't. That's the point. We have to control the flow of information for all sorts of operational and legal reasons. It transpires that he checks out and will be useful to us. The cold reality is that we have to *use* people to get where we want to be. It's perfectly okay because it's not for personal benefit. It's so we can get the job done. Does that make sense?'

His blinking slowed for a touch as the information sank in. 'Just because I think they're on our side, I shouldn't be overfamiliar. Yes, it makes sense.'

'Good. Run things by me or Kate for the time being. I don't want you to crawl. Keep running, but just watch out for stumbles. There's a lot to be aware of. Use your initiative as you have been doing. But keep your eyes wide open. okay?'

'Yes, Sir. No worries. I was a bit too keen maybe.'

'Maybe.' Mahoney led his DC back into the incident room. 'Anything on the van?'

'Zero. Nobody clocked a numberplate. We don't even have a clear idea on the make. There's no business listed as "Electric Eric" or anything similar. None of the other firms or contractors have heard of it.'

'Get an officer back down there and speak to Boxhall and the couple at the shop. Get them to recall as much as they can about the van they saw: size, shape, what they remember about the signage on the exterior—stencil size, lettering, anything they can think of. Get an image made up and we'll go with a public appeal through the media. What about Newcrest?'

'Dunstan's all over that, Sir.' Gibson pointed to the officer who was scanning a computer monitor.

'Right. Sort the van stuff and I'll talk to Dunstan. Oh yeah, one more thing: Hellyer's mobile. Alice Cheung received a text on Friday evening from the victim's phone. He wouldn't have sent it himself, I'm guessing, so how did his killer do it?'

'Must have known the four-digit code.'

'How?'

'Observation. Yours, I think, is 1-4-7-8.'

Mahoney's eyes were saucers. 'How do you know that? You're not hacking me, are you?'

'Just a little observation game I play. It's not that hard to follow the pattern that people swipe or tap. You go vertically down the left and then across with your right index finger. Simple.'

It surely was. Mahoney realised he'd been tapping a capital L for Loser. Time for a change.

'Are we still meeting as a group this afternoon?' asked Gibson.

Mahoney checked his watch; it was after five already. Shit. He still had the Forensics material to read, assuming it had been done. Where did that day just go? He called out to the room.

'Guys, good work today. We'll leave the round-up for now. Meet again tomorrow morning at eight. We can gather our thoughts then. If you've got somewhere to be, then go.'

There were a few nods, but everyone continued what they were doing. Not a bad sign.

Mahoney headed over to Dunstan. 'Andrew, anything?'

The burly officer held up a sheaf of papers. 'Would you like the short version?'

'Yes, I think so.'

'Nothing. I mean it's all quite interesting in terms of a business model. Sound investment strategy. They were good on the public consultation process. Really ticked all the boxes. Nothing untoward at all. Textbook stuff.'

'Bugger.'

'Well, it is for us. Hellyer's death will require some corporate tinkering, but there doesn't seem to be anything here that opens up a window on that death.'

Mahoney hoped Cortese would shed more light. It was still early days but the longer the clock ticked, the shorter the fuse.

CHAPTER NINE

Mike Kitchener from the Forensics team rang. A report on the crime scene at Opossum Bay wouldn't be ready until the morning. His preliminary findings weren't anything to write home about, he'd admitted. The pool of congealed blood on the floor did indicate a time of death earlier in the weekend. There were traces left by bodies other than Hellyer but that's all they were. No identifiable links to actual people. Of course, those traces were catalogued and could be matched against any suspects later on. The investigative team just needed to dig up those suspects.

Mahoney thanked him and decided to call it a day; there was little to be done that couldn't wait till morning, and he had promised his partner he would be free this evening. The peak hour traffic to Kingston had subsided so his run up the Southern Outlet was brisk. He took the exit for Tolmans Hill and wound his Toyota round Woodcutters Road to Susan Hart's address. As he got out of the car, he tried to leave his detective persona in the driver's seat. A homicide case could be all-consuming but he wanted—*needed* perhaps—to have a personal life and leave the blood and guts shut outside. It was a forlorn hope.

They were coming up for almost two years together; a few potholes had been negotiated and they seemed to be in a good place together. He was gradually getting better at going with the flow. In this part of his life he'd realised there was little to worry about if he decided not to worry—not an easy thing for a man so used to turning things over in his mind.

Almost as soon as he was inside he felt relaxed. She was pleased to see him and he was glad to be here. He knew domestic life couldn't always be as solid as it was for Ruth Rendell's good old Inspector Wexford. One thing a lot of writers did get right with their fictional detectives, though, was the depiction of pressure. Even in his hometown he'd witnessed the debilitating effect of the job on colleagues, so if a detective in Edinburgh or Los Angeles drank too much to help block out the detritus, it was believable. Alcohol was not really an option for him. He was certainly not teetotal, but he'd found he couldn't function even at half-speed if he'd had too much booze the night before. A glass of wine or two, but that was the limit when he was on a case. He didn't need a furry head to go with a furry tongue.

It wasn't till after the meal that the subject of work was broached. He was stacking the dishwasher when Susan brought it up.

'Is this one a triple A?'

'Looks it. What's come through to your lot?'

Hart was a journalist at the *Mercury* newspaper. They did their best to demarcate their professions, but he'd learned that he could trust her. Her loyalty to him overrode any instinct as a newshound. Besides, she was back to editing the weekend lifestyle magazine, and her fellow crime reporter also acknowledged the boundaries.

'Suspicious death. Notable businessman. Awaiting a fuller briefing from the constabulary,' she replied.

Mahoney returned to the dining room table and gave her an edited version of that fuller briefing.

She sipped some Riesling. 'Whoever did it knew plenty about him. The tennis bit particularly.'

'How so?'

'You know how I played a lot of competitive tennis in my youth?'

He didn't know that, must have missed that bit. 'Yes, I think you've told me.'

'I was pretty good. Made the Wilson Cup team two years in a row.'

'How did you fare?'

'Very good down here. Different story at the National Champion-ships. It put all my hopes in perspective. One sixteen-year-old from Queensland walloped me in straight sets. Needless to say, she kicked on and I opted for university.'

'Still, it must have been great to get that far.'

'It was. Hours of practice and years of fun in the sun. We had a ball … pardon the pun. Tournaments, camps, trips away. That's how I knew Scott Hellyer.'

'Really? He did all that?'

'Oh yes. He had lots of coaching, the best racquets and flash gear. A bit of a hotshot in many ways, on our little circuit anyway.'

'So he was good? Aside from looking the part.'

'Very much so. But, like all of us, once he got to the nationals he'd get smashed against the seeds. He kept playing club pennants. Once you saw the difference in standards, you realised pretty quickly that the path to professionalism was just too steep. Still, as you said, it was a good way to spend your teenage years. It gives you a confidence that you carry into the other phases of your life.'

'I guess that was the case for him.'

'Undoubtedly. Mind you, he didn't need too much of a boost. Good-looking and funny. His parents thought the sun shone out of him.'

'Golden child?'

'For sure. Scott had an elder sister but you wouldn't know she existed. She didn't play tennis. You never heard anything much about her. His parents came to all the tournaments and it was Scott, Scott, Scott. He got all the attention.'

Mahoney felt the detective creeping out of the car, but tried to keep the conversation casual. 'Mmmmm, the special one. I wonder what happened to the sister. It must be hard to put up with all that in a family.'

'I'd imagine so, but it doesn't seem to have unhinged her. She's now the Federal Commissioner for Equal Opportunity. One of our heroes.' She patted her chest and smiled. 'The sisterhood, that is. I doubt the old buffoons in their grey suits are as impressed by her.'

'She's Gail Ogle?'

'Yes. Didn't anyone tell you?'

Mahoney shook his head. 'Hellyer's estranged wife mentioned only that the parents had passed away—some sort of motor accident I think it was. No mention of a sister. Bit curious.'

'Perhaps. But finding out the father of your kids is dead wouldn't help the mental processes.'

Mahoney stored his new knowledge away: a task for the morning. For now it was more important to find out if Susan still had any of her tennis dresses stored away.

CHAPTER TEN

The morning briefing was a consolidation of progress made. There was a consensus that the killer had a deep personal motive for the murder, and that none of the persons interviewed thus far seemed to have that motivation. If anything, despite the incongruities of their personal relationships, they would all much prefer Scott Hellyer to be alive.

The forensics report was detailed, a marvel of technical ingenuity, and it reinforced what they knew already. Hellyer had been executed sometime on the Friday evening, after dusk and before midnight. Analysis of his stomach contents and blood showed traces of Rohypnol in sufficient quantity to have rendered him defenceless. He'd presumably ingested it from a laced stubby of beer found at the scene, although the bottle had been wiped clean of any prints.

Mahoney had delegated the task of bringing the group up to speed to Kendall. She concluded the summary with the acknowledgement that some material at the crime scene did not match clothes or samples belonging to the deceased.

'All evidence is secure at the New Town Lab, and whoever we run down can be matched later. As the boss is going to say, we need to unearth some persons of interest.'

She resumed her seat and Mahoney took centre stage; he knew he had to work the latent enthusiasm in the room. It was always akin to a coach addressing his team. The result they craved was never in dispute—to apprehend the killer—and to do so required each member to focus on the process. Forensics were like the backroom medical staff of an elite sports club: incredible support, but the detectives in this room were the players who could really determine the outcome. They must be simultaneously geared up for the challenge and reminded of the necessity of covering all the bases. Perspiration and inspiration. His gaze swept the room. All eyes were on him.

'This execution is deeply personal. It matters a great deal to the perpetrator that it was done in a specific way. We have been fortunate to secure the services of an expert profiler, one Adriano Cortese. You may have seen him in here yesterday. He's down from Melbourne to help us understand the psychology of this crime. His initial report will be available later this afternoon. Please do not share any of his thinking with anyone outside this room. The same rules apply as for any information we use on any case. Our employment of a profiler is staying in-house. We don't need the media going off on some Hannibal Lecter fantasy. My view is that his input will be crucial. We have a cruel and unusual act. It has to be admitted that this is not your run-of-the-mill criminal. We have to proceed as per our regular strategy, but solving this requires an X-factor. I'm confident Cortese will provide that.'

Mahoney stepped sideways to the Perspex board and tapped the photo of Hellyer trussed up on the beams. 'This man was killed for a very particular reason. By process of elimination, we need to discover that reason. His ex-wife did say he was something of a philanderer, but this doesn't look like the work of a cuckolded husband. It's too extreme. Hellyer was conducting an affair with Alice Cheung but her husband is a very unlikely suspect. Firstly, he doesn't seem overly fussed that it was going on. Secondly, and more crucially, Hellyer was an important business partner in the golf course development. Cheung has a lot to lose from this death.'

Mahoney raised his arm again to indicate a digitally enhanced photo of a white van.

'Whoever was driving this vehicle over summer, and especially on Friday evening, is our guy. A hell of a lot of planning went into this venture. Gathering exactly forty-eight brand new tennis balls to be belted at Hellyer, scoping the place out, knowing about Alice Cheung, sussing out the victim's favourite brand of beer ...' He slapped the board with the back of his hand. 'A masterclass in planning.'

Mahoney looked to find Gibson. 'David, can you share your earlier thoughts.'

Gibson stayed seated but swivelled around to address the group. 'Hellyer weighed in at eighty four kilos, so to manipulate that dead weight must have taken some strength. We can assume the killer offered Hellyer the stubby that was laced with Rohypnol, so perhaps they had a beer together. Boxhall, the neighbour, is pretty sure it was not a female he saw driving the van. Without being sexist, you'd think it was a male who was doing all this.'

'It does make sense,' interrupted Mahoney. 'Sometimes we have to make assumptions. Do we have anything more on this van?'

Dunstan raised his hand. 'As you can all see from the image on the board, we've pieced together a fair idea of what it looked like. Mr Boxhall and the couple from the shop went through various permutations with one of our techies. It looks like it was a Ford Transit van, late model. No idea on number plates unfortunately. One other resident I spoke to on the phone earlier today noted down the mobile number printed underneath the Electric Eric logo. Said she wanted some work done. I tried the number but got a "not in use" message.'

'So, he makes the van look authentic but doesn't want anybody making contact.'

'Yes, Sir. It looks that way. I've put the vehicle details out on social media, and there's a segment organised for the television and radio today. As soon as we're done here, I'll go through hire companies and the auction sites to try and trace it. Constable Herrick is going to comb through the records for traffic infringements and stolen vehicles.'

'Good man. Okay, Sergeant Kendall has the remainder of the tasks for today. Check in with her once I've finished speaking. Some if it is humdrum. Tracing the ropes, tennis balls, beer stubbies and so on. Quite possibly thankless, but it needs to be done. We developed some momentum on the back of this sort of fact-checking yesterday. Let's keep it up. Anything that jumps out, anything at all, let either Kate or I know. Same bat-time, same bat-channel, tomorrow.'

Officers resumed their work stations and started working the phones. Mahoney turned his back on them to consider the board. *What did you do, Hellyer? What did you do for someone to believe you deserved this? Who did you drive so far down the road that they could imagine such an act?* The input from Cortese looked to be increasingly important.

CHAPTER ELEVEN

'Thank you for acceding to my request, Inspector.' Cortese was standing next to Hellyer's BMW on the gravel outside the house of horrors. 'This viewing will augment the information I have gleaned from the various reports.'

Was it a profiler thing to be lexically ornate? Mahoney did wonder if the incomer was taking the politeness aspect just a little too far, or maybe it was all part and parcel of the man's persona. Fashionably attired, immaculately groomed and smoothly spoken. Even his e-cigarette looked designer made.

The request to personally view the crime scene had come right after the morning briefing, and Mahoney had agreed immediately. The drive down had been quick: minimal traffic on a cloudless day. In other circumstances it would have been a pleasant jaunt, but not today. As Mahoney drove he shared the salient facts of what the investigative team had learned. For his troubles he got some nods and an occasional 'indeed' from the passenger seat. Only on the final stretch, past Clifton Beach, did Cortese sit up and show an interest. Mahoney was sharing the tennis conversation from the night before, but saying he couldn't see why the victim being good at tennis was that interesting. Sure,

Hellyer was tortured with tennis balls, but wasn't that merely a nifty way to inflict damage?

'You don't wait decades to avenge a straight sets loss in a junior tennis match,' Mahoney commented to his passenger.

Cortese didn't sound so sure on that point. 'I think the lawn tennis feature is one of the most important aspects of this case. It's about families, Inspector. As Tolstoy said, "Happy families are all alike; every unhappy family is unhappy in its own way."'

Cortese did not expand on his comment as they entered Opossum Bay, and remained silent until they reached the house.

As they stood at the rear of the dwelling, Mahoney asked, 'Is there anything you can determine out here? I mean, any more information you need?'

'No, thank you. Access to the stage is what I now require.'

Once inside Mahoney assumed the position he'd stood in with Kendall two days before. From there he watched the profiler walk through a choreographed routine. As he did so, Cortese voiced several observations onto a hand-held digital recorder. After fifteen minutes or so he stopped and joined Mahoney, who waited for enlightenment.

'The good news is that you don't have to unduly rush your investigation.'

'Meaning?'

'It will be at least a week, possibly a fortnight, before the next execution. This murder doesn't have to be solved today.'

Cortese looked completely serious, and Mahoney decided he wasn't being wound up.

'Your reasoning being?'

'Nowhere near as complicated as you might imagine. You know most of what I'm drawing from this scene already. You already know the perpetrator to be an intelligent, calm and patient person. The planning took weeks, months probably. This is an individual who functions successfully in our society, holds a position of responsibility and is financially comfortable. He is either divorced or never married. I'm inclined to the former. His occupation affords him sufficient time to undertake reconnaissance. Self-employed I would say, possibly a business consultant. He is in his forties, physically very capable and, to all intents and purposes, quite sane.'

'Take me though it.'

'The intelligence and patience you already understand.'

'Yes, it's a meticulously planned and methodically executed crime.'

'Then you comprehend that this man has a good job and moves easily in our society. The anger behind this crime has been kept in check for a lengthy period. He is raging internally, but that rage is controlled. Even here, in the throes of the act, he is purposeful and calculating. The killer blow is not delivered until the theatrical construct has been played out.'

'You mean that even at the climax of this scene he never actually lost it?'

'Correct. When you find this man—and you will—it will be a complete surprise to those who interact with him every day. They will never have witnessed him losing his temper. He is very controlled.'

What Mahoney was hearing tallied with what Kate had said on seeing the body. More importantly, it fit with the evidence of the scene.

'Why will he kill again?'

'Because it is not this victim who must be eradicated. It is the revenge tragedy in the perpetrator's consciousness that must be played out. His retribution is, I believe, linked to what Hellyer represented. There will be another like Hellyer who needs to be vanquished. The killer's crusade is deeply personal to him. Whoever is the next victim in his sights has been selected, not because of a personal dislike, but because that person is emblematic of the problem.'

'That problem being …?'

'Something I must think further on.'

'Fair enough.' Mahoney glanced at the beautifully crafted rafters in the ceiling space. 'How do we know that the perp's got money?'

Cortese looked askance. 'Think, Inspector. Our man drives a late model largish van. It wouldn't have been stolen because the owner would have alerted your colleagues, and it's unlikely to be hired. No, he has purchased this van and, crucially, he has somewhere to park it where it won't garner undue attention. Therefore, I conclude he has access to a parking bay that is not part of his primary residence. Attached to a rental property perhaps.'

'Terrific. That makes sense. And he'll do something like this again you think?'

'Certainly. He wants to be recognised. Presently, he has the upper hand. Nobody knows it is he, the intelligent one, who is behind this. The satisfaction of carrying this off is partial. The conveying of an indisputable message to the deceased is also not enough. He must be recognised as a force to be reckoned with. He craves that. Craves your respect, Inspector. You will recognise his brilliance. A recognition that has been denied him for much of his life.'

'So, he is a nutter then.'

Cortese laughed. 'Perhaps.'

□

On the return journey Mahoney quizzed his passenger. 'What led you down this path? Not just boredom with private practice I'd guess.'

'That is a correct assessment. I may have misled you yesterday. Helping members of the public modify their thinking is worthy in itself, and there is a good living to be made. And the government supports people through the Mental Health Scheme, so there is less reluctance for those experiencing anxiety and depression to seek help.' Cortese turned his gaze inside the vehicle. 'But I wished to resume academic research. A fellowship at Victoria University became available and I saw my chance.'

'He who hesitates …'

'… forsakes the opportunity. Forensic psychology is of increasing interest to undergraduates. Qualified lecturers were thin on the ground a decade ago. I wouldn't say I surfed the zeitgeist but the timing of my move was fortuitous.'

Mahoney decreased the car's speed as they cruised through Lauderdale. 'Has television sparked that interest in students?'

A small raising of the eyebrows. 'No doubt. And it is not necessarily a bad thing. One would also hope David Attenborough's documentaries have spurred a generation to see the biological sciences in a new light. I like watching Tony Hill on television as much as anyone and if a fictional profiler stimulates interest, it would be churlish to ignore it. The effect, whatever the cause, is beneficial. The sooner we reconfigure the dark arts and begin to comprehend the complexity of our minds the better.'

'Agreed. You could pop down there sometime.' Mahoney pointed to his left where the Police Training Academy sat stolidly on a headland. 'Guest lecturers are always welcomed.'

'I shall. Once I have helped you with our conundrum.'

'Great. I'll give you the contacts and set something up. It would be beneficial for the cadets to hear from a practitioner in the field. Textbooks are all well and good, but real experience is gold. I reckon you'd present a good lecture.'

'I trust so. I've witnessed some of the best.'

'Whereabouts? In the States?'

'Precisely. I utilised an overseas study grant to spend six months at the FBI's justifiably famous Behavioural Sciences Unit at Quantico. It was the most intense period of my life. My knowledge and methodology improved immeasurably.'

'I assume you have an established procedure. That isn't a piss-take. I just want to know how best to mesh things together.'

'No offence taken. Your willingness to involve me is commendable. It's much better than being left on the periphery.' He sat a little straighter in the bucket seat. 'Some of these elements have been covered slightly out of order but at least they're being implemented.' He tapped the dashboard as he specified the stages. 'First, I evaluate the criminal act and the specifics of the crime scene. Then, I evaluate the preliminary police reports and the autopsy protocol. And there is also analysis of the victim. We have, to a greater or lesser degree, been doing those first five stages. Naturally, I will need to revisit that material and keep up-to-date with developments in the investigation.'

'Of course. Hang on a sec, this is a bugger of a roundabout.' Mahoney took a gap in the Mornington traffic and shot through to the Tasman Highway. After he'd eased across the feeder lane, he was free to concentrate again. 'Then comes?'

'I develop a profile with an outline of the critical offender characteristics, and make some suggestions for the investigation on the basis of that profile.'

'Which you've been doing already back at the house. Even your informal observations are an eye-opener.'

'Thank you.' The profiler's eyes widened as the car crested Rosny Hill. The bridge was in the foreground with Government House standing regally on the hill behind. Mount Wellington loomed in the distance. 'My word, that is an arresting sight. I arrived in the dark on Sunday night. I missed this spectacle.'

'I suppose you're right. You get used to it, I guess. Now, where would you like to work today? You're welcome to use my office to write up your findings. You'll have access to all the relevant material and I'll sort out one of my officers as a liaison type.'

'You won't be needing the space?'

'Not till much later this afternoon. If I spend too long in there, I atrophy. The leads we need aren't in the incident room. I'll be out talking and chasing things down.'

'Then I accept your offer.' Cortese glanced at his watch: a Breitling no less, the DI noted. 'It is almost midday. I can have a preliminary document available for you at five o'clock.'

'That will be perfect.'

CHAPTER TWELVE

'Early lunch suit you?' asked Mahoney. He had decided to catch up with Kendall in the central business district.

'Sure. I rushed out the house this morning without even a coffee.'

They walked half a block up Collins Street and into the Fullers Bookshop Café. Tables were at a premium but Kendall saw a couple of elderly ladies leaving one. She grabbed it while Mahoney ordered drinks and muffins.

'How did things go at Tiger? Was the Jones woman in?'

'She was, but it was pretty much as yesterday. No great insights, but I do have Hellyer's desk diary. What about Cortese?'

'Different story there. That is one switched-on guy. He's a bit foppish, but his being in town is the best break we've had thus far.' He related their profiler's thoughts.

Kendall pursed her lips. 'That is insightful. The bit about Hellyer being a representative of something is interesting. It fits with the one useful thing Jennifer Jones told me.'

'Which was?'

'Hellyer has really tidied up his act in recent times. She's worked pretty closely with him for six or seven years now. When he initially got the job she was expecting a bit of a smart aleck, bit of a sleaze, someone in the job for the benefits more than anything.'

'I'm sensing a "but"?'

Kate smiled. 'But he turned out to be a big asset. Tiger Brewing were new to Hobart eight years ago. They're well established up north, and they decided to set up an office here to boost market share. Jones was here from the start and the first eighteen months were tough. Then Head Office got Hellyer in as a marketing manager. He worked hard and implemented clever campaigns. He didn't hit on colleagues and didn't seem to have any kind of negative reputation.'

Mahoney dabbed at some crumbs on his plate. 'Model employee. Doesn't quite tally with what Sophie Hellyer told you.'

'No, it doesn't. Gibson visited her while I went to the Tiger office. He told her it was a courtesy call to check how she was getting on.'

'Nice move.'

'It was. Mind you, he did sanction it with me first.' She paused for a second or two. 'By the way, have you had words with him recently?'

'I may have. Was his manner rather formal this morning?'

'Pretty much. Straight down the line.'

'He's still finding his way. He'll settle. It doesn't seem to have dampened his initiative.'

'Not at all. He called me while I was waiting for you and told me a few things about his visit. Mrs Hellyer is coping. The funeral is scheduled for tomorrow, unless we object.'

'That should be fine. Pitney is dealing with the coroner. We'll attend. There may be something of interest and it's nice to show some support.'

'It's to be held at Turnbull's in Letitia Street at ten o'clock tomorrow morning.'

'Lock it in. And the other things?'

'About Hellyer's family. His parents died in an automobile accident seven years ago. The coroner's verdict was that the father nodded off at the wheel and their Lexus veered across the Midland Highway into an oncoming semitrailer. Both the driver and his wife were confirmed dead at the scene.'

'Christ, that's horrible. I think I remember the Automobile Club lobbying for protective barriers in the aftermath.' Mahoney massaged his temples. 'And that was when their son decided to start taking his career seriously?'

'The prodigal son grew up.'

'And what about this elder sister Susan told me about?'

'This is interesting. According to Sophie Hellyer, she barely knew her husband's sister existed. Her husband never mentioned her and she wasn't at their wedding twenty-five odd years ago. But she was at the parents' funeral, and that's when the estrangement ceased. She never became a visitor at Christmas, but she and Scott did maintain regular contact, Sophie thought. She is that Gail Ogle.'

'So Hellyer, influenced by a sudden jolt as to our mortality, initiated a new phase in his life. He worked harder, then success in other areas of his professional life followed. Fronting the golf course for instance.' A few stray crumbs brushed off the table and he dropped them on his plate. 'Did Mrs Hellyer happen to say if his recreational activities altered?'

'Funnily enough, yes. One of the first things she did was to apologise to Gibson for giving us too strong an impression that her husband played around. Apparently after the death of his parents he knuckled down at home as well. Drove the children to their sports activities at all hours. Came home straight after work on a Friday.'

'Wow. He was reformed. And they still split?'

'Ah, well. She explained it was mutual. They had grown tired of each other and, once the children left the nest, there wasn't much to keep them together. All quite placid.'

Mahoney swirled the remains of his cup and sipped some cold coffee. 'It is rare for anybody to deserve to die. It appears more and more certain that Scott Hellyer certainly didn't call for his fate. Thinking aloud here, and borrowing heavily from Cortese, but it looks like our victim is dead because he fits the strange schema for our killer.'

'Granted, but what do we do to catch him?'

Mahoney stood. 'Find that bloody van.'

□

As they were leaving the café Mahoney's mobile phone rang. He tapped his sergeant on the arm in a gesture to wait, then bit the side of his lower lip as he listened intently.

'That was Dunstan. Someone needs to bottle his research skills. He's a gun.'

'What's he found this time?'

'Only a lead on that ruddy van. We'll get my car and shoot up there.'

'Where? And where's your car?'

'Just round the corner. After I dropped Cortese off at the office, I couldn't be stuffed walking so I drove.'

From the parking meter in Victoria Street Mahoney drove his still newish Toyota out of the CBD and up to South Hobart. En route he instructed Kendall on the personnel she should call. If this was the van, immediate scrutiny was required. Just short of the soccer stadium he turned right and took the car down a side street that became a bridge over the Hobart Rivulet. On the other side of the stream in the lea of the wooded hill was a large corrugated iron warehouse. They stopped right in front of a portable office. As they got out, a woman in blue King Gee clothing and a green high-vis jacket walked across to them with a clipboard in her left hand—the art of always looking busy.

'I'm Jill Hansen. Are you the police? You're pretty quick.'

Mahoney did the introductions. 'I hear you've got a vehicle that's unaccounted for?'

'Yep. And it's a bit suspicious.' She walked them briskly into the warehouse: concrete floor, steel girders and a few skylights in the high ceiling. Even with the mild autumn weather, the temperature inside wasn't all that welcoming. Mahoney supposed the eclectic collection of vehicles didn't mind the cold; he guessed there must be almost a hundred automobiles of varying types parked in front of them.

They walked down a transit lane and Kendall asked, 'Whose are all these? They don't look like work vehicles.'

'Because they're not.' Hansen's tone was curt. She made it sound as if she was being distracted from important work in her cabin— more like she didn't like having to leave the radiator that was no doubt by her desk. 'Private ownership. Whole lot of reasons they're here. Cars confiscated from the anti-hooning legislations, some impounded 'cause the owner's run foul of you lot, and a few that were in the wrong place.' She halted at a white van. 'Like this one.'

'Are you state government?' asked Mahoney.

'Nah, private contractor. Some Greek guy with a big shed and nothing to use it for owns it. The three city councils and the State government pay to store motors like this here. How's that for a piss-easy way to make money.'

The detectives agreed.

'How did this van get here?

Hansen checked her clipboard. 'Hobart City Council responsibility. Collected from Salamanca Place at five forty-six on Saturday morning. No attempt to contact owner.'

'Because there aren't any rego plates?'

'Yep. Reckon so. Brought up here by Ferguson Towing and dropped off at ten past six. Been here since then.'

Mahoney nodded to her notes. 'Any parking tickets on the windscreen or a voucher on the dashboard?

'Nup. You know all I do. That it?'

Obviously the heater beckoned. 'That's fine. Ta. Can you direct our colleagues down here when they arrive, please. And make a photocopy of your paperwork.'

'All right. Good luck with it.' She set off back to her own compact little headquarters.

Kendall circled the van; it looked to be the make they were after. 'No plate on the rear either.'

'Clever way of doing it.'

'Why not torch it?'

'He wants it to be found, I reckon. To let us know he's a step or two ahead.'

'Why Salamanca? It's a busy strip.'

'Not for cars on a Saturday. From half past five in the morning any car still there gets towed away. The whole roadway becomes the market. Plenty of warning signs, but a few still get caught out. Park there on a Friday evening, go out to the bars, have a few too many and cab it home. Come back too late the next day to collect the car and the council has had them dragged away.'

'Presumably he banked on that. Did the deed at Opossum Bay and dropped the van off minus the plates in the wee hours. No-one is contactable so it ends up here indefinitely.' She nodded to herself. 'Good plan.'

'It is. A beauty. And this place has served its purpose. He couldn't keep it where he'd been storing it before as it's now a liability. Needed to distance himself from it. If he'd lost it too far from the city, he would have had to get a taxi which is traceable. If an accomplice had collected him, then he would have had another person who could become a weak link. Dropping it at Salamanca meant someone else did the disposal for him. Rather neat.'

'It would still turn up but he got some distance from it. He could saunter off without attracting undue attention. What about his gear?'

'The gear he used at Hellyer's?'

'Yeah.'

'If it's not inside the van, it's been dumped somewhere within a fifty kilometre radius of Hobart.'

'Or he took it home.'

Footsteps echoed on the concrete behind them: Kitchener and Donna Givens from Forensic Services. 'Seems we're about to find out.'

Mahoney waved at them and shouted. 'Mike, drive your car in. Saves lugging all your stuff.'

Kitchener acknowledged that and they turned back; a couple of minutes later they parked nose up to the van and got out.

'John, Kate, how are you?'

'Optimistic.' Mahoney tilted his head to the Ford. 'Turn her inside out. I reckon this is the vehicle our guy used.'

Without any further chit-chat, the FSST officers suited up. Givens started on the exterior while her supervisor used a master key to open up the rear doors. The option of returning to base was open to the detectives but they remained—at least until some sign that this was a legitimate lead.

It didn't take long. Givens called them over to the side where she was tapping her gloved fingers on the upper rear panel. 'It's sticky to the touch. You can see how dust particles have attached to the residue.' She traced her finger along the sides of a rectangle. 'A latex film has recently been detached from the surface. Approximately a third of a metre high and one metre long. Probably a clear plastic background with the design stencilled on. It's a quick and effective alternative to spray painting on the duco.'

Kitchener clambered out of the rear and took a quick look. 'Sounds like what we're after. Look right to you?'

Mahoney agreed it did. 'Much inside?'

'To the naked eye, it's clean as a whistle. But don't worry, I'll find something.'

'Good. This has to be it. Mike, go through it like the proverbial. As soon as practicable check the engine and stuff. Even without the plates we can establish the provenance, as they say on the Antiques Roadshow.'

'No problem. We'll sort it. Where will you be?'

'Out and about. Ring anything through to HQ and ask for Constable Dunstan. He'll be working on a trace at our end.'

'Righto. Allow us a few hours. Talk later.'

'Thanks, Mike. Cheers, Donna.'

As they turned to leave, Mahoney held his head up and sniffed the cold air.

'Is that a whiff of progress, Sir?'

'It could well be.'

CHAPTER THIRTEEN

Mahoney turned the car back into Macquarie Street. There were a few patrons basking in the afternoon sun outside Ginger Brown Café. He recognised one man in an olive-green suit.

'Was that Rex Chambers over there?'

'Possibly,' replied Kendall. Her voice was dead flat and her eyes looked straight ahead.

'Want to stop?'

'No, thank you. I'd rather not see Rex-the-ex if that's okay with you.'

'Oh.'

There wasn't much he could say to that, so Mahoney remained quiet. It took till they were down to Molle Street for her to elaborate.

'The short version is that Rex is exploring his options and they don't necessarily include me.'

He slipped the car into the near left lane, turned down the hill and pulled into a car park next to an impressive triple-storey brick building.

'Is he leaving Internal Investigations? I thought he enjoyed scrutinising other police officers.'

His colleague sniffed, pulled out a tissue and gently blew her nose and wiped her eyes. Mahoney waited.

'I'm sorry, Sir. I thought I'd be fine.'

'That's okay. Take your time. I mean, we don't have to discuss it.'

'But I want to.' She looked through the windscreen. 'Can we walk on the rivulet trail for a bit?'

'Sure. Bit of a saunter can't hurt.'

Within moments they were on a tended gravel path going upstream, shaded by a grove of trees turning colour with the season. It was Mahoney's favourite time of year. Generally clear days with a crisp edge to the early mornings.

Kendall wiped her nose with another tissue. 'Do you remember the chat we had about relationships a while ago?'

How could he forget? Kate had been incredibly supportive as Mahoney tried to deal with a serious fissure in his own relationship with Susan. 'Yes, of course.'

'I might have been a bit assertive about my resilience that day. Rex has clearly indicated he's leaving and it's more upsetting than I thought it would be.'

'You don't have to be bulletproof. You have feelings. You can express them.'

'Thank you.' She smiled slightly. 'Do you want to know what he's up to?'

'You don't have to tell me. Your call.'

'He's taking a year's leave, without pay. Going up to Sydney to test his thespian ambitions … among other things.' The last phrase was squeezed out through a clenched jaw. Mahoney desperately tried to formulate a tactful question; Kendall continued before he could.

'He thinks he wants to join the other side.'

'Organised crime?'

Kendall laughed. 'Nice one, Sir. No, he, apparently, has long felt he is "not your average bear" so he's off to live in Sydney's inner-west to "explore that option". Leaves a girl feeling a teeny bit deficient.'

'Which you're not. You know that.'

'Sometimes I wonder. There's a side to this job that you don't see. Being a woman in this job can be wearing. Sexism lays not far below the surface. Nothing concrete, but there's always that feeling that if you don't stand to piss, you don't belong in the force. I deal with it. I have to. Rex was my buttress for some of that silliness. And now he's going.'

They turned and started walking back. 'Well, I can't solve much for you but you can rest assured that you're my best officer and you have my unqualified support.'

'Thank you. I do feel that and it's much appreciated. Don't worry, I'll get through this hiccup. We all have to dust ourselves off every now and then. Being right smack in the middle of a case will focus my thinking.'

'Works for me. Speaking of which, I'd better admit why I stopped down here.'

'So we could check out the Stensilset operation? I guessed that.'

Sprung again. 'Yeah, that's right. They've got most of the ground floor of that heritage building. According to Susan, they're the premier bunch for getting publicity banners and the like done. Could be that our guy used them.'

'That would be handy. A change from working our way through a pile of leads and not getting anywhere till the last but one.'

They headed back to the car park and went over to the display office entrance. Mahoney approached the receptionist and told her their business. She picked up her phone and, almost straightaway, a young male in denim jeans and a lurid t-shirt came into the room.

'Thanks, Josie. Hi guys. I'm Nick Marios. I do the designs for those types of clear stencils. What are you after?'

The detectives showed him their ID badges and Mahoney drew a shape in the air.

'Rectangular transferrable sticker you could put on a van. Working was pretty simple. "Electric Eric" on there for certain and a contact phone number. Made up sometime in the past six months.'

Marios went to a computer screen, logged on and brought up an image.

'That look right?'

'Yes, that's it. Did you meet the client?'

'No. It was an email query with the specifications. I mocked this up and the client agreed. I never met him.'

'He didn't come in?'

'Nup, all done electronically. Payment was into our business account at Westpac.'

'Electronic Funds Transfer?'

'Josie, how did this snoozer pay?'

The receptionist clicked into the accounts system. 'No record on our statement of a sender's account. So I guess he paid cash to the teller and told them our account details. That's it. Sorry.'

'No problem,' Mahoney assured her. To Marios, he asked, 'Are there any client details in your database?'

A few more clicks. 'Bit of a strange one. Original query and the agreement was via a gmail address. Once the payment was in our account, I gave the go-ahead for production. Couple of days later I sent an email letting him know and requesting delivery instructions.'

'And he sent you a post office box number. You sent them off in a carboard tube and later on when you followed up your message to the gmail account it bounced back.'

'Yeah, that's right, Inspector. Exactly that. Is this some sort of scam? The mobile number he gave for the signage doesn't work either.'

'It wouldn't. Just any old ten numbers that looks like a valid contact. Not your fault. Whoever did this worked out the best way of getting what he wanted while leaving almost no trail. I doubt very much there'll ever be any more work from Eric's business.' Mahoney scratched his scalp. 'If we can have the postage details and a printout of the design and your emails, that would be helpful. For all the good it will do, but we'd better give it a try. Australia Post will have some record, I hope.'

Kendall spoke to the receptionist. 'Josie, does it show what day the money went in?'

A lacquered fingernail traced down the screen. 'At the Sandy Bay branch of Westpac on the 4th of January this year. Into our account the next day.' She looked up and smiled. 'I hope that helps.'

Mahoney slapped the counter lightly. 'Thanks for your help. Please keep this confidential. We'll be in touch if anything else pops up.'

Once back in the car with the small sheaf of documents Kendall said, 'The PO box is Sandy Bay too. The Post Office is next to Dome Café and that oriental food shop.'

'Yeah, I know it. The Westpac branch is in Magnet Court so that's easy. Ready to go?'

'Yep.'

□

The high obtained from their luck at Stencilset lasted just over an hour. While Kendall checked the local bank, her boss took on the lead at the Post Office in King Street. They arranged to rendezvous in the Dome Café at around four o'clock.

Kendall was ordering a small pot of tea and considering an Anzac cookie when Mahoney entered, looking frustrated. She altered the order to a large pot with two cups and joined him at the semi-enclosed booth near the far window. 'You look like you had as much joy as me.'

'Most likely. How was the bank?'

'Bit of a dead end. I spoke to the manager, Clark Haas. A tall guy with a solid jaw, and boy, could he use it. I got a full history of how his is the highest performing branch in the state. No shrinking violet that one. We had to wait for a bit in his office to speak to the teller … sorry, *customer relations officer.*' She paused as the tea was served. 'Anyway, the bank does have excellent security, including a schmick new set of digital recording cameras.'

Mahoney poured his beverage and waited for the 'but'.

'But any records for January have been wiped. Haas was very helpful though. He brought up the data for January 4th. He found the transaction and identified the employee who received it. Got her in and explained what I wanted.'

'And ...?'

'She was as much use as she could be. She confirmed it was her transaction, but she couldn't remember anything unusual. The guy paid four hundred and fifty dollars cash into the Stencilset account. The depositor wouldn't have needed ID. He would have been given a receipt, but there's no record of who he could be.'

'It was over two months ago, and if he was a nondescript sort of bloke on a busy day after the Christmas and New Year break ...'

'That's what she said. Almost word for word. She's got no idea if she's seen him since because she barely remembers the first encounter. So, he's not a regular customer. How did you fare?'

He took a mouthful of tea, then snorted his frustration. 'Worse, if anything. The bank not having anything is understandable, but the Post Office should. And they didn't. The procedure for securing a PO box is simple and, you'd assume, foolproof.'

'Don't you just go in, provide a valid ID, set up a payment and you're good to go? Assuming there is a box free at that branch.'

Mahoney opened his hands. 'Exactly. And what happened next door? Our chap circumvents it.'

'How?'

'Used a stolen driver's licence as I found out. It's taken a few calls but here's the gist. The man who set up the post box did it on the 4th of January. As we've already said, a busy day after the holiday break. Lots of small businesses opening their doors for the new year of trading. The clever bugger chose that day.'

Mahoney poured more tea into his cup. 'The account was set up under the name of Gary Oates, as per the plastic ID card. And, before you ask, I have contacted Mr Oates. He had been blissfully unaware that his driving licence was missing until he came back in early January from a week on a friend's boat and found it among his mail at the family home. He assumed he'd misplaced it and that a do-gooder had returned it to the address on the card. Thought no more of it.'

'Really?'

'Yeah. Sounded perfectly genuine. How often do you check if you have your licence on you?'

'Never. Unless I'm doing something that requires an ID validation.' Kendall's eyes narrowed. 'This may mean our man looks like Oates.'

'The Australia Post employee does remember the actual transaction. She checked the photo and apparently made a comment to the guy, along the lines of how much a holiday beard changes one's looks. The customer kept a straight face and said he was on long service leave so he was having a break from his razor.'

'And she accepted that?'

'No real reason not to. It was a busy morning and the guy otherwise looked like the photo. Bear in mind the image on your licence is thumbnail size. It was astute of her to even notice the difference.'

'Would she recall enough of this customer for an identikit?'

'Possibly. She's agreed to come in early tomorrow morning and sit with one of the computer people. We could get some decent images: a bearded and a clean-shaven version. The Oates chap agreed to pop in as well so we could photograph him and see if that jogged the Post Office lady's memory.'

'That's good of him.'

'Sounded like a good guy. I explained that his licence is part of identity theft so he's keen to help us as much as possible.'

'Am I right to presume the PO box next-door is no longer linked to our person of interest?'

'You are. The guy asked for a one month trial, paid cash and hasn't been seen since. The whole thing has lapsed.'

Kendall's brow furrowed. 'This seems like an awful lot of bother to avoid picking up the stencils in person. Almost a bit over-the-top.'

'I agree. The whole process is over-the-top: the van at Salamanca, the tennis balls … This guy is painstaking in everything he does. The only blip—and it's tiny—is what we discovered this afternoon. We now know of someone who has actually spoken to him. But all that tells us is that he's around six foot and has dark hair. He may or may not have a beard, and he might look a bit like Oates. It ain't much.'

Mahoney's phone buzzed. He took the call, sat into the backrest, listened and rolled his eyes once or twice.

'That was Kitchener calling from the van. We still ain't got much. A few fibres and prints but no matches at all. It has been cleaned very thoroughly. The cab, in particular, is pristine.'

Kendall tapped the table. 'It's like the Fotheringham case then. The more expert the method, the narrower the range of suspects. That's something.'

'Cortese did say it would be a very particular individual we're looking for.'

'So it becomes a matter of when.'

'At the moment I'm kind of hoping he reveals himself at tomorrow's funeral. And dances on the grave.'

CHAPTER FOURTEEN

Mahoney had intended to let Gibson down gently, explaining to him that he was required elsewhere so his presence at the funeral wouldn't be necessary. But the young blood nut had taken it well. He said he was fine with overseeing the identikit process and reckoned it would be better for him to gain some first-hand experience in this area of investigations. He even suggested they ask the Westpac teller in as well. Reckoned she may not have remembered much yesterday, but today with the assistance of the facial imaging software could be a different story altogether. Mahoney could only agree.

'David, a couple of things to remember. Make sure the witnesses don't get a chance to meet. We can't afford for one to influence the other. That corrupts the process. The Post Office lady, Jill Ikin, is the first one in at half past nine. Get the lass from Westpac in later.'

'What's her name?'

'Umm, not sure. Kate will know so check with her before we leave this morning.'

'Sure. No problem.'

'Later on, after we've viewed the images, we can get them both back in and place the other witness's image in a catalogue of faces. See if anything comes of that.'

Gibson's hand went to the phone before he realised the tutorial wasn't quite finished. 'And the other thing?'

'Let the police artist direct the cognitive interview. You've got Mike Eather today. He's excellent with the little prompts that bring memories out.'

'Of course. That's a given. I'm riding shotgun. I know my place.' He gave his superior a grin that Mahoney couldn't decipher as knowing, cheeky or enthusiastic. He decided to let it slide.

Kendall was on the phone herself as Mahoney sauntered over.

'That was Sophie Hellyer with an offer of assistance.'

'Of what kind?'

'Unfortunately their son, Simon, can't get back from the Northern Hemisphere. It turns out he's not green keeping anymore. He tried out for some athlete development program at the university in Scotland. He did well at the interview but if he wants the scholarship on offer he has to card a number of good scores in a series of satellite tournaments. The first of three starts tonight, our time. If he misses any of the three weekend cuts, he's out, and the opportunity of the scholarship goes. Given he's classified as an overseas student the fees for study are horrendous. He wanted to come home anyway but his mother counselled against it.'

'She argued that his father would want him to pursue the scholarship?'

'Exactly that. Lord knows how the boy will go missing the funeral, but he's accepted her advice on two conditions. Firstly, his sister Maggie will read a short eulogy on his behalf. And secondly, the ceremony will be recorded so he can watch it properly in a few weeks.'

'Seems reasonable. Does the assistance have to do with the recording?'

'Yes. She's hired a specialist through the undertakers as part of the package. And—here she admits she may have watched too many English crime shows—she wondered if we wanted to send someone in civvies along to film the event as well. In case any suspicious figures turn up.'

Mahoney rubbed his hands together exuberantly. 'Brilliant. That really could work. Leave it with me.'

Overnight Mahoney had read Cortese's detailed analysis. A strong theme was that the perpetrator was seeking some sort of recognition. Of obvious concern was the profiler's belief the slaying at Opossum Bay would not be an isolated incident. And of immediate relevance this morning was the linked hypothesis that whoever did that deed would want to witness the full repercussions of his actions.

□

There's a funeral today: his funeral. From where I'm sitting you can see the melee of mourners swarming into the remembrance hall. Looks like Hellyer was well-liked, no Willie Loman. No long painstaking struggle to get anywhere in life for him. I wonder if amongst all the gush of the eulogy anyone will admit that he'd had it all gifted to him on a plate. Doubt it.

How I'd love to go in there and smack those hypocritical fools with a short sharp shock of reality. I bet someone, some guy in a smooth suit who drove here in a smart car, is claiming Scotty was a winner. A winner in the game of life. Right then I'd remind them what old Holden Caulfield reckoned about that. I always loved that bit where he puts scorn on that little dictum. Life is a game. Yeah, if you're on the side of the hotshots it's dandy. If you're on the other side, it's no game. Just a slow sad shuffle through the crap. I'd set them right on that.

And that's what I'm doing. Showing the smug ones that everyone counts. We all have a voice. It's taken a while for mine to be heard but they're paying attention now.

It's a risk being here, but an acceptable one. I thought about attending the service and loitering at the back, hanging around for the refreshments and having a look at the photos of his life pinned up on a board. Scotty as a junior sports champion. Scotty as a proud father. Scotty as a successful businessman. Scotty trussed up at his shack with a knife in his groin. The last one won't be there. Pity. Would 'make a statement' as they say.

Discretion overrode my curiosity to witness the send-off. The coppers would be there, hoping their prey will slip up. No chance. So I'm sitting in this pissy little corner shop across the road. Nursing a coffee and pretending to read the paper. Dressed in a flannel shirt and overalls looking like a tradie on his morning break. Bit of grease on my cheek and grubby hands. Nice touch that. Just another run-of-the-mill guy going through an ordinary day. Another poor sap. That's what the bitch behind the counter thought. Didn't even think I was worth chatting to. Don't know what she's got to be so snooty about. Stuck behind a counter in a shop so ratshit not even the wogs want to set up here. So stuff her.

Funnily enough, it was a funeral that kicked all this off. In June last year my mother went to her final resting place. Except she couldn't rest, could she. She'll still be fretting over something wherever she is. I was the only immediate family member left to organise everything. My father died three years ago. Adrian, my younger brother, no longer around either. Muggins got to sort it all out. We had a nice little ceremony at the Launceston Crematorium. Lots of people saying it was such a pity and they hoped I'd be okay. Haven't heard a peep from one of them since.

A month later, the crowning glory. Probate. Some joker from Perpetual Trustees informed me I was to receive the balance of the estate after the proceeds from the sale of the family home went to some research group for acquired brain injury. So I got a fifteen-year-old Nissan car and an assortment of goods and chattels. Stuff no sane person would want unless they fancy pokerwork. I considered contesting the will but let it go. It came to me that there was a better way of making people acknowledge your presence.

That's what I'm doing now. Leaving my footprint. People won't overlook it, that's for sure.

CHAPTER FIFTEEN

The detectives arrived half an hour before the designated start of the memorial service. Mahoney's feeling was that a large number of mourners would attend. Looking at that morning's paper and copies from the preceding three days, he saw that the initial announcement of Scott Hellyer's death had been posted on the Monday with details of the funeral placed in the following day's edition. On the Tuesday there were also quite a number of bereavement notices from extended family and friends, including a joint expression of sadness from the Cheungs—the DI could only wonder how the dynamics in that relationship were playing out. By Wednesday the stream had become a torrent, with expressions of sympathy filling almost four columns of the classifieds section: business associates, hospitality groups, sports clubs and old friends. The picture showed a man who was widely known and well regarded. Mahoney's revised impression was that Hellyer, despite some arrogance, was a figure who would be much missed by his community. Yet someone hated him enough to kill him.

Kendall found a parking spot at the bottom end of Wignall Street. As they crossed Letitia Street the funeral centre came into view from behind a row of oak trees. Constructed as the original

Hobart High School a century before, its architecture illustrated the changed nature of schools. Then, when not many continued their studies beyond their early teens, it had been the principal secondary school for the city. Over the next few decades other institutes and high schools were established but this remained the elite institution.

They walked up the steps and through the large sandstone arch of the official entrance. Off to the side of this grand centrepiece were some gaudy annexes, but nothing could dull the sense of grandeur once you were in the entrance hall. The current custodians, a funeral company, could not have selected a more suitable venue for services of the dead. Although secular in nature, it was a space that automatically made you consider your place in the greater scheme of things. The vaulted ceiling and generous proportions made the enormous room feel like a small cathedral.

Aside from a few Turnbull employees they were the first ones there. Kate turned to her boss. 'This must have been an imposing venue for school assemblies.'

'I'd imagine so. My uncle came here. He was pretty bright. This was all before the baby boom changed schooling in Hobart.'

'How's that?'

'With successive increases in population after the war and changes to the Education Act, more high schools had to be built. If you drive around the suburbs, you'll see the evidence of two waves of prosperity. In 1961 at least five new high schools opened their doors. It's why Clarence High looks just like Taroona High. Then again, in another burst of building in the early seventies, you get Rokeby and Kingston. It was a boom in almost every respect.'

'What happened to this place?'

'It became a matriculation college for a while, senior secondary students only. Then it became hopelessly outdated and they moved to the site at Mount Nelson. Nobody knew what to do with the main building until this firm got their inspired idea. Mind you, I'm not sure how I'd feel turning up to a service for an old friend in the very room I had to sit through addresses by the Headmaster.'

'At least it would inspire memories.'

'That it would.'

Two men in dark suits wheeled the teak coffin up the aisle to the front of the room. When it was in positon by a lectern, Mahoney stared at the gleaming bronze handles. There were whole days now when he didn't think of his deceased parents; he told himself he was too busy. An old mate of his recently told him that, as he drove to work every day, he said a quiet prayer to his father up in the celestial sphere. It didn't strike Mahoney as a mawkish thing to do, but rather a simple and heartfelt act of respect and gratitude. After all, where were you if your parents hadn't brought you into the world?

He took Kendall by the arm and guided her to a row of chairs. 'Kate, we need to alter our approach. I think we're being a bit … desperate.'

She nodded. 'And possibly intruding on the grief of his family?'

'Yep. As well as everyone else who turns up today. We have a duty to find the murderer alright. But at what cost to dignity? I'm not saying we shouldn't be ruthless if we have to be, but this seems a step too far.'

'She did offer.'

'You're right, but it doesn't mean we are compelled to accept. Hers isn't such a bad idea, but I can't help feeling we'll be trammelling over the mores of this memorial. There's a time and place to hunt the killer down, and this isn't it.'

Kendall glanced towards the entrance. 'There's McLeod now. I'll let him know.'

'Thank you.'

As she went across to their colleague, Mahoney took out his handkerchief and wiped his nose. He'd started second-guessing himself. Was he being sentimental? Was this decision an impulsive feeling or a considered thought? By the time Kendall returned, he'd settled on the latter. They were doing the right thing. Respect was due and being there as observers was sufficient. He cocked his head toward the departing McLeod.

'Was he okay with that?'

'Yes. Turns out he couldn't have done it anyway. There's been a nasty accident on Clare Street near the Catholic school and he has to get over there and do the photos. Your moral quandary was solved anyway.'

'Never hurts to examine what you're doing. At least we haven't wasted his time. Let's take a seat before it fills up.'

Very soon all the chairs were occupied and, by the time the celebrant welcomed the mourners, there were plenty of people standing at the rear. Mahoney guessed there were around two hundred in the main room and another fifty or so in the room behind, straining to see the front.

The ceremony was dignified but not maudlin. Hellyer's daughter, Maggie, gave the eulogy. Undistracted by the sadness she must be feeling, her conglomeration of memories was delivered with fondness and a touch of wit. Their marriage may have been over, but Sophie Hellyer could be proud of their efforts if the maturity of their daughter was any guide.

Mahoney never felt comfortable at funerals. It was the only time he really worried about his own mortality, and it opened the stopgap on a flood of memories. He concentrated on keeping it together—it wasn't even as if he'd known the deceased—but his stolidness went out the window with the concluding phase of the service. A PowerPoint display of images from Hellyer's life was on the screen, accompanied by one of Mahoney's all-time favourite songs, 'For a short time'. The Weddo's ballad of the untimely death of a young woman always took him to a deep place, which was why he rarely played it—just too powerful. Tears pricked his eyes, but he wiped them away roughly as he turned his head to the side. It wasn't his time to show emotion. As he watched the pallbearers carrying the coffin out to the waiting hearse, another emotion surfaced: anger. What right did anybody have to put their ego above the life of another? They would have to catch the bastard who did this. There really was no other option.

□

Little was said in the car as they returned to headquarters. Mahoney was mulling over strands of the case in his head, while Kendall drove as assuredly as she did everything in life.

Once inside the incident room Mahoney made a beeline for Dunstan. 'Andrew, any luck with the van?'

The burly constable looked up from his screen. 'Some. Even without rego plates there are ways of tracking it. Donna Givens from Forensics phoned through what they had on the vehicle ID and dashboard. The odometer reading was a tick over 73,000 kilometres and the vehicle number was intact so that helps a fair bit.'

'Really?' Mahoney knew how to start his car and where to get it serviced, but not a whole lot more.

'Yeah, for sure. Motor traders have had to clean up their act the past few years. Details on a vehicle in a commercial yard are subject to spot checks by the Trading Authority, so the car yards keep proper records. Still a few shonky trades, but mostly it's legit.'

'So how does that help us?'

'Geason and I did a database search, and hit pay dirt in Argyle Street. Johnny Morrison at Vroom Motors sold that van back in October. The right make and model, and the correct vehicle number. At the time of sale the odometer reading was in the low seventies.'

So, not a lot of usage since. That fitted with a vehicle used sparingly for a few day trips here and there. Mahoney felt they were getting closer.

'It was a cash sale. Bloke by the name of Gerard Ogden wanted a vehicle to move some furniture about. Morrison said it was a good deal for him. He offloaded the van at the full whack, no haggling. Easy money, he reckoned. This Ogden guy said he'd inherited a car from his mum and it didn't suit him so he wanted a quick sale. Probably why he accepted the sod all that Morrison offered. That side of the paperwork fitted. Ogden then said he'd noticed the Ford Transit in the yard and he wanted that. It was a done deal.'

Mahoney stood vertical. Was it another false start, or were they off on the trail? He glanced behind him, saw Gibson at his desk, and made a snap decision. He took the printout from Dunstan. 'Lovely work, Constable.'

Mahoney walked over to Kendall's desk. 'Kate, I'm going to take Gibson with me for a bit. Have to visit a car yard. Could you look over the report from Cortese and give me your perspective.'

With a straight face Kendall said, 'I thought I mentioned my concerns about inherent sexism in the job. Take a male for the stuff about cars and leave me to give a female perspective on the profiler's dossier.'

Mahoney stammered something inaudible. Before he could come back with a proper reply, she smiled. 'Just kidding, Sir. You were so intense after the service, that I thought a leg-pull might help.'

His shoulders relaxed. 'Oh, right. Yep, I was a bit affected by this morning. So, you're fine with this?'

'Of course. I overheard what Dunstan said. David's the obvious choice seeing as he's been working with the identikit artist this morning.'

'Of course.' That hadn't occurred to Mahoney but it was a good point. 'We'll see you in a while.'

He called across to Gibson. 'David, we're off out. Bring the laptop with the images from Eather.'

CHAPTER SIXTEEN

In Mahoney's car the DI passed Gibson the printout. 'Read this so you're up to speed when we get there.' They set off up Argyle Street to the car strip, and a few minutes later stopped outside Vroom Motors. As they entered the compact showroom, Mahoney's face lit up. Just short of the lone desk he dropped into a crouch with his hands out in front.

'Skeeter, get ready!'

The wiry man behind the desk raised his head in alarm, then broke into a wide smile.

'Honeybear, you're going down!'

He leaped out of his chair and grappled the detective while Gibson looked on in astonishment. Had he strayed into a random schoolyard? The grapple became a handshake and Mahoney gestured to his colleague to join them.

'Johnny, this is one of my up-and-comers, Detective Constable Gibson. David, meet Johnny Morrison.' Gibson shook his hand but still looked confused as they took chairs by the desk. Morrison resumed his perch; he was too big for a jockey, but the man was lithe. He had sandy hair and pointed ears. If you wanted to buy a car from a bloke who looked like a fox, he was your man.

Morrison was still grinning. 'Constable, you looked concerned before.'

'Just trying to get a handle on the nicknames, I suppose.'

'That's easy. At high school we had a wrestling club. Not really a club, more a piss-take of the stuff on TV. I'm Morrison, Moz, Mosquito, Skeeter. The lean, annoying one. Your boss was the gentle enforcer so instead of Grizzly he was Honeybear. Plenty of others in on it, including the mighty Difalco twins who were shaving by grade eight. That was quite early in the seventies. Great fun.'

Mahoney nodded. 'We must catch up. The Ocean Child is only a few blocks away from here. One Friday soon? Anyway, first a police matter.'

Mahoney placed the printout on the desk. 'We're after a driver who did some business here.'

'The Ogden fella. I won't ask what he's done because I don't want to know. Mind you, I tell that to all the snoozers who walk in here but they tell me anyway. Yesterday, this joker from the Huon started …'

'Ogden.' Mahoney tapped the sheet. 'It's kind of important.'

'Geez, alright. That was one of my quickest deals ever. Either he was in a fair old rush or he's a complete numpty.'

'I don't think he's thick. Tell us what he wanted.'

'Trade-in on an ancient Nissan Pulsar, late nineties model. I had a quick squiz at it and looked pretty good. Put it through the PPSR.'

Gibson had his notebook out. 'Sorry, the what?'

'PPSR. Don't ask what it stands for. It's a national database that gives you vehicle history. Didn't give the historical owner but it wasn't showing up as stolen so I offered him three hundred for it.' Morrison saw the look on the detectives' faces. 'I know, but who's going to buy a fifteen-year-old Pulsar? I knew he'd take it.'

'How so?'

'While I was on the phone just before he came in, he'd been sticking his beak into the Ford van. Not many of those around in the yards so I was pretty sure of a sale. Anyways, we got to talking. He wanted the van bad enough to agree to the stupid price I had on it, and to the peanuts I paid for his old car. He didn't query any of it. Not my fault if he's a sucker.'

Mahoney avoided the obvious mosquito joke. 'And the form of payment was …?'

'Cash. But then about sixty per cent of customers use the folding stuff. Even on a twenty grand car, they won't pay the bank fee for a cheque. Suits me.' Morrison looked at Gibson and grinned. 'You're not with the tax blokes, are you? Anyway, he showed me his driver's licence and it was sorted.' His bony fingers flicked through a receipt book. 'Here you go. Gerard Ogden, 94 Melville Street, Hobart. That help?'

'Phone number by any chance?'

'Nah. That's all he needs to give me. No finance or warranty arrangement. Pay the cash. See you later.'

Gibson tapped his pen on the notebook. 'What about on the vehicle registration form?'

'Same. Name, address of both parties and the handover price. We keep a docket of that and the buyer takes the larger sheet to Service Tasmania to register the purchase and changeover.'

'The onus is on him to get it recorded. It's out of your hands at that stage.'

'Yeah. It's meant to be done in the first fourteen days. If it's not done, they send out reminder notices.'

A thought shot into Mahoney's head. 'Which, if he chose to, he could have ignored easily enough for the period the vehicle was registered for. When's the van covered to?'

Morrison glanced at a separate book. 'Next month, so until then he's pretty clear. He's driving a registered vehicle so it's not illegal. Technically, a bit iffy but not so bad. What makes you think he hasn't told the Rego Board?'

'Just a hunch. 94 Melville Street has been part of a building site for six months now. The new TAS Mutual offices are replacing a row of terraced houses. This guy's no numpty.' Mahoney rubbed his forehead.

'It makes me wonder why he didn't scratch the engine number off. Bit of a silly mistake.'

Gibson leaned in and pointed to the printout. 'But he did. He's actually bloody clever.'

The DI held his hands up. 'I give up. Cars aren't my thing. What have I missed?'

'Well, Sir, our guy did scratch out the number on the engine block, that's the engine number. There's also a vehicle identification number which is stamped on an ID plate somewhere in the car, which was also gone. But Givens found another somewhere else.' Mahoney looked searchingly to Morrison for help.

'On the chassis underneath the spare tyre. Reckon that's the one they found. Varies from make to make. The Mercedes ones are absolute pricks to find. Put that number in the database and the rest of the details pop up. Your bloke at the station did that and then got onto me. Sharp fella.'

Mahoney sat forward. 'Is the chassis replica common knowledge?'

'Doubt it. Never been asked by a punter about it. Why would you?'

'Exactly. No point.' So they had a slight edge; Mahoney doubted the perpetrator could have expected the lead on the van to have occurred so quickly. It was time to try for some recognition. 'Johnny, I was going to ask you to look at a couple of photos, but I'm going to ask you another favour instead. If I send one of our identikit guys up, can you help come up with a likeness of this Ogden guy? You sat with him for a bit so you'll have a good idea.'

'No worries. I'm better with names but you've got to be good with faces in this game too, reading them and remembering them. I guess mum's the word.'

'Too right.' All three stood.

The men shook hands again. 'And I'll get that beer with you soon.'

'Absolutely. I owe you a few for this. Cheers, Johnny.'

□

Back in the car Mahoney drove up the one-way street into North Hobart, passing five car yards in a couple of blocks. It was a garish section of the city but it made sense for the major car retailers to congregate here. It suited the tyre kickers as well. He ignored the first chance to turn back into town, continuing to the State Cinema car park, where he was in luck; just as they entered, a blue Fiat was reversing out of one of the prized parking spots. Mahoney snapped it up immediately and they took the stairs to the café at the rear of the complex. He gave Gibson a ten dollar note and his coffee order and told his offsider to meet him on the top level.

A few minutes later Gibson ascended the stairwell and joined his boss. 'Two skinny caps on their way.'

They sat in two enormous chairs which had been nudged around so they faced away from the rest of the mezzanine.

Mahoney pointed out to the south. 'One of my favourite vantage points in a city full of them. And a good place to catch our breath.'

'Not bad at all, and doing a good trade by the looks of it. Downstairs is full.' The chatter of the patrons drifted up through the atrium space. 'I came here for a film last week but didn't realise this was out the back. Good design.'

Mahoney hooked his thumb over his shoulder. 'The owner has a snug office over there, behind us. He's probably in there now working on his next means of squeezing every last drop of value out of the space. There's even a rooftop cinema. He's a shrewd bugger.'

A young brunette delivered the drinks and left with the metal number holder. Gibson held off while sweeteners were stirred in and then asked why they were taking a breather.

'Two reasons. Firstly, I'm conducting a professional development session and we're then having a strategy update.' Mahoney scooped some froth into his mouth and sat back. 'Number one. Your performance. Very good.'

'But ...?'

'No buts. B+, bearing in mind you're in the formative stage of your investigative career. Any mistakes you've made have been down to a lack of experience. You can hardly criticise someone without years of experience for not having it. Like a lot in life, you can't be taught some things. You have to go through them to understand what's going on.'

'A catch 22 of the profession, as you'd say.'

'Exactly. Mistakes are inevitable. When you make them, do your level best not to repeat them. Learn from them for the future. Next, hasten slowly. In a way, that's what we're doing here. With what we've learned, if we rush helter-skelter after this Ogden, we could stuff it up. We need to get our ducks lined up. That also applies to your career.' Mahoney caught Gibson's eye and held the gaze. 'Your trajectory in the force is upwards, there's no doubt about it. That is not due to naked ambition or desire for rank, in my opinion. It's because you believe you can do a better job than most. Over time that will prove to be the case. Attitude and aptitude. Both big ticks. But I guess there is a "but". There is no fast-track in Tassie. Kendall went to Sergeant quickly once she was in our squad, but she had ten years in, and there are plenty of other officers who reckon it was still too quick—not me, but it's a conservative force. From recruitment to retirement, for the bulk of our colleagues anyway, is roughly a forty-year period. The modest pay structure and the pension scheme dictate that many are in for the long haul. There might be the odd time-server but most want to do the job. Maybe not with great zeal, but they're conscientious.'

'Aside from natural attrition and redundancies, there's not a huge amount of upward movement?'

'Pretty much. There are opportunities that you can grasp, but they won't happen as quickly as you might like. What to do? Again, hasten slowly. You're not arrogant so working with those less capable shouldn't be a problem. It will be frustrating to remain at the same rank as someone like Herrick for a couple of years, but I can assure you that when the openings appear, it will be you going up.'

Gibson said nothing for a while, just stared over the rooftops to the Domain. Was it bitter disappointment?

'Don't worry, Sir. You've hit the nail on the head. As you said, it's early days so the chance to hoover up the experience is there. Sound fair?'

'Sure. I'm good with that.'

Mahoney gave a slight nod of relief. Management involved some grey areas, but it looked like this wasn't going to be an issue. On with the case.

'So, what would you do now with the fresh material we have?'

'Given the theme of our tutorial, I'm buggered if I know.' Gibson smiled. 'Seriously, I'd include the photofit Eather's doing with your wrestling friend in a portfolio of images and show it to potential witnesses.' He counted them off on his fingers. 'The post office lady, the bank ladies, Boxhall, the shop couple at Opossum Bay. Maybe put it up on our social media platforms and in the paper—unless you don't want to alert Ogden to what we know. Then perhaps we should keep it close to our chest.'

'Yes, good. Then?'

'A lot of legwork this one. Take it around the other local bank branches. Ogden paid twelve grand in cash for the van. That's a fair whack. Unless he had it in a shoebox, he had to get it from somewhere. Cash machines have a limit on withdrawals so he either used ATMs over a period of time or he got it in one go over the counter.'

'Or he's got a number of accounts with different banks and visited a few. This guy covers his tracks. The reason we've got a lead on the van is due to a tiny oversight that almost nobody would have picked up. So my guess is he's a multiple account holder and he spread out the withdrawals.'

'Can Sergeant Dobosz get a line on that?'

Mahoney laughed. 'There is very little Dicky Dobosz can't do in that realm. He's worked minor miracles in tracing a money trail before. Assuming the accounts are in the name of Gerard Ogden, that is.

'He probably thought he was safe to do that, working on the assumption we'd never find out because we wouldn't trace the van.'

'That's a fair call. Next?'

Gibson bit his bottom lip. 'Get to Service Tasmania and check the car registration info and the licence details. Possibly dead ends, but you never know.'

'The devil's in the detail. Right, let's get back. Time to hasten.'

CHAPTER SEVENTEEN

Back to the smartboard, not to start over but to kickstart the next phase. A briefing had been called for five o'clock and, as an incentive, Mahoney included the promise that all could be out the door by six o'clock at the latest. The only absentee was Constable Herrick; for this particular update, he was of more use to his football club at training than he was at HQ.

Mahoney stood to the side of the screen, reknotting his tie as if physically recomposing himself to address the troops. A little thing like that could subtly reinforce the impression that the senior investigating officer was presenting a professional front. It was vital, a few days in, to maintain momentum.

'As I promised, short and sweet. We have made some breakthroughs and I want your input as to where we go in the next twenty-four hours. I'll start with a quick rehash. The first item is the van. DC Dunstan must take credit here … again. Ringing around to council car parks bore fruit. A Ford Transit van, likely to have been the one used by the perpetrator, was tracked down. Traces on the external panels were found by Forensics. The next jigsaw piece was getting lucky on the firm that produced the Electric Eric stencils. We then tracked down the payment and delivery details for the sticker signs. As you've hopefully noticed from reading the progress log, whoever did this was determined to leave as small a trail as possible. The email exchange with Stencilset, the cash payment at the bank, and the use of a stolen licence to register a post office box, all indicate a desire to avoid being traced. They also represent two other things. One, the collection of incidents cohere with the theory it was a single scheme. By luck and graft we have recognised a distinct trail. Second, this is the work of a devious and meticulous mind, completely in sync with the act of the murder. The method used to offload the van was damned clever. Nonetheless, and I sincerely hope our villain doesn't realise this, there was one small identifier in the van. The second vehicle ID number led us to the relatively recent purchase of said van. So, well ahead of the killer's intentions, we have an identity to go with the scheme.'

Mahoney tapped the keyboard on his computer tablet and three photo images appeared on the screen. 'Gerard Ogden. All three images have been assembled from witnesses interviewed today. Their veracity is in ascending order. Furthest from me is the recollection of the teller at the Westpac branch. By her own admission, it was very vague as she can't really recall the transaction. We can all but ignore that one. Next is from the lady at the Post Office. She can recall the interaction, but it was a brief one a couple of months ago. Hers is an improvement but not that much. Our suspect had a beard at that time, which I'm assuming he doesn't usually. If you're thinking this is all getting convoluted, you're right. It is. All done deliberately by our guy. This third image is our best bet. Not because it's the most recent—it isn't—but owing to the fact the witness sat with our man for over half an hour. This is based on a car yard interaction, and the witness is reliable. Like a gambler, he makes a living out of reading people's faces. Morrison sold him the van and looked very carefully at the driver's licence used for ID. So it is him. This is Gerard Ogden's face. We aren't meant to know this, obviously. The bank and post office were calculated risks. He got away with the bank, and nearly got away with the post box, leaving no traceable identification.'

Mahoney signalled to the centre of the image with a flat hand. 'This was a risk. Stealing a vehicle was perhaps too much for him. Maybe he was stingy and wanted the trade-in on the old Pulsar so he went to a used car yard. Who knows? But it's come unstuck and we know who he is. Tracking him down will be another matter. The transfer of ownership papers were not lodged at the Motor Registry. His last known address was as per his licence, bank details and pretty much everything Sergeant Dobosz could think of to check. It was a terraced house, but it's now reduced to rubble at a building site. No phone, mobile or landline registered to him. No email address that hasn't been deactivated. Poof! Gone, just like that. But we don't think he's left the state. Since Friday nobody under that name has left by air or sea, and the bank cards haven't been used in the past week. He's gone to ground and we need to flush him out. Urgently. Because, as those who read the profiler's report will know, he is certainly capable of murdering again. Here's the nub. Do we hit the media with what we've got and risk igniting the publicity blaze that could sidetrack the investigation, or do we softly softly catch our monkey? It's over to you.'

Geason spoke first: a senior constable who could single-handedly organise a festival, but wasn't a great lateral thinker, his was a voice rarely heard in this assembly. 'He's our guy. I've seen convictions with weaker chains of evidence. However, we still don't have sufficient evidence for this case. I'm not suggesting you're after an arrest this instant. What I am saying is we don't want to go public too early. As soon as we proclaim this guy as a person of interest, the witch-hunt will start and that could retard us. Softly, softly maybe.'

As a mark of respect to the officer, or due to general agreement, no-one put forward the counter argument. Kendall swivelled in her chair. 'The boss is basically telling us we've done well so far. The crime scene gave us nothing much of immediate value forensically, although it was very telling as an insight into a deviant mind. The careful work done since then has led to these advances. Keeping this in-house has two advantages. The first is the absence of distractions from the media. The second is that this perpetrator desperately wants recognition. If we starve him of that and creep up on him, we may be better off.'

The decision was made.

Half an hour later Mahoney was still in his office. His tie was loosened and he was hunched over his desk trying to list the next set of strategic actions. The decision not to show their cards was playing over in his mind. It was right to delegate actions to his colleagues, but what about crucial decisions? Shouldn't he make them? No matter how good the team on game day, it was still the coach who had the final call on tactics.

Avoiding a media frenzy was all well and good, quite sensible really, but was he letting people's sensibilities override his one compelling aim: to apprehend the killer? Surely that trumped all other considerations. Displaying respect at the funeral was one thing, but letting considerations of sensitivity have too much sway was altogether another. They had incriminating information. Surely he should use it. But how?

Making up a list of pros and cons wasn't really helping; jotting down notes was getting him nowhere. He leaned his head onto his hands and massaged his scalp.

'Watch out for splinters.' It was Dunstan at the door. 'Got a second, Sir?'

'Sure, Andrew. Come in.'

The burly man took a seat. 'There's a snag.'

'Tell me about it. I've been stuck here trying to unravel this for ages.'

Dunstan glanced at the pad. 'It's to do with the van.'

'Go on.' It didn't sound like good news was coming.

'I've just been on the phone to a few suburban stations. I had a hunch. Early on Friday afternoon a man called the Kingston station to report the theft of a white Ford Transit Van. He said he'd discovered it missing from where he'd parked it in the Channel Court car park the night before. He'd gone there to do a spot of shopping and when he came out the battery was flat. He didn't have Roadside Assistance so decided to come back the next day and pick it up.'

'Having renewed with the RACT Assist scheme in the meantime?'

'Yeah, exactly. That's what he told them at Kingston.'

'What name did he give?'

'John Doe.'

Sweet Jesus. Someone was taking the piss.

'Why did we only just hear about this?' Mahoney fought to keep his voice level; it was hardly Dunstan's fault.

'The officer at Kingston who is responsible for the stolen vehicle database was on leave until today. He came back to a stick-it note on his desk.'

'A stick-it note?'

'The call was picked up by the receptionist at the front desk, a temp finishing off a two week placement. She was about to head to lunch so she jotted it down and left the note on Constable Mitchell's desk. He returned to work today and put the information in the system this afternoon.'

'Let me guess. There's been nothing further heard from the caller, and the contact number didn't produce a response?'

'Yep. He's a crafty bugger. The temp did ask for the rego details, but the caller said he wasn't sure because he'd only recently bought the van.'

'This is doing my head in.' Mahoney breathed deeply and looked at the sheet of jottings. 'Okay, executive decision. We put out an appeal for information. Radio, television, newspapers and social media. Can you help me do that now? We need find Ogden.'

'Sure. So we're releasing the photo ID?'

'Yes. We've got to. This is starting to spiral away from us. There's a time to think and there's a time to do.'

CHAPTER EIGHTEEN

It had not been a night Mahoney would wish to repeat. Sleep had finally come after midnight but it had been fitful. As she'd drifted off to sleep, Susan had murmured 'sweet dreams' to him—if only. Immediately before waking at five o'clock, a familiar dream had come to him: he was trying desperately to get home in time for something important, stuck without clothes and zig-zagging through the streets before anybody saw him.

How he hated that riff in his subconscious. At one stage last year, he'd finally made an appointment with a counsellor. It went relatively well so he'd made time to see the psychologist once a fortnight. On one visit they'd tackled the area of disturbed sleep, particularly during times of intense workload. Mahoney outlined his pattern of sleep deprivation. The counsellor, looking over the top of half-moon spectacles, had explained it all rather simply. 'Most of the time your subconscious is a country lane with a few ramblers. You sleep soundly and experience minimal anxiety. But, during a disturbing case, your mind and emotions, particularly controlled anxieties like fear of failure, are in overdrive. Accordingly, when you do sleep your subconscious is more like an autobahn, hence the dreams.'

Put like that it made perfect sense. On a homicide case his mind was never still. In fact, it was always racing so much that it was unrealistic to expect it to switch off. And the dreams themselves were variations on the idea of self-worth.

'Do you feel that you'll be revealed as a lesser being? Somehow not worthy of your status? These dreams reflect that. As if you are frightened of being exposed.'

Mahoney had admitted that was a submerged concern. Running a successful crime squad was obviously a results-oriented job, and doubts about your own capability seemed quite normal. And now here he was in Susan's kitchen considering just that proposition. Was he up to it? If he cognitively assessed his capacity for the task, was he still good enough? Time marches. Was he keeping up? With mug in hand, he went through to a recliner in the lounge room. Dawn's tendrils were creeping over the horizon. Intermittently sipping on his strong coffee, he stared out the window and ran through the case in his head. Blessed with a sound memory he paced out the investigation hour by hour.

A crime of this sort could not be predicted. Naturally, then, the investigators were reactive. All participants had been on-task from the word go. Kendall, despite her own woes, was as good as ever, Gibson was firing, Dunstan was a rock: incredibly dependable, Forensics were meticulous. Progress had been made—but how much really? Plenty, in truth, but still a long way to go.

□

Showered and dressed, Mahoney was sitting at the window bench in Ginger Brown: water, latte and a Spanish omelette. Mind already in fourth gear, he was planning the day. The public appeal would generate loads of material, and he had a good team to sift through it all.

At bang on eight o'clock, Gibson and Kendall entered. Neither required food but coffees were ordered. Mahoney gestured for them to sit either side of him. They formed a tight triangle with their backs to the rest of the café. After a brief explanation of his decision to go public with Ogden's image, he moved straight into his proposed itinerary. Both his subordinates sat up in order to take notes.

'We'll sort out who does what as we go. In no particular order, here are some ideas. One, we see if there's been any usage of Hellyer's mobile phone and credit cards. Neither were found at the scene. If Ogden, assuming the perpetrator is of that name, has them then there's nothing to prevent him using that stuff. It's unlikely he's stupid enough to keep the phone turned on as that would allow us to locate him, but he may have used it, so we get the service provider to release that information. Alan Wagin is always good for that sort of job. Credit cards. At most places the contactless limit is a hundred dollars. He can feasibly use them without being required to show any identification or know the pin number. As with the phone, we don't put a stop on that, but we can put out an alert so any usage of the cards is highlighted. Dobosz for that one. Gary Oates's licence. It was returned a while ago, but it did its job in getting the PO box for our perp. The visual identification there is too sketchy to rely on, but it's still a very useful link. As we learned yesterday, a cash buyer for vehicles only needs a licence at point of sale. Ogden, with a beard in place, could have bought another vehicle around that weekend in January. Not a huge task to bluff his way through.'

Kendal looked up from her pad. 'Sir, did you sleep at all last night?'

He smiled in return. 'Some. This is mostly from a bit of thinking earlier this morning. I felt we were short-stepping a bit and we need to be striding. Okay, next is to comb through the list of public service redundancies from the middle of last year. This, I admit, is fishing in the lake but the profile does lead this way. See if there's a Gerard Ogden anywhere. If there isn't, see if there's a male getting out after a long, steady career. Our guy's got financial resources, time, patience and a long-held grievance. Cortese's suggestion is that the murderer has functioned as a normal social being for a significant period of time, his whole life really. A fairly anonymous figure, probably single or divorced. He hadn't scaled the heights, but went about life without causing any notable upheaval. Mostly kept himself to himself. All the while harbouring a massive grudge. Any queries?'

Kendall did. 'Remember in the Sproule case, you cornered him by detailing the mobile records to show where he'd been? If Ogden has used Hellyer's phone in the past few days, we could work out some locations and specifically show the image around there. If he's shrewd enough, he won't have activated it wherever he's holing up, but it could assist us.'

'Yes, yes, good. David?'

'Do we know for sure that the image we have and the name of Gerard Ogden is our guy?'

'Short answer is no. It's still circumstantial. Ogden could even be an assumed name for all we know. The van purchase at Vroom Motors is pretty concrete, though. What I'm outlining now is a lot of work, but we've got the personnel for it. Our aim is to transition from chasing the guy to encircling him. I had a few other ideas spitballing around, but this is the short list. We do this and our weight of intelligence increases.'

CHAPTER NINETEEN

Kendall drove back to Letitia Street for the second time in as many days. She passed the funeral home on her right and parked around the corner in Ryde Street. She was here because, amid the flood of information coming in from the public appeal, a couple of gems had surfaced. Gibson was off chasing one out at Glenorchy, and she was here.

It was warming up so she left her jacket in the car. As she entered the corner shop, the smell of fried food hit her. Why did crap food have to smell so good? To the side of the bain-marie was a woman who looked to be about her own age. She had pale skin and the roots of her hair could do with some attention, but she wasn't unattractive. Her fat-splattered blue garment hid whatever figure there was to display.

Kate approached the counter. 'Are you Jenny Stevenson?'

'Yep. And you're either the estate agent or a copper.'

'Police. Is it going on the market?'

'Sort of. Some wog's got the freehold. I'm hoping to get out of the lease. No-one wants the business, but they might want to take the lease on.' She looked around the space. 'God knows why. Anyway, that's not your worry. This bloke is.' She pointed at a copy of that day's paper.

'That's right. We appreciate you calling.'

'It's what you do. He was here around this time yesterday. Odd bugger.'

Kate glanced at the paper. 'You're pretty sure it was this man?'

'Oh, yeah, that's him alright. He had a strange way about him. He ordered a coffee and a toastie, then got a bottle of water to bring it over ten dollars.'

'So he could pay-wave the purchase?'

'Yep, happens a lot these days. People buy something extra for the convenience of using their plastic without a fee.'

'How long was he here for?'

'Three-quarters of an hour. He pretended to read the paper, but he was just flicking through. Most of the time he was staring out the window at the big funeral that was on. That was the Hellyer bloke, wasn't it?'

'Yes, it was.'

'And this is to do with his murder, isn't it? This could be the bloke who done it.'

'Possibly. We don't know anywhere near enough yet to identify suspects.' It was best to be circumspect.

'Yeah, right,' she said with an obvious tinge of sarcasm. 'You can't say much. I get it. So, he was there for a fair while, keeping tabs on things. I knew there was something off about him.'

'How was he dressed? How did he appear?'

'That's what was a bit odd. He had work gear on, King Gee overalls, but they were clean. His hands were grimy and he had a splash of grease on his cheek, but that was it. I reckon he was dressed up to look like a tradie. He wasn't though.'

'How could you tell?'

'What sort of tradie drives around in a pissy little Mazda? Joker. It was parked across the way, faded blue with those stupid black stripes down the side.'

'Thank you. We may need to call on you again. You've been a real help.'

'It's no hassle. Good to have a smidgen of excitement in here.'

'Anything else you can recall?'

'Not really. He weren't real friendly. Bit of an attitude.'

Kendall reiterated her thanks and left. It looked as if Ogden did have alternative transport. She pulled out her phone to call Gibson.

□

Gibson listened to Kendall's news, catching the enthusiasm and agreeing it sounded good. His search among the car yards was a bit trickier, but having a possible make to propose to people could help. The PSSR was designed to give the full history of a vehicle, not the owner, and Dunstan had drawn a blank with the Motor Registry Office; no vehicles were registered under the name of Gerard Ogden, but—as Kendall had just discovered—that didn't mean he wasn't using one.

While Herrick was trawling the showrooms in North Hobart, Gibson was out on Main Road Glenorchy where the rest of the city's car yards were located. Both had tablets with them so they could show the photofit image around. The first couple of businesses couldn't help. No-one had seen the guy, and there were no sales to anybody by the name of Ogden or Oates. Gibson was wondering if Herrick was having more luck as he walked across the bitumen to the office of Elwick Motors. He tapped a knuckle on the sliding glass door and a stocky figure waved him inside.

As soon as Gibson showed his ID, the man started swearing. 'About fucking time. I rang those bozo pricks down the road yesterday morning. Busy, my arse. They're doing school visits instead of catching crims and protecting local business. We show bit of discipline and where's the help? Useless.'

The dark-haired man ranting from behind the desk was slobby. When he stood, a doughy pillow of lard hid the buckle of his trousers. His shirt collar was undone—it had to be, to accommodate the wad of flesh beneath his chin, Gibson supposed.

'I didn't catch your name, Sir.'

'Figures. Those dumbfucks round the corner are useless. Tits on a bull. Can't even pass on a complaint. And they want extra numbers. Fuck me.'

Gibson couldn't imagine anyone wanting to.

'I'm here now. How can I help you?' Hide the doughnuts maybe?

'Jeez. You don't even know who I am.'

'I presume you're Geoff Toohey.' The name was stencilled on the business cards near the phone.

'Yeah, that's right.' He sat down and the chair wheezed. 'Well, now you're here you can sort out this speeding fine.'

Gibson wasn't sure what the expectations were of the local police around here. If this was typical, there was little wonder they'd ignored Toohey.

'I'm not sure …'

'That fucking Oates prick. Got a motor off me, dirt cheap. I practically gave it away. Not only does he not bother to switch the rego over, but he goes and gets a speeding ticket. And he's got the hide to reckon it wasn't him. Fucking disgrace.'

Bingo. This was how it had felt when football was going well for him.

'Just to check. You sold a used car to a Mr Gary Oates back in January?'

'Yep. Bit of a shit box. Mazda 323. The duco was rooted, but the engine was alright. Good little buy.'

Gibson nodded as if acknowledging the charity of the man.

'Oates showed me his driver's licence, paid cash and drove away.'

Gibson flipped the cover off the tablet and brought up the Post Office lady's image. 'Did he look something like this?'

Toohey leaned across the desk and peered at the screen. 'Pretty close. He kept scratching at his beard. I felt like telling him to shave the bloody thing off if it was that annoying.'

'Did you chat much?'

'Nup. All done in twenty minutes, from him walking in to driving out.'

'Did you study the licence closely?'

'Doubt it. It was cash for a small car on its last legs.'

So much for the alright engine. Gibson bit his lip.

'So, he was meant to do the paperwork for the transfer? But he didn't do it, so any traffic infringement caught on camera comes back to you?'

'It came to me, yeah. But I matched the car to the buyer and rang the sod. And you know what?' His face was reddening again. 'He reckons he wasn't speeding in any Mazda 323 because he never bought one and he's never driven one. Lying prick.'

'Actually, he may be telling the truth. It's odd but we think the man who bought that car was impersonating Mr Oates. I'll get this sorted with the Justice Department, so you needn't worry.'

Gibson reached for the notice of the fine and read the details: a fortnight before, a Mazda 323, registration OYE 415, had exceeded the speed limit by more than ten kilometres per hour on Sandfly Road. So, down past Kingston. Traffic would know exactly where the trap was set.

'I know this has been an inconvenience to you, but it's going to help us a great deal in a major enquiry we've got on.'

'Oh, well. Okay then.'

Gibson could almost have hugged him. If he wasn't such a whining slob.

□

Back at headquarters there was a renewed sense of energy in the room, almost a hum. Gibson went straight to the DI's office. When he'd rung Mahoney with the good news, he'd been told to come straight back in and deliver it in person. Kendall was already in the sanctum when he knocked and entered.

Both his superiors looked up as he strode in with a pep in his step. A drone task had turned out to be pretty satisfying.

'What news from beyond the flannelette curtain?'

Gibson skipped over the expletive-ridden rant and delivered a straight summary of the situation. Every so often Kendall would nod as if he was confirming her findings.

'As you predicted, the Oates licence was put to further use.'

Mahoney headed over to his white board, but before he got there his desk phone rang. He'd barely said his name before he held the receiver away from his ear and put the speaker on. His colleagues could hear a man shouting, '... and whatever else this man has done.'

Mahoney interrupted. 'Mr Oates, please stop. I hear you. We've sorted it. Now listen. We know the Mazda and the fine have nothing to do with the real you. The fine will disappear. The Justice Department is aware of this travesty.' Mahoney pointed his finger at Gibson who nodded in recognition that this had better be done. 'Your help is appreciated. The person who stole your card and used it for illegal purposes is being chased for even more serious reasons. I don't wish to alarm you but, believe me, we truly want to get this guy. Bizarrely enough, this identity theft is helping us.'

The voice on the line was more subdued. 'Alright then, fair enough. And can you do me a favour?'

'Perhaps.'

'If you ever need a character witness against that moron from Elwick Motors, let me know. The man's a menace.'

'I'll see what I can do. Thanks again for letting us know. We appreciate it.' Mahoney put down the receiver. 'We should recruit him. He's motivated to close the case.'

Mahoney went back to the board and looked at the diagram with a circle in the middle containing the word 'PERP'. There were a series of short spokes coming out from the middle like spider legs and, at the end of about half, there were snippets of information the team had gathered. Mahoney inked in a few words to summarise the fresh material from Elwick Motors. On the next spoke he wrote, 'Mazda/ funeral/Ogden?'

'Kate has a reliable identification of the man we think is Ogden observing yesterday's funeral. He drove the Mazda 323 you've just traced. The next two tasks go without saying. Put out an alert for that Mazda to all officers. If he's out and about, he'll be seen. Approach with caution and all that jazz. Second, action that idea to locate exactly where that speed camera was. That could narrow it down to the vicinity he's holed up in. Now, onto the other stuff from Ginger Brown. Wagin and Dobosz should have the respective phone and bank records by close of business today. Geason is dealing with the public service angle, but not having much luck. The State Service Commissioner's office agreed but the union got wind of it and are kicking up a fuss. Right to privacy or some such nonsense. I sometimes think the main interest they're trying to protect is that of their leader to get on television and moan about the government.' Mahoney sighed his disgust. 'Now, where was I before that little snippet of vilification? Ah, that's right, the case. Forensics have cross-referenced their findings from the van and Hellyer's shack. There are hair, fibre and DNA samples from the same organism found in both places, which is good, but …'

'Only when we apprehend someone,' Kendall finished. 'I'm presuming it doesn't match anybody in the system or this discussion wouldn't be happening.'

'Exactly. When we run this guy down, it will stick. I've got a feeling we'll be dealing with him very soon.'

CHAPTER TWENTY

If I gave a shit, I would say this is cute. Mummy dropping her teenage daughter off to school. Not your average school, mind you. St Hilda's, a prestigious independent college set amidst leafy grounds in Dynnyrne. As close as you'll get to a finishing school in little old Tassie.

The daughter dear, Chloe, is unloading a humungous backpack from a silver Toyota Prado, still the preferred vehicle for yummy mummies to ferry their offspring around. She's off to camp. Good weather for it, slightly crisp now but warm sunshine later. Away from Thursday till the following Friday. It's part of the Grade nine course designed to produce 'resourceful young women' and it's good of the school to put this material on their website for my research purposes. Very sporting of them.

Chloe hoists the backpack onto her shoulders and, looking like a turtle on its hind legs, waves goodbye to her mother. Patricia Heath waves back and flashes her delightful smile; courtesy of the Bayside Dental Practice, it is bright and cheerful—like her whole demeanour. Life is good: mansion in Sandy Bay, apartment at Port Douglas, ski holidays in New Zealand. Son Jack is studying business at Melbourne University, aiming to evolve into a facsimile of his father.

Daddy, Ian Heath, runs his own communications consultancy company: one of the success stories of the local economy, apparently. Whenever he receives some pissy award or other for his entrepreneurial acumen, he never mentions how the whole operation is feather-bedded by a series of long-term contracts with the State Government. Jobs for the boys. He's away now in Utah or somewhere with his lad mates on a ski trip. Good of him to update Facebook to let me know his whereabouts and what a great time they're having.

This leaves pert Patricia to steer her grotesque SUV home for a cuppa and a little rest before popping out for lunch with the girls. Except there'll be a place set that won't be occupied today.

Following her along Churchill Avenue is dead easy. She turns right and our two-car convoy winds its way into Beddome Street. She parks in the driveway of a substantial double-storey brick residence: tiled roof, white walls and lots of elegant foliage in the garden. I cruise past, turn into the cul-de-sac and pull up opposite. My little Mazda is pretty inconspicuous, so I won't draw much attention.

As I get out of the car I reach across for the clipboard and parcel— my excuse for calling. Grey short sleeved shirt, cap, sunnies and dark green shorts. Plenty of pockets, one of which holds my surprise buzzer. I'm good to go.

I knock on the door and Patricia answers quickly. I feel I know her well enough, not that we've ever met. God, no, I don't belong in her circle. She's dressed in a sleeveless red dress with buttons all the way down the front. If I were a bull, that could get me going. Very convenient dress for access—but that's the furthest thing from my mind. When the shrinks disassemble my scheme, they won't discover a single sexual angle. This is a program that is all about social justice, but they won't understand that.

For a moment she doesn't register what a man is doing at her door—a plebeian looking man at that. I hold up the parcel. 'Delivery for Mr Heath. I'm with Transit Couriers.'

The smile covers her ignorance. 'Oh, yes. Do you want me to sign for it?'

'Yes please, madam.'

I hand the clipboard over. She unclips the pen and props the plastic against her lower ribs for purchase. Perfect cover. I whip out a taser and next thing Trish is jolted back into the hallway. I'm no expert with these things, but it looks like I've got it right. The electric kick slams her on her back and her head thunks on the polished oak floor. She's doubly stunned so it's easy-peasy slipping the chloroformed rag under her nose.

I gently push the heavy front door shut and do a quick reccy of the house. There's nobody else around. Perfect. Plan A can continue unhindered. It's time to run a bath in the 'capacious en-suite leading off the plush master bedroom.' That's how it was described in a weekend supplement a few months ago. As I said, it is so accommodating of people to lay their personal lives open for the benefit of others.

The roll-top bath takes about five minutes to fill sufficiently. I keep an eye on her and an ear out for any noise. Compared to Hellyer, this sacrifice is more perfunctory. It has to be. The release of that pic to the media has meant the schedule is being brought forward. I've still got time, but not as much as I'd hoped. Hey ho. At least I can still do some good today.

Off with the taps and I lift Mrs Heath into the bath. Archimedes would be proud; the displacement is perfect. I leave her clothes in place. That will confuse the profiler who probably thinks I still have issues over my first wet dream. Then it's just a matter of gripping her ankles and lifting her legs vertical. She's deceptively light. I count to one hundred. One minute she's unconscious, the next without consciousness. I hold her in place for a bit longer, just to make sure. Any air bubbles have dissipated. Life has left her body. My work here is done. Credit for my efforts may take a while. It depends how worried the girls are when she doesn't front for lunch.

Taser in one pocket and rag in the other, I collect the parcel and clipboard from the floor in the hall and take a peek out of the glass pane set in the door. There's no-one about. I wipe the internal door knob and use my pen to pull the outer handle towards me, closing the door behind.

Back into the Mazda and off. It takes till I'm on the Southern Outlet before I start breathing calmly. I'm not being followed. I got away with another one. And so I should. I've earned this.

CHAPTER TWENTY-ONE

The woman sitting opposite Mahoney was beside herself. A potent cocktail of shock, grief and lingering fear were afflicting her. Kendall was with her on the couch, soothing her back between the shoulder blades, and a paramedic knelt in front and talked softly. It would be a while before Anna Vagianos could help them further.

Mahoney exited the living room and joined Gibson in the kitchen. The DI noticed a uniformed officer sitting at the bench writing up some notes, her brow furrowed in concentration.

'David, is this the attending officer?' Mahoney gestured to the bench.

'Yep. Constable Troncone. She was here first with her colleague. He's outside directing traffic past all our vehicles. You wouldn't believe it but the bloke opposite complained about the inconvenience of having us here. He wanted to know when we'd be gone as he was expecting guests for dinner and wanted the parking spaces.'

Mahoney started for the door. 'I'll go and tell him what he can do with his parking spaces.'

'Don't worry, Sir. Gav Miller already has. That's Constable Troncone's offsider. He told him they could park their Audis up his arse.'

'Excellent. That's the brand of community policing some people need. I say we leave it about an hour and then venture over to interview everyone. Should put them off their hors d'oeuvres. I don't know. Some people.'

'I know what you mean. Katrina over here was telling me the same guy rang in last week because someone knocked over his rubbish bins and they weren't all left standing straight after the weekly collection.'

'He rang us?'

'Apparently.'

'What's his name?'

'Alistair Montgomery.'

'Pity we can't bring people in for being dickheads.' Mahoney nodded towards the female constable. 'What brought her up this time?'

'Anna Vagianos made a distress call. Patricia Heath was meant to have been with her and some other friends down at the yacht club for a fund-raising lunch. Mrs Heath didn't make it, which was unusual for her. There was no response to Anna's voicemail messages and texts, and the landline wasn't being picked up.'

'So she popped by to check?'

'Yep. She knew the rest of the family was away and was worried that her friend had slipped over or something. They're a pretty tight group. There was no answer at the front door so she walked round the balcony. That's when saw the body in the bath, still in her dress. She rapped on the window, but she knew something was badly wrong. She got straight on the phone. Troncone and Miller headed up here immediately. Miller broke in through a lounge room window, surveyed the scene and made the next call. The cavalry arrived, but too late as it turns out. The rest you know.'

Vagianos had gabbled her story to Troncone as the initial symptoms of shock hit her. In the interest of discretion, Kendall and Gibson had then taken Vagianos into the lounge when they arrived at the scene—they couldn't leave her stunned in the front garden.

She was hardly a suspect and her prints could be eliminated from whatever Forensics found. The worker bees were already at their tasks in the hallway.

Doc Johnson stuck his head through the doorway. 'John, do you want to come in now?'

He certainly did. He followed the pathologist down the hall, through the bedroom and into the ensuite. Outside, the light was fading but the bathroom was lit up. The lip of the roll-top bath was at the same height as the lower edge of the window, designed so you could gaze at the river while soaking in comfort. Not that Patricia Heath would ever enjoy that luxury again.

Johnson padded over to the bath while the DI remained at the entrance.

'As you can see, the body is clothed. That suggests a suspicious death right there, regardless of whatever else is discovered.'

Mahoney agreed. He quickly went back to the lounge room and togged up in the pale blue overalls and plastic booties prescribed for the immediate crime scene. Back in the bathroom, he ventured over to where Johnson was kneeling. The doctor pointed to the victim's nose as he spoke into a small recording device. This was for the dual purpose of recording initial observations and as a prompt for further forensic pathology checks.

'The upper lip and nostrils smell as if chloroform has been administered. It's faint but discernible. In the right nostril are cloth fibres that I won't disturb now.'

He edged back so that Mahoney could get a clear view of the chest. 'The stitching around the third button down has some slight scorching. My early guess is that something like a taser gun was used.'

'Sufficient to kill her? Or just to stun her so the chloroform cloth could be forced on her?'

'Unless she had a weak heart, it would probably only stun her. There's a slight bump to the rear of her skull. She was knocked over and then the chloroform rag was applied.'

'Then carried in here and placed in the bath. The rest of the bathroom looks pretty dry. What do you think happened then?'

'My guess is that she was drowned. There are slight marks at the ankles. The perpetrator gripped her there and raised her legs, thereby submerging the upper torso and head. As you said, there's no evidence of water being thrashed about, so she was out cold as this was done. Water entered the lungs, breathing became impossible and death occured quite quickly.'

'Could she have regained consciousness?'

'Unlikely, I'd say. There are no obvious signs of a struggle. Her hands are unmarked. She was drowned whilst still unconscious. The body's reaction capability was overridden by the fact she was artificially incapacitated.'

'Could she have been already dead?'

'That is a distinct possibility. Have you heard of diatoms?'

Mahoney shrugged. 'I think so. Best refresh me.'

'They're microscopic algae found in almost all forms of everyday water. If they're not present in the lungs and the blood, then she was already dead. If detected, we know she was still alive when the water started entering her system. That can't be determined here of course. If I had to say now, my appraisal would be death by drowning, but the autopsy will be the clincher.'

Mahoney looked out of the window for a few moments. Lights were coming on as dusk moved into night. It was almost serene. The body below him triggered a forgotten memory of a painting he'd seen in a gallery somewhere. London?

Johnson interrupted his reverie. 'It's not exactly Millais's *Ophelia*. Hardly poetic.'

That was it. Mahoney hadn't known Johnson to be an art lover. 'As in the famous painting?'

'Yes, one of the pre-Raphaelite paintings. Possibly the best artistic depiction of the paradox of death. One minute you're living a life of hope, all the while unaware of the close proximity of death.' He looked down at the body. 'In reality, there is precious little art in what we see. Rather more blunt, unfortunately. I'll alert Madeleine Pitney so the autopsy can be done as early as possible.'

Mahoney patted the medic on the shoulder. 'Thank you, Sam. In a way, the manner of death isn't quite so important as the fact that it is very obviously a murder.'

Back in the kitchen, Kendall had joined Gibson; when Mahoney came in, they stopped their conversation and looked at him expectantly. Troncone was no longer there. The DI shut the door behind him before speaking. 'It is homicide, to confirm what we already knew. And I think it's our guy. For no other reason than it's so bizarre.'

'Perhaps not just that,' added Kendall. 'When Mrs Vagianos had calmed a little, she said it was a sick ending for someone who was once a water baby. Mrs Heath's maiden name was Whittey. Patricia Whittey swam for the country at the 1998 Commonwealth Games. Made the final for the butterfly and was in the gold medal relay team. Quite an achievement for a Launceston girl. Retired soon after and studied up north. Moved down here for her first teaching job, married and stayed.'

'Ignore what I said. It is definitely our guy.' Mahoney was suddenly more intense. 'Right, this is a stream of consciousness. First, the deceased will have a sibling who didn't garner anywhere as much attention. This sibling has led a happy life but the focus in the family was always on the champion daughter and her swimming.'

'Like Hellyer and the tennis,' Gibson said.

'Exactly. Cortese strongly suggested that families were at the heart of this. Our murderer was one of those siblings whose needs are met while growing up but who knows they're not the favoured one. The attention and affection of the parents rests squarely on the golden child. At least that's how it is perceived.'

'Our perpetrator is enacting a revenge fantasy where he dispatches the once young high-flyers.'

'Yes, Kate. That could well be it. Our problem is that motive is not a great way to identify suspects. No, strike that. Our major problem is that our killer is accelerating. This execution is nowhere near as elaborate as Hellyer's. It was planned and carried out with a degree of expertise, but it was quicker and there isn't the same sense of theatre.'

Kendall voiced what they were all thinking. 'The release of the image precipitated this action. He planned to kill this victim, but not quite so soon and more elaborately. However, now he knows we're onto him he pressed the fast-forward button.'

'Seems that way. More than ever we have to go into overdrive. I hope you two didn't have plans for tonight.'

□

Mahoney didn't have to go far to complete his first call. Constable Miller was still outside the house helping to monitor comings and goings to the crime scene.

'Constable, is it safe to make a house call over yonder? I hear you dumped oil on troubled waters. Can't say I blame you, but best tell me what exactly was said.'

'His nibs came over waving his arms about and complaining about the extra vehicles in the street. Told me to fix it up or he'd be on the phone to the big boss.'

'And you said he could shove it up his rear end.'

The laughter transformed his face. 'Nah, I was just winding Gibson up. Now he's in a suit he's lost his sense of humour. What I told Mr High-and-mighty was that it was a serious crime scene and that took precedence over his entertainment plans. The way he reacted you'd think I said a lot worse.'

'Right, okay. It seems he has issues with the messenger. Some people don't want to be placated, especially pushy people. I'll see how I go. If I'm not out in fifteen minutes, send in reinforcements.' Mahoney smiled to make the levity clear.

As Mahoney crossed the street, he took in the array of late model imported cars that now filled the kerbside: well-heeled guests. He climbed the steps and rang the bell. The front door was opened by a portly man in a dinner suit.

Before Mahoney could ask for a cocktail, the ugly face above the bow tie launched into a volley of abuse. 'It's the militia, is it? Jack booting in to harass peaceable citizens. What right do you have to impinge on our liberties? Disgusting plebs. Especially that stupid fool directing traffic. I've a mind to call the Commissioner right now.'

The penguin paused; he was awaiting a reaction, but when met with a deadpan look, started up again. 'So they've sent a deaf mute. Just brilliant. I pay my taxes so a spastic can parade about in a suit.' The man stepped over the doorstop and jabbed Mahoney in the chest. 'What's wrong? Too embarrassed to speak?'

'That, Sir, is assault. Please desist.'

'It knows a clever word.' He poked his finger into the officer's gut.

Mahoney smacked the arm away and grabbed the man's suit lapels. He jerked the abnoxious man towards him slightly, swivelled, then slammed his back into the brickwork. As he held the buffoon in place, Mahoney whispered, 'And that's self-defence.'

When Mahoney loosened his grip, the suited man slid down the wall and held his right arm up as if to ward off a blow. His tone was now snivelling. 'Don't hit me. I've got guests.'

'Then act like a host and be civil. My rank is Inspector and I expect to be made welcome. Now stand up.'

He stood up, albeit gingerly. 'I'm going to complain, you know. You can't do that.'

'As you wish. However, bear this in mind. In plain view of a commissioned officer of the law you jabbed me in the chest. Twice. That constitutes a threat. Naturally, I defended myself. With minimal force. I'm prepared to call it square. As for your earlier attempt to obstruct a police investigation, my next step depends on your next step.' Mahoney held his hands open as if weighing up his options.

'That's ludicrous. I was simply telling the young chap what to do.'

'Sir, you do not tell a police officer what to do. You have rights as a citizen, but bossing around the constabulary is not one of them, whatever their rank.'

A voice called from the hallway. 'Monty, what are you doing now? We're about to be seated.' A face appeared at the doorway. 'Oh, are you police?'

'Yes, madam. Monty was just assisting me with our investigation. Are you aware a serious incident occurred across from you today?'

'No. I was busy inside most of the day preparing for this evening. We don't know them very well. They've only been here for six months. They had that ghastly article published about their house. Very foolish. An open invitation to burglars that sort of thing.'

'Did you notice anything at all today?'

She smoothed her dress and lowered her voice. 'Well, I did think "while the cat's away ..."'

'As in?'

'Well, you know ...' She came out onto the porch and whispered conspiratorially. 'Her husband's away so she gets a bit of rough in.'

Neither had yet asked what the incident was; it didn't seem to matter.

'Did Mrs Heath have a visitor today?'

'Some sort of dodgy looking character. He parked right in front of our house and went in there this morning.'

'What time was this?'

'A bit after nine, or thereabouts. She answered the door and in he went.'

'How long was he there?'

'How am I meant to know?' She seemed genuinely affronted at the suggestion she was a nosey parker. 'His little rust bucket was gone an hour or two later. That's all I know.'

'This is very important, so please try to remember. Can you describe the car or the visitor?'

'The car was a little blue thing. Pockmarked. No clue as to the make, sorry, but it was certainly an eyesore.' She stopped suddenly, as if struck by a crucial thought. 'Inspector, do you mind if my husband goes back in? Our guests must be wondering what on earth's going on.'

He'd had enough of Monty's company anyway. 'Certainly. And I shan't keep you much longer.'

After Monty traipsed in, she smiled and offered her hand. 'Cynthia Montgomery.'

'Detective Inspector John Mahoney.'

'Don't mind my husband. He can be rather self-important. I appreciate you taking him down a few pegs. Don't worry, it was self-defence. He is his own worst enemy. Now, where was I?'

'The visitor today.'

'Ah, yes. Six foot or so. Green cap, grey shirt with short sleeves, darker green shorts, fair skin, cheap sunglasses. He was carrying a parcel and clipboard, but my impression was that it was a front for some steamy suburban sex.' A telling pause. 'She invited him in.'

'You saw that?'

'Not exactly. As you can see, those poplars hide the line of sight. I just assumed she'd let him in because the car didn't leave straightaway. But it was gone by eleven o'clock because when I came out for the mail, there was no sign of it.' She smoothed her dress again. 'Now, is there anything else? It's just that …'

'No, that's fine. You've been very helpful.' He turned to go. 'Oh, by the way, don't you want to know what happened?'

'Yes, but we have guests and I'd rather not have their evening spoiled. It's not as if I knew the woman well. I dare say all will be revealed. Goodbye Inspector.'

Mahoney skipped back down the steps to where Miller was still in position by the Toyota Prado. 'Looked like you didn't need assistance, Sir.'

'Not as it turns out.' He looked back up to the Montgomery house. 'That was one of the most strange doorstop interviews I've ever done.' He shook his head in amazement. 'Very helpful though. Are you posted here for tonight?'

'Until ten. Then someone else takes over—if you need someone here that is.'

'Yes. The SOCO team will be here for a fair while. Could you, and whoever takes over from you, also keep an eye on the Mongomery's mansion. I don't imagine they're in any danger but you never know. Keep me posted of anything untoward. Whatever time.'

'Sure, Sir. Nice work with the slam.'

'Thank you. I don't think he'll be quite so rude to us next time.'

□

'Are you alright, John?' The soft voice caught him by surprise; the click of heels on the tiled balcony had sounded like Kendall approaching. It was a female colleague who had approached and stood next to him, but much more senior in authority.

'Commissioner, good evening. My task force is expanding.' The quip suggested an optimism he didn't feel.

'For the moment, it's Christine. I've instructed the other officers to give us some time alone. Now, my original question.'

With her searching eyes on him, he wasn't sure how to respond. At his rank there were few who would regard him in quite this manner.

'Knackered. Hopeful. Apprehensive. Proud.' It sounded glib but he believed he could trust her with a frank assessment. She was too shrewd to be blindsided by flummery.

'I'd be tired too. You've had some long and intense days. It's that effort that gives us all hope that a result is not far away. I'm given to understand from DS Kendall that a lot has been discovered very quickly and that Constables Dunstan and Gibson are standing tall. So, I'm wondering why you are apprehensive.'

When had Kate briefed the Commissioner? That was an interesting take on the hierarchy. The Commissioner seemed to read this thoughts.

'Let me assure you that Kendall isn't my mole in the team. I happened to arrive as you were going across the street. I came straight in and DS Kendall gave me a clear and succinct precis. And I read the case log earlier this evening, which is very thorough. As you may know I was in Adelaide from Sunday for a national conference. Instead of going home this afternoon, I went into the office and AC Westbrook updated me on happenings. This strikes me as a very unusual case. I'm here to obtain a sense of it for myself and, more importantly, to assure you of support.'

Mahoney chided himself for his brief bout of insecurity. This wasn't his old nemesis, former Assistant Commissioner Newman. Christine Baker was the real deal.

'Then thank you. I think the apprehension is not that we're incapable of solving this. The resourcefulness of everybody has been great. It's more that we're faced with an antagonist who has prepared thoroughly for an extended period of time.' He gripped the rail as he searched for the right phrase. 'The killer isn't acting emotionally or impulsively. These deaths are determined by his deeply suppressed emotions though. He's giving vent to rage, yet doing it in a thoroughly controlled and ingenious manner.'

'As the profiler explained. Interesting report.'

'Yes, he did. That does help us to understand the killer, but it doesn't necessarily enable us to catch him. I think I'm beginning to glimpse his motivation. I've got some ideas I'll run by Cortese, the profiler, tomorrow. But it's the physical detection that is going to lead to an arrest.'

Baker nodded. 'As I thought. You have nothing to be apprehensive about.'

Mahoney tapped his watch. 'Time. What if our pursuit is propelling him to commit his planned murders more quickly? We've got to work faster.'

The Commissioner started laughing abruptly. 'You need to see this shrink. What's his name, Cortese? And get some sleep.' She reached into her handbag. 'Here, take these.' She slipped two small white pills into his hand. 'They'll help you rest tonight.'

'But I need to be here …'

'No.' Almost a bark. 'Listen to me. You, Kendall and Gibson need to leave this site to the Forensics team. Whether you admit it or not, you are overtired, to the extent that it's verging on anxiety. A minute ago you pretty well suggested it's your fault this murder happened because you're doing your job quickly and effectively. That is grotesque nonsense. This calamity has been a long time in gestation. Even hinting that you and the team are at fault for today is like blaming me for these murders.'

Mahoney's shoulders dropped. He realised he'd been holding his upper torso rigid. Baker was right—they hadn't dropped the ball. He breathed deep into his abdomen and exhaled slowly.

'Thank you. I am getting close to running on empty.'

'Good. Rest tonight. Is there a briefing tomorrow?'

'Nothing scheduled yet.'

'Good.' She glanced at her watch. 'It's now almost nine. If you can't get a decent sleep in tonight, I'll change chemists. All personnel state-wide are on the lookout for the Mazda vehicle and the Ogden man. There is nothing that has to be done by you tonight. Go and rest.' She patted him on the arm and left.

Mahoney fingered the pills in his jacket pocket. One night without his mind whizzing couldn't hurt.

CHAPTER TWENTY-TWO

Mahoney woke with a start, straight from sleep to a rousing chorus of Flight of the Bumble Bee. The incessant buzzing of his mobile phone was hard to ignore. It was Kendall.

'Sir, we've got that lead on the car. Traffic have produced the details on the speeding ticket. It was on Sandfly Road near Longley last Sunday.

He blinked as he sought some focus. 'Okay, what time is it now?'

'Ten past eight.'

A ten hour sleep, and he could have gone on slumbering. Thank God it was just the one tablet he took. 'Can you collect me at my place in half an hour? We'll head down there.'

'Sure, Sir. Double shot latte?'

'Yes, thanks Kate. See you then.'

He still felt a little slow as he eased out of bed. Christine Baker's pill had done the job—a sound sleep without the dreams. Once under the steaming jet of the shower, he began to feel awake. He reminded himself to call Susan; it would be another night without catching up, but he hoped they might have some time on the weekend. Unlike most of the working population, Friday was not on his mind—the rapidity of the week's passing was.

Once dressed, he bundled an assortment of socks, jocks and shirts into the washing machine and set it to the economy cycle, hoping he would get back sometime soon to hang the load out to dry. Everything went on hold during an investigation. No wonder the accumulated stresses fractured the domestic lives of some officers.

Out the front of his apartment he saw Kendall approaching with a takeaway coffee in each hand. She was on foot.

'I'm back in my place. It's only a few blocks away. Remember?'

Of course. She would hardly still be at Rex's place.

'Right. Of course. We'll go in my car. Perfect.'

They got in his Toyota 86, not quite a sports car but at least a sporty car. Kendall placed his coffee in a cup holder.

'You alright this morning? You seem preoccupied.'

'I took a sleeping pill last night. It was very … effective. Usually I'm bolt upright first thing but there must be something of an after effect.'

'Probably. They can knock you out.' She took out her phone. 'I've got our location. It's near the Longley Hotel.'

'Good.' He flicked the indicator. 'We'll take the scenic route, up Huon Road and through Fern Tree. It may even be quicker.'

It was a winding road that suited his car beautifully. In the break between the morning school run and the early tourists to the mountain, there was little traffic. Kendall seemed content to let him concentrate on his driving. Once past Neika the road straightened.

'Well, that's woken me up. Good to test the old skills once in a while. You can drink that coffee with confidence now.'

Kendall took a sip. 'It's still warm enough. A bit longer with boy racer and it might have turned cold. You should be a match for a little old Mazda.'

'You'd hope so.' He took a swallow himself. It was tepid; his sergeant was a good fibber. 'Now, today's schedule.'

'We discover Ogden's hidey-hole and arrest him?'

'I wish.' He noticed her deadpan delivery was getting very good. 'Texts received while I was waiting for you: autopsy is at noon, forensics prelim report due by lunchtime, meet the press at two this afternoon.'

'Really? Do we need the last one?'

'Yes and no. Commissioner Baker has called for it. Word will leak somewhere and then all hell could break loose if we don't exert some damage limitation. If we're proactive, the media could assist us.'

Kendall sipped again. 'As we discovered, the public appeal did help. It's a lot to sift through though.'

'Agreed. But it does help for people to be alert for our guy. You could argue that with a macabre killer on the loose, people have a compelling right to know.'

'As long as it doesn't become a circus like the Finch investigation.'

'We've learned from that. I think we can control the flow of information better in this case.' He slowed the car. 'Hold on. This bit's gravel.'

They were quickly back on the bitumen and passed the Longley Hotel. 'Nice pub. It's the one they use for that show *Rosehaven*,' offered Mahoney.

'Can't say I've seen it.' Kendall checked her map and pointed right. 'The speed camera wagon was perched about a hundred metres up the rise. They put one there in response to local complaints that hoons were doing highway speeds on a quiet country road.'

Mahoney turned the car right and crawled past where they figured the automatic camera must have been. As he accelerated smoothly away he said, 'This helps us. The section of road we're on only goes for about a kilometre or two. It's effectively a loop, with both exits on the Huon Highway. This used to be the old winding road to Huonville. There's only a dozen or so properties to check.'

Kendall looked left and right at the rolling hills. 'It's a beautiful spot. We're thirty minutes from town and it's Shangri-la.'

'I know. A very quiet location for a bolthole. We'll drive the route first for a quick look-see, then double back.'

The road rose and dipped through paddocks of parched grass, the tinges of green testimony to some recent rain. In late summer it had bucketed down for a few days as if to signal the end of the season. Since then it had been clear sunshine with little humidity.

As they rounded a curve to the left, Kate spoke, 'What a perfect retreat.'

Mahoney glanced over at the cedar-clad house Kate was pointing at. It was shaped like a hexagon with a cylindrical skylight in the roof. 'You can stay there if you like.'

Kendall's voice was immediately enthusiastic. 'How so? Is it a plush bed and breakfast?'

He pulled into the verge. 'Not exactly. The main building you can see is part yoga room and part meals area. Down below on a ridge that we can't see from here are about six or seven nifty little huts that guests stay in. There's another pavilion down the hill for massages and all that stuff.'

'A bush health retreat.'

'Yeah. You can do as much or as little as you like. All meals or some meals. Lots of yoga or none at all. The owners aren't didactic. Believe me, I tested the limits of the regimen. Susan and I had four days in early February. I'd rented my shack out to people for most of the summer for some handy cash. Susan was here on assignment, so to speak, and I tagged along. The deal is you pay the basic tariff for accommodation and then add on the various extras like spa treatments that interest you. Susan tried a bit of everything and really liked it.'

'And you?'

'I sat in the picture window and caught up on my reading. Tore through that Nick Hornby radio comedy one. Bit slower with *Girl on a Train*. Spooked me out a bit that one.'

'That's it. No facials?'

'Nup. Walked about a bit and had a remedial massage. And read some really good books. It was perfect.'

Kendall seemed unconvinced. 'I think I would want to do a bit more. I've got some leave coming up, so I might give it a try.'

Mahoney pulled out and accelerated up the rise, braking as the road narrowed. After a few minutes they reached the junction with the highway. He did a three-point turn and they retraced their path. Mahoney had counted five dwellings visible from the road. It was time for some old-fashioned door-to-door work.

An hour and a quarter later: zilch. The final call was the bush retreat. Mahoney eased the car up the gravel drive. As they got out, a female exited the Hexagon and came towards them. 'If you'd park in the guest area, please. There are signs.'

And a warm welcome to you too, thought Mahoney. He whipped out his ID. 'This is official business. I'm DI Mahoney and my colleague is DS Kendall. I'm hoping you can assist us.'

The woman pulled up short and stared at them for a few seconds. 'I'm sorry. What business?'

The DI couldn't figure out why she seemed so distracted. 'We're searching for a person of interest in this area. We know his car was on this road recently. This morning ...'

'What type of car?'

'A blue Mazda 323. Not in the best condition.'

Her face was a mixture of shock and concern. 'Oh dear. You'd better come inside.'

She hurried back to the glass sliding door. As they followed, Kendall shot Mahoney a quizzical look to which a shrug was the only response. Inside, the sense of lightness was dominant. Beams radiated from the perimeter to the raised skylight, and four of the six wall panels were floor-to-ceiling glass. Sunlight flooded the space. The sprung wooden floor and glazed windows added warmth to the large area. Right now the area was quite empty. The woman signalled for them to come over to a bench where she held up a sheet of paper.

'My apologies for being abrupt. I'm Jodie Brenner, one half of Bush Yogi. This retreat was my baby for a couple of years. I had two huts and a sports massage service. My husband, Rob, came on board as my business partner a couple of years ago with some new ideas and since then all we seem to do is expand.' A quick smile. 'But not in a rushed way. I work fewer hours now than I did then. We hired some great casuals and offered more services. The turnover is unbelievable and we get to take the yoga classes.'

Mahoney hadn't asked about any of this, and he was unsure why he needed to be told. He wasn't offended that she didn't recall him as a guest; he didn't remember her.

'It looks lovely. Could we get to the business I mentioned just before?'

'Oh yes, sorry. I'm a bit flustered this morning. I thought I should tell you who I am. Coming out and shouting at you like that was not very Zen.'

'That's okay. You seemed quite concerned about something I said.'

'When you mentioned the car, I suddenly thought of second sight. I think one of our guests was driving a car like that.'

Mahoney felt his pulse tweak. 'Is that guest here now?'

'No. That's what's spooked me. Well, partly.' Her hands danced all over the place. 'It's all a bit weird.'

Kendall stepped forward. 'Jodie, let me get you a glass of water. Sit down and take the inspector through it. We're not rushing.'

Mahoney sat next to Jodie. 'One step at a time. The car is still here. Correct?'

'Yes. Down in the guest car park. Rob checked this morning. It's a blue Mazda 323 which has seen better days, as you said.'

Kendall put the glass on the teak surface and sat across from their hostess. 'Was there a reason for checking, Jodie?'

'We think he's gone missing. He borrowed one of our hybrid push bikes yesterday afternoon to go for a ride, but he wasn't back this morning.'

'Did that alarm you?' Kendall's voice was calm.

'To be honest, we'd forgotten about him. Thursday night is our time out. Rob and I get off site and eat out somewhere. We went to

Woodbridge and got back at about ten thirty. We just assumed the guy was back.'

'What prompted you to check this morning?' Mahoney doubted an inventory of the bikes was done each day.

'His credit card wouldn't process. We put a deposit on file when a guest checks in and then put the full amount through on checkout. He was meant to be leaving today. After it bounced, Rob went down to his hut. He had a feeling the guy had done a runner.'

'And the guest wasn't there, the car still was, and the bike wasn't back?'

'Got it in one. We thought the worst, so Rob has gone out in our van looking for him in case he got knocked off the bike on one of the side roads. We changed our minds on him scarpering without paying because his car was still there.'

The detectives stood; they didn't have to ask to know how Rob's search was going.

'Mrs Brenner, if you could show my sergeant the car park, I'd like to take a look at the accommodation.'

She stood as well. 'Of course. Is this man in some sort of trouble?'

'He isn't in immediate danger. However, we do need to contact him urgently.'

'By the way, what name did he register under?'

'Scott Hellyer.'

Their man didn't mind taking risks. 'Was that the name on the credit card?'

'Yes. Visa. It all seemed legitimate.'

As Mahoney walked down to the hut, he considered the charge sheet they could draw up. Somehow credit card fraud didn't cut the mustard compared to the main game. He wondered again if they were keeping pace with the momentum. Again, they were hot on the trail but that trail was meandering and could stretch a lot further.

The bluestone crescent path brought him down to where the man they thought to be Ogden had been staying. He stood in front of a rammed earth building which he knew from his previous stay would be akin to the Tardis: deceptively large on the inside. Behind to his right was the guest car park containing the Mazda.

Upon entering, he was struck by the warmth; it wasn't stifling but pleasant enough not to require a jumper. Across the floor tiled with dark flagstones was the living area with its two seater table and some easy chairs. To his left was a compact kitchenette and to his right was the bedroom with ensuite. It looked to his naked eye as if the place had been cleaned, ready for a new guest.

As he was donning his plastic gloves, he heard Kendall's footsteps on the crushed bluestone. She entered and also slipped latex gloves on. 'It's the right car. Rego checks. I told Mrs Brenner to call her husband back. He's not their worry now.'

'No, he isn't. Anyway, it's not as if he'd find anybody. My belief is he's dumped the car here and made his getaway on the bike, bizarre as that seems.'

'Yes, on the surface. But again the only reason we have a lead is luck—that speeding infringement. It's like the second vehicle engine number. We're onto him, but it seems fluky how we're doing it.'

Mahoney snorted. 'Don't I know it. We're doing all the right things though. We can't forget that this guy has planned his whole operation carefully. Take this place, for example. He came here to stay on Saturday, driving the Mazda after successfully dumping the white van. He checked in for a week and could come and go as he pleased. Remained fairly anonymous by pretending he simply wanted some peace and quiet.'

'It's a risk using Hellyer's card though, isn't it?'

'A calculated one. If the Brenners twigged that it was the same name as the deceased man at Opossum Bay, so what? Their guest is alive and well, so they would figure it's just a coincidence. I don't know if you noticed but there is no media here at all—no television, radio or newspapers, and no internet. There's no embargo, but connection to the outside isn't encouraged.'

'What if someone here recognised him from the public appeal?'

Mahoney frowned as he turned that over. 'We know the image is reasonably accurate because the woman in the shop opposite the funeral venue recognised him. So, on Wednesday morning he still looked much as we thought. Yesterday he was wearing a cap and sunnies so picking him is harder.'

He walked into the ensuite. Kendall followed and stood at the doorway as her boss rummaged in the compact tidy bin. He held up a small white plastic bottle in his hand and flipped open the orange cap. It had no labels on it, so he took a sniff and then handed it over. 'Not being sexist, but I'm hoping you'll know what this is.'

Kendall held it to her nose. 'Hair dye.' She shut one eye to peer at the aperture. 'It looks like some hue of red.'

'Right then. He's dyed his hair sometime in the last forty-eight hours. We'll check with the Brenners to see if they noticed that, although they may not have seen him. If you don't venture up to the main room, you're pretty much left to your own devices.'

She shook the bottle lightly. 'If he used the whole lot, that's a hefty application. I'm no expert but the tone would go from dark to something much lighter. Not as strong as Gibson but sort of rusty.'

He took the container back and placed it on the wash basin. 'We'll get Kitchener and the gang down. They can comb through here and the car.'

'And they'll discover the same traces again.'

Mahoney caught the frustration in her voice. 'I know. But at least the conviction will be solid.'

'Do we release more information this afternoon?'

'At the press conference? We'll have to. It makes us look a bit all-over-the-shop but we've got no choice. I've never felt so close yet so far from a culprit. It's all a bit maddening.'

'I know just how you feel.'

□

Kendall made the call to New Town. Manning and Givens would be down right away, although in practical terms that meant at least forty-five minutes. They decided to wait on-site; it was possible that useful information might be available from the car or hut immediately.

It was now almost eleven fifteen. With the autopsy scheduled for midday, Mahoney made two more calls: one to Dunstan to get down to the hospital and observe, and the other to Cortese. Fortunately, he was still in town and also agreed to attend Pitney's examination of the body. So far so good.

Back at the main building they found that Rob Brenner had returned. With the introductions done, Mahoney asked him if he'd seen 'Hellyer' over the past week.

His voice was low and gravelly, almost as if his larynx was damaged. 'Bugger all, Inspector. Our bungalow is off to the other side of the complex, about eighty metres from that hut and the guest parking area. Unless he came up here, there would have been little chance of us bumping into each other.'

'He didn't include himself in any classes or meals?'

'None at all as far as we know. We offered him all the services when he arrived, but he said he wanted quiet time, pure and simple. If that's a guest's preference, we abide by it. Seems a pity but some folk are odd like that.'

Kendall glanced at Mahoney. 'Can you describe what he looked like when he arrived last Saturday?' she asked.

The Brenners looked at each other before Rob replied. 'Just another fella. About six foot, normal sort of face, no striking features really. Only thing was that his hair looked a bit luxuriant. You know, like a bit dark. He had the faint beginnings of stubble and that looked much lighter, as if the beard would be greyish. I reckon he must have dyed his thatch.'

'Some people aren't so keen on the inevitable process of time. Me, I'm happy with the salt and pepper advance.' Mahoney kept his voice light. 'Have you by any chance seen or heard our public appeals recently?'

'Fundraising?'

'No, not really. Appeals for information.'

'Nah, too busy running this show. We're in our own little cocoon down here. That's why we love it. We don't even have to advertise. All our business comes by word-of-mouth.'

Kendall had unobtrusively slipped out to the car and was now returning with an iPad. She propped it on the bench and turned it slightly so the couple could see the screen. 'Could you cast your eye over a few portrait shots for us? Stop me when anyone recognisable appears.'

After considering a random selection of Caucasian males, they halted the slide show on number eight. 'That's him,' said the husband. 'Well, near enough. His hair was a bit darker when I met him but that's really close to the face.'

Kendall showed them another dozen, but there was no reaction. She took the collection back to number eight. Brenner was adamant. 'That's him. Can I see one of the early ones again?'

'Sure.' Kendall went back until the image provided by the post office worker brought a reaction. 'That one. I didn't notice it first time through, but that looks like him if he had a beard. Is it?'

Kendall stayed neutral. 'There is a resemblance. I can see what you're thinking.'

Mahoney took over. 'Mrs Brenner, just to check, the credit card was fine last Saturday but today it was rejected?'

'Yes. The holding deposit went through fine, but today it didn't work. I rang the bank and they said the card was deregistered at the owner's request on Wednesday. I don't know how we'll get the payment now.'

'I'm afraid I can't help you. The brutal truth is that you probably won't get the payment. You see, the man who stayed here was not Scott Hellyer. Unfortunately, Mr Hellyer died last weekend and we believe the card used here was stolen from the deceased.'

Rob Brenner croaked, 'This guy was a serious crim then? Hang on, how did that Hellyer bloke die?'

'He was murdered.'

'Shit. By this bloke? The one who was under our roof? Why weren't we told?'

How in God's name could anyone answer that?

'That's why we made our public appeal. This man you identified is a suspect, but we had no idea he was staying here. I can assure you that if we had known, he'd have been in custody days ago. We're very, very keen to get hold of him and that's why we're here. We were following a lead on that Mazda being in this area in the past week. We couldn't action anything until today. Believe me, I wish we'd got here yesterday but circumstances prevented us.'

As he said it, Mahoney thought it strange to label the bathroom drowning a 'circumstance'.

Jodie Brenner found her voice. 'Gosh, that's scary. We weren't harbouring him. This is all a total surprise for us.'

'No-one's suggesting that.' He knew it didn't fit for their lone wolf to have any accomplices, however peripheral. 'You were unwitting hosts, that's all. And your co-operation today has been hugely appreciated, especially with that identification. We are going to have to inconvenience you a bit further, I'm afraid'

Rob Brenner coughed and then said, 'As long as we're not in danger, or our guests.'

'I won't make an empty promise, but I'd say this person is long gone. Right, here's what we need to do. First, some Forensics officers will be here very soon. They'll be unobtrusive, but the hut that he stayed in will be out of action for the rest of today. They'll do their stuff and return the hut for your use tomorrow. The car will be inspected in situ and then towed away to our compound. I doubt you'll see the bike again. We'll take the details of the make for our purposes, but it's probably ditched somewhere.'

He turned to Kendall to see if she wanted to add anything, but she shook her head. Mahoney continued, trying to sound upbeat. 'Whatever insurance doesn't cover, we'll try and make good somehow. I'm sure we could get some of our team down here for a few professional development days during winter. Here's my card. Let me know when projected stays are light, and we'll book you out for a couple of nights. I have a budget I've barely dipped into, and it would be a good cause all round.'

Rod Brenner's eyes lit up. 'You're on. August is generally slow. We take a fortnight off and get the odd job people in for the first two weeks of the month. After that's done, you'd be really welcome.'

A hand was offered which Mahoney shook. 'Done deal.'

'Will you two be staying now?'

Kendall answered. 'I will be. The Inspector has to get back to town for a press conference. That's right, isn't it, Sir?'

'Thanks, Kate. That's the plan. You'll be right to oversee the dynamic duo when they arrive?'

'Of course.'

CHAPTER TWENTY-THREE

Gibson had decided to take a punt. The investigative team was making steady progress, but he believed that what was needed was a breakthrough moment, something that could speed up the chase. So, he took himself out of the main building to visit the Forensic Accounting Unit. He had an inkling that social media would be a sure path to the killer.

Once across Argyle Street he entered the administrative centre for Tasmania Police, nodded a greeting to Constable Dyson on the reception desk and took the lift up to the fifth floor. He went in through the sliding glass doors and over to the guru's desk. Sergeant Richard Dobosz looked up as he approached.

'Gabster, welcome. What do you need?'

A promotion, a modest pay rise … Gibson doubted Tricky Dicky could assist with either of those.

'Hi, Sarge. I want to draw on your tech savvy. I've got an idea on how our culprit may be scoping out his victims, and I need you to help me draw a line.'

Dobosz motioned to a chair. 'Sure thing. Fire away.'

Gibson opened a folder on the desk. 'Okay, the second victim first: Patricia Heath. I'm thinking that for a perpetrator to accomplish what he did, there has to have been a fair amount of preparation, as in backgrounding the victim.'

'And how does a stranger acquire such information?'

'Exactly. I'm thinking her life was more of an open book to outsiders than she realised.'

Dobosz nodded. 'Because she's sharing her life almost constantly with the Facebook world. Or on Instagram.'

'Yeah. "Look at me. Look at my happy life." That sort of thing.'

'Let's look at her Facebook activity.' Dobosz opened his own Facebook home page and typed 'Patricia Heath' into the search bar he. A short list of names appeared, with what looked like the recent victim second on the ladder. Dobosz opened the page and they saw a photo of a smiling woman in overalls at the start of the Sydney Harbour Bridge climb—big sunglasses, windswept hair and a cheesy thumbs up for the camera.

'Looks like her. What's she got on there?'

Gibson's colleague scrolled down the page and intermittently clicked on various posts and photos. Neither spoke; the material spoke for itself. It did indeed seem as if Patricia Heath had placed a great amount of her daily activity online for all to see.

The phone on the desk trilled. Dobosz picked up the receiver and listened.

'You'll have to excuse me for a short while. One of the new civilians in the help desk area needs a hand. Won't be long.'

Not a problem for Gibson. There was enough to be going on with on Heath's profile. He shuffled his chair in front of the work station and scrolled through the page. In the 'About' section were the essential facts of her life: age, marital status, education, employment status and interests. Until her untimely death at forty-three years old, Patricia Heath had been married to Ian, a management consultant, and mother to Jack, at university in Melbourne, and Chloe, a student at St Hilda's.

His mobile rang. 'Yes, Kate.'

'David, where are you?'

'At Dobosz's desk, backgrounding Patricia Heath.'

'Oh, right.'

'Problem?'

'No. That's just what I was going to suggest.'

'Good.' Gibson didn't want to end the call. 'How's it gone with contacting her immediate family?'

'Fine. Dunstan's spoken to the husband who should now be on his way back from the States. He was in Utah on a trip with some mates. He'll pick up the son on the way back through Melbourne, but that whole thing will take a day or two.'

'What about the daughter? She's local, isn't she?'

'Annette Masters from Family Support has it covered. The father agreed for her to contact the girl and escort her back from the school camp she's on. That lady from the other night, Anna Vagianos, is going to care for her until the rest of the family arrive.'

'What about other relations?'

'Well, Patricia Heath was originally from Launceston. Her parents are still alive, a Mr and Mrs Whittey. Annette has broken the news to them and they're driving down in a few days to help where they can. She had one other sibling, Phillip, who lives up that way too. He will surely help them.'

All the while Gibson's gaze was fixed on the screen picture of the Heath family, seated around a picnic table somewhere by the sea— bright, healthy and loving life. They could barely have imagined the prospect that now befell them.

'Do you need me to do anything?'

'No. Keep at that. Family support will manage the Heaths. I'll sort the forensics stuff, and the boss is going to the media briefing. How long will you be?'

'Not sure. I had a feeling whoever did this knew a lot about the victim, and it looks like her social media activity gave just about anybody a direct line on everything she was up to.'

'So could you maybe track who was interested?'

'It's a possibility. I've just started going through her Facebook page and Tricky Dicky will hopefully help me delve further.'

'Okay. There's a briefing at five, so I'll see you then.'

'Sure thing.'

Gibson hung up. All business, two colleagues just doing their jobs. Probably the best way forward. Back to Patricia. He moved the cursor to the 'Friends' tab and clicked the mouse—you never knew.

□

Before going into the press conference, Mahoney only had time for a fleeting phone conversation with Dunstan. The autopsy was still in progress so any conclusions were preliminary, at best. Testing of the fluid in the lungs was the priority, but that didn't happen at the snap of one's fingers. The report on the crime scene should be ready by close of business.

But what information should they give to the public? The release of the image had been a spark. How to fan the flame without setting off a wildfire? They had a name, but could he be sure it was correct? The killer had to know the police were on his trail, so there wasn't a need to hold information back. Perhaps by releasing more intelligence than usual the perpetrator could be spooked into thinking the investigators were close. Maybe, just maybe, he would go to ground. It would make him harder to find, but it would stall the executions.

Ten minutes before the lights went up, Mahoney checked his options with the Commissioner as they stood huddled in the corridor outside the briefing room. She was dressed in full parade uniform and looked imposing—precisely the desired effect.

'Do we release the name?' Mahoney asked.

'Ogden? Yes.'

There was little argument there. 'What about Oates?'

'As in the misuse of his licence for nefarious purposes?'

'Yes. I'm inclined not to, but it could help.'

'Why are you inclined not to?'

'My thinking is that it refracts the focus, possibly slurs the man's reputation and gives away that we're onto the Longley hide-out.'

Baker pulled her jacket straight. 'Yes, leave him out of it. He's been very co-operative, has he not?'

Oates had certainly been helpful—justifiably angry but certainly willing to assist. Mentioning the link would add insult to injury.

The dilemma now was how much laundry to air in public. If only they could work undercover as a secret service and close in on their prey like a phalanx of stealth bombers, but Mahoney put that 'if' in his mental waste basket. The initial media appeal had borne fruit. Besides, the press conference was obligatory; the public had a genuine right to know. Didn't the police have a duty to serve *and* protect?

Mahoney followed Baker into the media room, allowing himself a sideways glance at the scrum. It was a full house. He assured himself that he knew how to play the hand they'd been dealt. Sitting on their cards and letting the killer dictate play was no longer an option. They must bet aggressively; it was ultimately winner takes all.

There was a short hiatus as sound and lighting levels were checked before the Commissioner opened proceedings.

'Ladies and Gentelmen, we are calling on the co-operation of the citizens of Greater Hobart for assistance. In the past week two brutal murders have been perpetrated in this region. I want to assure you that all the resources of your police force are being devoted to apprehending the person responsible for these diabolical acts.'

As she continued with an outline of the case, Mahoney was quietly staggered by her analysis. Her faculty for mastering the breadth and depth of the investigation was impressive. At this rate, he would barely have to contribute anything. Five minutes later the questions started being fired. The opening shot was from a familiar figure, although Mahoney noticed that Paul Hicks now wore silver-framed glasses which made him look more like an academic than a journalist from the local paper.

'Inspector Mahoney, are you hunting a spree killer?'

It was the obvious question, so it was best to deal with it early.

'We believe it may have been the same person responsible for both atrocities. I baulk at the term "spree killer" not so much because it generates hysteria but because it isn't emblematic of these particular deaths.'

'That sounds like just the sort of response a seasoned officer would give while attempting to maintain calm.'

Hicks was canny; that's exactly what it was. 'Without wishing to underplay any threat, I must make it clear that there is not a maniac on the loose in our community. The person we are seeking is highly unlikely to engage in sporadic killings in an attempt to make a statement.'

Hicks broke in. 'I'm not suggesting this is akin to Martyn Bryant and the Port Arthur massacre. So, rather than considering a mass murderer, are you instead accepting you have a serial killer?'

Someone had done his homework; it was exactly what Cortese's profiling suggested.

'The short answer is yes. Given the killings were in separate locations over a period of time, then that would be a reasonably accurate assessment.'

Hicks must have felt he'd prised the door open. 'So, it is a serial killer then? You appear reluctant to admit the very real danger on our doorstep.'

Here was the rub: how to avoid alarming people while honestly acknowledge what they were dealing with, and how to communicate to the perpetrator that they possessed strong leads without causing him to panic.

'Your questions are astute, and very much the ones we are asking ourselves. But can I just make a point regarding terminology? With what we would term a "serial killer" there is often a sexual motivation in the mutilation of the corpse which is not apparent in these two murders. Furthermore, our initial profiling suggests there is a connection between the culprit and the victim. Serial killers tend to be more random in their selection of targets.'

The rest of the pack seemed content to let Hicks dictate proceeedings. With the manner of a bright pupil grilling an authority, the journalist continued.

'Then you admit the killer knew his victims?'

'Or knew *of* them. We believe the killer selected the victims not because of who they were but because they fitted into his schema of wanting to achieve a certain goal. What that goal is precisely may not become known until an arrest is made.' Mahoney sat forward in his chair; he wanted to give the impression of sharing vital information. 'And an arrest *will* be made.'

The time for guardedness was over. 'The person we are pursuing is a Mr Gerard Ogden. We have strong reason to believe he was in the immediate vicinity when both attacks occurred. If anybody has any knowledge as to his current or recent whereabouts, they should contact the police immediately. Please do not approach him or alert him in any way. We have recent images of Ogden, but it is possible he is altering his appearance regularly. Please do not feel you are wasting resources if you merely think you've seen a man who looks like this. Contact the police immediately. If you have had any dealings or interaction with Ogden in the recent past, contact us. It is a matter of great urgency.'

The direct appeal seemed to put a stopper in Hicks's bottle, and nobody else took up the reins. Mahoney glanced at his superior; her look assured him that enough had been said. It was time to go and track their man.

□

Back in his office, Mahoney took a moment. Was there anything aside from the case that required his attention? He opened the desk diary in which he catalogued his personal engagements. It was Friday now and in capital letters across the weekend section he'd written 'SUSAN / LAUNCESTON'. What for? Then he recalled they were both meant to be attending a golden wedding anniversary party for her parents. Fifty years! How did a couple manage that? He would be rapt if he and

Susan could clock up just five years without turmoil. There had been discussions of late about Mahoney moving in with her and renting out his apartment. He'd be sure to get good money for a dwelling in South Hobart, and it wasn't as if he needed his own bolthole to escape to these days. The compulsion to have his own space was diminishing, and they would hardly be on top of each other in her home in the hills. When this case was concluded, he'd do it—when this case was finally over. If and when. To ensure it was the latter he would have to skip this trip north.

'Honey, how are you?'

'Peachy. All packed and ready to go. What time suits you for pick-up?'

Bugger. 'Umm, it's going to be ...'

'I'm kidding. I hardly expect you to drop everything and come up. Nor does Mum, particularly now.'

Phew. 'Right, thank you. This is one of those times we've talked about. Thank God it's not always like this.'

'Absolutely. You'll get there. Don't worry.'

'Easier said than done. Why did you say "particularly now" about your mum?'

'They know Mr and Mrs Whittey. Very well, in fact. They were meant to be coming to the party tomorrow night. They may not be coming now, understandably.'

The parents of the second victim—small world. 'Poor things. So they were informed earlier today and your Mum already knows?'

'Yes. Actually she's gone round to their place in Newstead. You know, the old school way. In times of bereavement, family and friends rally round to visit with cake and coffee, and try to keep the spirits up.'

Mahoney knew exactly what she was talking about. He had experienced that upon his own parents passing away. Talk of happy times to buoy the survivors through to the finality of the burial, phone calls, sympathy cards in the post ... a generation that followed form because it was fitting. The new generation set up memorial pages on social media. Not really the same, but you had to assume the emotions were genuine. The whole drawing down of the blinds was ancient history by now.

'John, are you still there?'

'Yes, sorry. Caught in a memory. I don't suppose you know if Mr and Mrs Whittey are coming down here?'

'I don't think just yet. What I gathered from mum is that Patricia's husband's folks will take care of the children down there for now. Her parents will travel in a few days' time. As you can imagine, they're very upset.'

'Of course.' He paused to choose his words. 'Did you know Patricia Whittey well?'

'Growing up, I'd heard of her. I was at Grammar and she went to Oakburn, but you tend to meet up at parties as you get older. We weren't family friends then. The olds became very chummy in retirement. Probus, golf club, all that type of stuff. Of course, most people up here knew of her. In a city this size, everyone takes pride in someone who does that well in sport.'

'I can imagine. Did you know she was down here?'

'No. We weren't close and, to be honest, I never heard much about her after her swimming success. We moved in different circles.'

'Okay. And just to continue our interrogation a touch further ...'

A laugh came down the line. 'Oh, John, don't be so self-conscious. Ask away.'

'Other children in the family? Any idea?'

'A brother, I think. I never knew him back then. Is it important?'

Families did seem to be at the heart of things, but Mahoney was reluctant to draw his partner into his sleuthing.

'No, not really. You know how it is. Backgrounding a victim is part of the whole scheme. If anything obvious jumps out, let me know, but I'd rather you have a grand time with your family. I'm sorry I can't make it. Give them my best.'

'I shall. And you know us journalists are always good listeners. I'll see you late on Sunday, I hope.'

'Yes, that should be fine. Go safely.'

'I will. Bye, honey.'

As he replaced the receiver, a knock sounded on his door.

'Come in.'

Gibson entered. 'Got a few minutes, boss?'

'For you, several. I was just talking to Susan about your hometown. Do you remember Patricia Whittey growing up?'

'Oh yeah. They called her Fish, not for drinking but because she was a great swimmer. She was years ahead of me at school, but I remember she was the talk of the town.'

'Did you know any of the family?'

'Nah. Launceston's not exactly huge, but it's not a village either.'

'Fair enough. So what brings you bounding in?'

Gibson held up an iPad. 'Bit of a hunch. Social media. You've heard of it?'

The DI held his sides. 'Oh, the wit. Yes, I think so. I don't bother with social media myself, but I think I've heard of it. Please enlighten this old Luddite.'

'Well, let's just say I wanted to search for particulars on somebody from a distance. I go online and, for some people, I can find all sorts of stuff there.'

'Such as?'

'For Patricia Heath, there's a massive amount: date of birth, education, family members, friends, interests, and pretty much everything she's been doing or has planned, *had* planned, including the lunch she missed the day she was murdered and what all her family members were doing that day.'

'Really?'

'For sure. It can be like a diary that you share with the world.'

Mahoney didn't even have a Facebook page. Professional discretion and a desire to remain private had held him back. He acknowledged that the Tasmania Police presence on social media was a step forward in communicating with the public, but didn't feel the need to venture there himself. Besides, a detective hardly wanted his presence too well known around town, for the very same reason correctional officers assumed dummy names at the prison: you didn't want aggrieved people knowing where you lived. No-one in the constabulary fancied a visit of retribution in the dead of night.

'And who has access to all this stuff?'

'It depends on your privacy settings, but in Patricia's case it was pretty much everybody. How about I give you a quick Facebook 101?'

'Fire away.'

'Okay, here goes. You go to Facebook's site and click here to create a page, you upload a profile photo and fill in the biography section with as much info as you like: birthday, email, phone contact, hometown … get the drift?'

Mahoney nodded. 'So far, yes. How do other people see it?'

'There's a couple of ways. If you've designated your page 'Public' anybody on Facebook can see it. Otherwise people have to search for your name specifically, or your name is suggested to friends of friends.'

The young constable was manufacturing an online identity in front of them. He had called himself 'Billy Lid' and used a photo stored on the iPad.

'You can also join any of the thousands of groups already established, depending on your interests. For example, you could join this one, Buy/Sell Hobart, and get regular updates on stuff for sale.'

'Slight tangent, but do our guys use this for stolen gear?'

'Yeah, sometimes.' A disbelieving chuckle. 'Some thick people try to sell stolen stuff this way. Anyway, back to Billy Lid. At this stage you can share whatever you like, apart from obscene material which would be taken down by Facebook. You can search for contacts you've lost touch with, sell products, publicise an event … the works really.'

'Can you go back to that one? I think it said Settings.'

'That's the crucial one for us. It's where you control who sees your posts, your friends list and your personal details. You can restrict access to your page or leave it as open slather.'

'Was Patricia Heath an open book?'

'As you can see, she has—had—a plethora of Facebook friends and she was very active ante-mortem. I'm able to access her friends list, contact details, photos, and all her posts which include her comings and goings and those of a lot of her contacts.'

'You might as well put your life on the front page of the paper.'

'You could, but I reckon more people can actually see it this way. Anyway, Snork—sorry, Sergeant Dobosz—and I went through her activity for the past month. Everything she was up to was on there: lunch dates, trips away, the lot.'

'And her family?'

'Same, same. She talks about her family a lot and tags them in her posts: her son's nights out in Melbourne, daughter's school expedition, and the husband's ski trip to Utah. All there for anyone to see. A lot of people restrict these kind of posts to friends. In that case you'd have to send a friend request to her and be accepted, but in this instance there's no need.'

Mahoney sat back from the screen and digested it all. 'It's a bit like someone gifting you a personal tracker, isn't it?'

'Yep, an open book.'

The DI scratched his scalp. 'A person, any person, could trace her movements, even her intended movements. God almighty, that makes it easier for him.'

'Absolutely. Our guy would know that the rest of the family were away and that she'd probably be at home getting ready for the lunch. He just needed to turn up and do the deed. If she had company, he would have had a cover story ready, making a delivery or doing market research, and left it for another time.'

'Bugger.' Mahoney's fist hit the table, jolting the iPad. 'It's almost too easy for him. I don't suppose there's a way of online tracking him.'

'Two words: snowflake and hell.'

CHAPTER TWENTY-FOUR

On Saturday morning Mahoney lay in his bed staring at the ceiling, trying to guess the time from the brightness of the light seeping through a gap in the curtains. He turned to his bedside clock which read 10:37 and gave himself two ticks: one for his guess being in the ballpark and the other for managing a long sleep. The past week had taken a physical toll; being constantly on the go was the only option, but it wearied the bones.

The whole team had been given the Saturday off; six days in and they needed a breather. It wasn't so much avoiding the accumulation of overtime as acknowledgement that pushing everyone too hard yielded decreasingly small returns. They were gathering leads all the time, but harnessing the strands into one conclusive rope was proving elusive. It was time for a lay day.

But what was he to do? Susan was away in Launceston. Perhaps he could make a belated attempt to join her. There may be information to garner there, after all. But she was doing that for him anyway. It was best to be here in case anything broke—no point being three hours away.

He rolled out of bed, determined to make a substantial dent in the small mountain of domestic drudgery that need attending to. His first task was the joy of cleaning the shower.

At around lunchtime Mahoney received a text from his former lieutenant, Munro, suggesting a catch-up. It had been a while. Half an hour later he entered the front bar of the Marquis of Hastings Hotel, and the place was humming. Both pool tables had games on the go and the gaming area was chock-a-block. The crowd was mostly middle-aged Anglo-Saxon males, yarning away, sipping beers and laying bets as if punting was going to be outlawed tomorrow. The pub was named after a convict ship from the early nineteenth century. In the room now there must be a few who were descended from the felons transported to Van Diemen's Land from the old country.

A familiar figure came into the view. It was Munro returning from the cashier with a betting receipt in his hand.

'Race 3. Randwick. Box Trifecta. Next holiday paid for.'

Mahoney smiled as they shook hands. 'Is that so, Tim? Nothing like a sure thing.'

'Exactly.' He held up the paper square. 'Probably nothing like it. Anyway, good to see you. Busy times I gather?'

'Absolutely. I need a break from it. Can I get you a drink?'

'I'm fine. In a round with Hendo.' He gestured to a man hunched over a table with a pencil in his hand making a series of tiny dashes on a card.

'Righto. See you in a sec.' Mahoney edged his way through the throng to the beer taps. Autumn Racing Carnival in Sydney certainly brought a crowd to any pub with betting facilities. As his schooner of Pale Ale was poured, Mahoney glanced left to a wall of screens. Race meetings in Sydney, Brisbane, Adelaide and Perth were displayed with the fields for each upcoming race. Perched on stools at the communal tables were numerous heads poring over the form in the newspaper lift-outs. A few were watching the TV screen above him which was showing the current race nearing its finish. A couple of shouts went up as an outsider careered away from the pack to win by three lengths. Someone was going to cash in.

Back with Munro, he was introduced to Paul Henderson. Henderson had a light smattering of capillaries visible on his cheeks but otherwise looked in fine fettle. Munro, as always, appeared as fit as a mallee bull. The trio agreed to contribute to a pot from which a series of trifecta bets could be made. Each chose a name hoping that they'd snare the first three in whichever race they nominated, usually the favourite, a solid runner and a medium to long odds runner—not all that scientific, but just maybe it could work.

As the afternoon wore on, Mahoney relaxed into proceedings. He caught up with Munro's news on his new position with the Drugs Squad and chatted amiably to Henderson about a cruise the recent retiree had been on; he'd returned the day before from ten days from Hobart to Melbourne, Sydney and across to New Zealand. Aside from the spectacular scenery of the South Island, Henderson's strongest impression was the amiability of the North Americans who made up the majority of the guests on the cruise. Well-travelled, well-off and great company.

Eventually Mahoney asked what Henderson had done for a quid.

'Public Service. I started straight after school in the Lands Department and pretty much stayed there. I started off in the Titles section and finished in National Parks. It sounds dry, but life in DPIPWE wasn't so bad.'

DPIPWE: Department of Primary Industry, Parks, Water and Environment. When you said it aloud, 'De-pip-wee', it was a silly acronym. Still, it was all work that needed to be done, although the Public Service didn't have a reputation for being a hive of activity. Mahoney never voiced this; he was also a public servant after all.

'How long since you pulled up stumps?'

'Just over a year. I reached that stage of life where the clock's on fast-forward.' He raised his eyebrows and drank a mouthful of lager. 'At least I'm here, above ground that is. A few of the intake I started with didn't see the distance. Here's a funny thing. One of them, who died from cancer a few years back, had the same name as your person of interest.'

'Gerard Ogden?'

'Yeah. Couldn't be him obviously.'

'How did he die again?'

'It started with malignant melanomas. He had red hair and very fair skin, and the cancer worked its way into his abdomen. He was a goner from that point.'

'How long ago?'

'About five years, I'd reckon.'

Mahoney nodded and then stared at the screen for the last race in Sydney. Names. There were so many names for horses; coming up with fresh ones must be an industry in itself.

Mahoney had released the name Gerard Ogden and received precious little response. Dunstan had found practically zero from an online search, and he was fastidious. What if their Gerard Ogden didn't exist?

Mahoney jumped off his stool and headed over to the bar. A blonde woman with glasses called Janelle came over, holding up a glass. 'Another Pale Ale?'

'Um, no, but I don't suppose you've got a current phone book.'

She put down the glass and glanced over her shoulder. 'I should have one. Let me check.' She disappeared and then returned holding a think A4-sized paperback. 'This do?'

'Yes, thanks.' Mahoney took it with him to a quiet spot in the corner. He flicked through the pages and ran a finger down the Os. He looked hard at the page, but there was no 'Ogden G' there—very few Ogdens at all, in fact. Perhaps their guy didn't have a landline; he certainly didn't have an address they could find. But what if Gerard Ogden no longer existed at all?

CHAPTER TWENTY-FIVE

On Sunday, Mahoney nosed the car into his underground parking space at headquarters. It was a day in the incident room for him, but the previous day's R&R, along with the emergence of a few new ideas, had invigorated him.

As he walked through reception, the duty officer was returning a set of car keys to a man in a panda suit. It was doubtful the sheepish looking guy had envisaged spending the night in station accommodation. Not stopping to gauge whether it had been drink driving or disorderly behaviour, Mahoney jogged up the stairs to the CIB suite and went straight over to the case board. It was time to take a considered look at proceedings and add some material.

He drew up an office chair and sat facing the jottings and crime scene photos. First off, he scanned slowly from left to right to get an overview. Remembering that he thought best when jotting things down, he dragged over a small table and grabbed a pad and pen from his office.

Forensics analysis for both murders was complete, as were the autopsy reports. The interview transcripts from all potential witnesses were up-to-date. But where were they in the investigation? In some respects well advanced, particularly the forensics material. Mike Kitchener must have cajoled a few colleagues to work late on Friday. They had a match—not to any person they could trace, but a couple of prints at Opossum Bay were a direct match for a hand print at Patricia Heath's home. Elimination prints had been assessed so, unless some random stranger had recently been in both houses, they had solid proof it was the same perpetrator at both locations.

Rigorous checks of the white van and the blue Mazda revealed skin particles and bits of hair, and there was a used tissue in the latter. Again, once the DNA analysis had come through, the FSST confirmed a direct match between human traces in both vehicles. There were no hits on the database, but they'd already assumed the murderer didn't have a record. The good news was that when they chased a suspect down, they would be able to conclusively prove he was at those places.

But chasing somebody down was the problem—the *who*. All through the week Mahoney had been grappling with the *why* as the squad discovered the *how*. But at the pub yesterday a chance comment had generated a hunch. What if their man had taken on the identity of someone deceased? It was a method used for decades by people intending to camouflage their identity. Sometimes all it took was a stroll through the cemetery looking for gravestones, particularly those of infants as it was easier if the identity you were assuming hadn't had much time on earth to leave a footprint.

Mahoney had a name, and it was not a common name in local circles. The first task in the morning for DC Dunstan would be to trawl the electoral roll, government databases and anywhere else in the online world for traces of any other Gerard Ogden. Nobody by that name was in the current phone book, but that was not necessarily a clincher with so many folks ditching their landline and purely using a mobile phone these days. But if they could find a listing for Gerard Ogden, public servant, who died five or six years ago, then that really would help.

Mahoney sat back in his chair and contemplated the ceiling. What was the reason behind using an unusual name? Why not choose a name with high frequency in the community? Anonymity in the crowd could be a plus, but there would be more chance of encountering someone else with the same name and a 'chances of that' conversation would be remembered—bit of risk there.

A thought hit him. Did the identity even have to be of a person who's dead? Of course not. The Oates scenario, with the purchase of the Mazda and the PO mailbox, demonstrated that. Mahoney shook his head and sighed. He could kick himself he was so frustrated.

He drew a line on the page and started listed pros and cons—the old ways were best. The disadvantages of assuming the ID of a living person were that you had to somehow steal a piece of proof (Oates's driver's licence), be reasonably sure they wouldn't miss it immediately (Oates was away sailing for ten days) and hope you wouldn't be recognised as an imposter ('Hey 'you're not the Gary Oates from the Rotary Club, are you? He lives down our way.') So, even though their perpetrator had done just that, it was a hugely risky tactic. It had worked for him, but only just.

Mahoney thought about the times at which things could have gone awry. Performing the crucial postal admin task on a busy day had been very shrewd, but even then it could have unravelled if the worker at Sandy Bay Post Office had known the real Gary Oates. Whoever they were chasing had balls—a capacity to take risks without any semblance of panic. The checking was a tad more perfunctory at the car yards, but the move was still pretty gutsy.

Therefore, adopting an identity with which the chance of recognition was more unlikely would be much safer, particularly if that identity needed to be used over a period of time. You didn't need to be an experienced criminal profiler to ascertain that this master plan hadn't materialised over the space of a few days; the actual strategy must have taken months to devise and the mindset sparking it years to gestate. With only what the police knew thus far, it indicated a long period of careful planning.

Where to now? On a fresh sheet of paper Mahoney wrote some reminders: Dunstan to check the Ogden identity trail, Gibson to continue looking at the social media activity of the two victims. Geason could reliably be given the task of bringing the physical evidence findings together. Kendall had already volunteered to collate and scrutinise witness statements; her calm demeanour would enable her to thoroughly cross-reference the information and pick out any inconsistencies or useful threads.

And what about the boss man? His hunch still nagged him. Perhaps unearthing more about the former Gerard Ogden would help. He was convinced the name hadn't been chosen at random, so their man must have known enough about the deceased's circumstances to select just that identity. But how on earth did he know that?

□

Mahoney spent the next few hours sorting through paperwork that had accumulated in his 'actions pending' tray. As much as he wished so much material wouldn't find its way to his desk, he knew this case wasn't the only work his division continued to be responsible for. Much of it he simply needed to read, before initialling the front cover and passing it on to colleagues. Other ongoing issues in the field, such as a spate of assaults in the North Hobart restaurant strip, were being dealt with by Sergeant Wagin. It was mainly mindless violence—but quite unlike the mindful violence that was his main priority.

All that done, he updated the incident board in preparation for the briefing tomorrow morning. He stepped back and made a final sweeping gaze of what they had. Progress? Just maybe. His phone beeped in his jacket pocket. When he flipped it open he was surprised to see the time, late afternoon already, and relived to see who the text was from: Susan.

'Darling, arrived home. Chances of seeing you are …?'

Mahoney smiled and jabbed a reply.

'Very very good. Be there by 5.'

Lights off and out the door. Not such a bad day all told.

□

'How did the festivities go?' Mahoney asked as he poured two moderate glasses of pinot noir.

'Pretty well considering the sad news the Whitteys are dealing with. They did attend the party in the end, but they were understandably quiet.'

Susan reached across the bench and took one of the crystal glasses.

'I'm surprised they felt up to it. I don't suppose you chatted to them?'

'No, it seemed a bit inappropriate.' She sipped her drink and sighed in appreciation. 'Oh, it's good to be home. The road building on the highway makes for a disjointed trip.' She took another slightly larger gulp and pointed an index finger at her partner. 'Mind you, I did have a good old chat with the elder sibling.'

'As in Patricia Heath's brother?'

'Yes. Phillip's his name. I hadn't seen him for many years. Admittedly this was a brief re-acquaintanceship, so to speak, but I'd have to say he came across as remarkably well-adjusted.'

'In what sort of way?'

Susan frowned. 'Well, he had a pretty balanced view of life and seemed content with his lot. He left school at seventeen, joined the bank and he hasn't left. He's the manager of the Burnie branch of Westpac. One wife, three kids. We had a little chat about how being a branch manager wasn't quite as impressive as it was back in the day.'

'You don't get the substantial house to start with.'

'Exactly. Still, he seemed fine with it all. It's a solid career that has given him time and money to provide well for his family. They used the preferential borrowing terms to invest in a few properties, the kids are at a good school and they enjoy idyllic holidays at their shack on the coast.'

'Very nice.'

Kendall caught Mahoney's tone. 'He wasn't parading stuff. I'm just condensing a long conversation and that's the gist of what we chatted about. It was a nice diversion from dwelling on his sister's death and his parents' dismay. He seemed a really nice guy actually.'

Mahoney nodded. 'Point taken. I look too hard between the lines. It's a peril of the job. Sorry.' He kissed her on the forehead. 'It's good to see you.'

'And you too, darling.'

They sat down at the dining table with a pizza in the oven—the lazy option but neither cared. 'So, Detective Susan Hart, is there anything else to report?'

'No, Sir. Phillip Whittey is genuinely distraught over his sister's fate and he never so much as hinted at begrudging her the success and fame she enjoyed.'

'Excellent report, Detective. Good work all round. But I'm afraid I am going to have to stand you down for the remainder of this investigation.'

Susan played her role and looked suitably disappointed. 'That's a pity. And I'd been doing such good research. You won't need the tennis stuff then.'

'What tennis stuff?'

'After your cute request to see my old tennis frocks last Monday, I got to thinking about those days. As I was staying at Mum and Dad's place, so I conducted an archival search.'

'Your mum's a hoarder?'

'You could say that. Actually, quite extreme. I went down into their basement and my pre-adult life was there: report cards and books from school, dolls and toys, and a stack of scrapbooks piled high in the corner.'

'No dresses?'

'They'd be a little small for me now. Anyway, if you don't want to know what I found, we needn't worry.'

'Sorry, being silly. What was it?'

'The scrap books. Big A3-sized things with thirty-two pages each. One for each year from the early seventies through to the mid-nineties.'

Mahoney did the maths. 'Covering the period from when you were an infant until you started your career in journalism? Approximately.'

'That's about it. In each one, in chronological order, she stuck in party invitations, event flyers, and any newspaper clippings about us—or anything our family was even tenuously linked to. I found them early on Saturday morning while looking for some old photos and ended up stuck down there for a few hours. I was transfixed.' She smiled at her partner. 'And I suppose you're wondering how all that might help your case?'

'Just a bit.'

'It comes back to the tennis. Each year there were five major junior tournaments: Burnie, Devonport, Launceston and two in Hobart. I played all of them, from under twelve through to under nineteen. For each of those seven years, Mum had clippings showing the draw and results from every day of every tournament.'

'And because you were really good and usually got through to the finals, the clippings were extensive?'

'Yes.' She stared at Mahoney as if waiting for the penny to drop.

As it did, Mahoney nearly leaped up. 'Brilliant! So, you're there, and so is Scott Hellyer … and maybe the name of somebody else who had a booming serve.'

'I acknowledge it's out there as a lead, but you never know.'

Mahoney tapped the table enthusiastically. 'No, not at all. This case is all about history. It's what's driving our killer. Stuff that happened way back when is a huge factor in this guy's life. He's carried some sort of baggage for years, decades. And now, for him, it's retribution time. Have you brought them back?'

'Of course. They're in the boot. Would you like me to get them?'

'Please.' He stood. 'I'll cut up the pizza.'

Susan went out to her carport while Mahoney busied himself in the kitchen. After two trips there were four stacks of bulging scrapbooks: mostly green covers with thickish internal pages which were yellowing at the edges. The longish day in the office meant nothing now that the glimmer of a fresh lead was there.

After a slice of pizza, Susan gave up on pursuing any other topic of conversation. She picked up her plate and glass and moved to the door. 'I'll let you get started. I can catch up on last night's *Agatha Raisin*. The years are on the cover of each book, okay?'

It was perfect. As much as he too liked a bit of amateur sleuthing amongst the cosy Cotswalds cottages, he was dying to go back through the time tunnel.

☐

At ten o'clock, Mahoney was in the same position, hunched over the scrapbooks. Susan had bade him goodnight a little while earlier; he'd briefly thought about joining her, but he was wired. Scrolling through the back pages of other people's lives was interesting enough, but the tie-in to the Hellyer death was a compelling reason to continue. Before opening the first book that would contain Susan's tennis exploits, 1985, he'd revisited the crime scene at Opossum Bay in his head: the welts on Hellyer's skin, the new tennis balls. That pummelling must have taken accuracy and power. The pathology report indicated a strike rate of around sixty per cent. Federesque.

As he trawled through the pages, it was hard to skip over all the other snippets and articles that made up this very personal social history, but he had to focus. It turned out Scott Hellyer had competed in the age group above Susan so most of his junior record was there. He too had played all through high school as a state representative and usually made it to at least the semi-finals. Mahoney scanned the typescript looking for names that figured regularly. A part of his analytical brain told him this could just be busywork, but his passionate mind overrode that easily. Digging into the past was what this particular case demanded.

By midnight he was done. He'd filled a dozen pages of his pad with names, disjointed flow diagrams and jottings. He'd taken a series of photos with his phone to be downloaded the next morning at the office. Was it all worth much? He wasn't absolutely sure, but a couple of names and articles did stand out. Whether it stood up or not was a matter for the scrutiny of his colleagues in a few hours' time.

CHAPTER TWENTY-SIX

'Everyone here?' Mahoney signalled the start of the briefing. Of course they were. A position in the Serious Crimes Squad was not taken lightly; an officer couldn't simply opt in. You applied, underwent an appraisal process and, upon acceptance, worked double-time to complete the six month probation period. This standard had been encouraged by Commissioner Baker in response to frustration that a few officers were in cruise mode; they'd been weeded out and the others survived. It didn't always mean the elite remained: Herrick, for example. He had appeared very keen initially, but recognition that it took much more than an eight-hour shift to do the job was obviously just dawning on him. Mahoney had already decided that Herrick would be better off in the Traffic Division. He would probably love a motorbike and leathers.

Standing to the right of the display board, Mahoney pointed to a sheet of A4 paper stuck to the upper corner with a large black question mark inked on it.

'First question for you all: good weekend?' Before the nods could even materialise, he continued, 'As they say in those US courtroom dramas: asked and answered. You all look fresh, although I know a couple of you put in some hours. Much appreciated. It won't surprise you, after reading your updated files, that I did as well. It may have been time well spent. Let's see. We'll use my question mark here as a focus, and the first of the W questions is why. Why choose these two specific victims? Kate.'

Kendall stood and walked to the photos of Scott Hellyer and Patricia Heath. She turned to face her colleagues. 'As far as we can ascertain, neither victim knew the other. We've talked to family, friends, business contacts, the lot. Being Tasmania they possibly, probably, knew of each other. And, before you ask, no they weren't related.' There were a few smiles around the group. 'From talking to the boss this morning it seems quite probable that each would recognise the other's name from sports circles. They both grew up in Launceston. They attended different schools and there was a few years difference in ages, but both were good—very good—at their respective sporting endeavours: Hellyer tennis and Heath swimming. So, in a small city they would have heard of each other. We can't see a connection here in Hobart, but it's their backgrounds that irrefutably link them. They were both brought up with advantages not available to most. Not wealthy families, but very comfortable by local standards. Private schools, nice suburb, you know the drill. Both were nurtured and encouraged to do their best. They were both the standout sibling in their families thanks to their sporting prowess. Patricia Heath's brother didn't set the world alight but, by all accounts, he is happy with his lot. There's no hint of resentment as far as we know.'

Mahoney nodded. 'I'd say so. A trusted source, namely my partner, spoke to him on the weekend. He leads a content and blameless life, with not a flicker of angst regarding his sister. Our colleagues up in the nor'-west discreetly checked and he was at his place of employment on Thursday, so certainly not a suspect.'

'Sophie Hellyer told us a bit about Scott's sister, and I spoke to her by phone after the funeral,' added Kendall. 'She acknowledged that her younger brother had been something of a golden child at home.

However, it was water off a duck's back. She just wanted to study hard and get out of Tasmania. She had no interest in sport but academically she was very able, and she's forged an excellent career in public service.' She held out her arms as if weighing two pieces of fruit. 'So, that's a slightly longwinded explanation of why the siblings aren't suspects. But it does help us see that the victims were of a general type: generously nurtured so they could shine in their teens before going on to have successful lives as adults. The boss will expand.'

Mahoney breathed deeply. 'The report from our profiler, Cortese, is invaluable in showing a way into the methodology of our perpetrator. Plus, it's very revealing in terms of delineating why these victims were chosen. Our man is a boiler of seething resentment, one of those people who continually think "what if?". "What if I'd done that? What if I'd had those opportunities?" Following, probably decades of cultivating his private poison tree, he now thinks "What if I do this? What if I recalibrate the injustice of my life by bringing down a few of those who were born luckier than me? What if I can topple these false gods and, in the process, demonstrate the cunning strength that should have seen me lauded by society?" Cortese's contention, in a nutshell, is that we're chasing a contemporary of our victims who has flown under the radar for most of his life. No publicity in the papers, no remarkable achievements, no celebration of his deeds. Also, markedly different to the victims in that his upbringing was not particularly nurturing. Cortese's educated guess is that this guy was the *other one*. The sibling who felt neglected because a brother or sister was afforded more attention. He took the bus to any activity he did while the parents went to watch the other child doing stuff. Unlike the siblings of our victims, he harbours bitter resentment: an emotion that now drives his daring strategy. He is a man with a plan.'

Mahoney walked back to his question mark. 'In general terms, we know why these victims were selected and why he murdered them. Of course this could all be gobbledegook, but the psychology of the case does make sense. So, how does the headshrinker stuff help us, bearing in mind there must be a few people who fit into this category? We take this information and we correlate it with the concrete material we do have. The forensic evidence is detailed. It doesn't give us a match to any database we can access, but that does mean any trial should be a slam-dunk. We've got that going for us. At present, he's almost certainly enjoying putting us through the hoops and revelling in how clever he's been, but the unnerving fact is that the murderer may eventually want to be caught. Obviously we need to ensure that happens before the tally increases.' Mahoney dropped his gaze to a desk at the front. 'DC Gibson, your go.'

Gibson tapped his keyboard and the smartboard lit up with a screenshot of Patricia Heath's Facebook profile. 'The short version is that our second victim was no shrinking violet. Like a lot of people, she was perfectly happy to put her whole life on display. If you wanted to track her, this is a very efficient hands-off means of doing so. Plenty of people, including strangers, could see it. Sergeant Dobosz and I went through her list of friends and the profiles of anybody who liked her posts. Nobody leapt off the page as being likely, and it's doubtful the killer would leave that sort of trace.' He waved the cursor across the screen image. 'All this shows us is that anybody could have co-ordinated her murder by studying her page. It won't assist us in finding who.'

Another click of his mouse brought up a fresh screenshot. 'Scott Hellyer also had a Facebook profile but he tended not to post material as much. However, he did utilise another platform a great deal. This is his LinkedIn profile page. On Facebook you can type in a name and, depending on their settings, anonymously view their stuff. With LinkedIn, a record of who viewed your profile shows up. It's the preferred form of social media for those in business and ideal for Hellyer given his roles in marketing and the golf course development. You want people you don't know checking you out because they could become useful contacts. Fortunately for us, Hellyer paid extra for the Premium package. Even more fortunately, his username and password were in his desk diary at Tiger Brewing. I logged in and, as expected, he had loads of contacts and a fair few people had viewed his profile. Of these, seven did not take the next step of becoming a contact. Sergeant Dobosz is looking much more closely at them this morning. Assuming our guy wanted to know more about Hellyer's dealings, this is one way to do it. The good thing for us is that he either didn't know or didn't care that a record of the viewing was catalogued, probably the latter but the crucial thing is it exists.'

Mahoney lifted himself up from the chair he'd taken. 'Good, David. Soon as, let us know.' He held up that day's newspaper. 'From new media to old. In times past, before some of you were even a glint in the milkman's eye, most people read these things. And they used to contain proportionally more local material than they do now. Thanks again to my trusted source, I have a pretty comprehensive record of Scott Hellyer's junior tennis career, and it got me thinking. We know our guy can belt a ball. You could say he possesses a lethal serve. What if he too had been a junior player? It's more tenuous than some of our leads, but it could establish a closer tie between killer and victim. My general hypothesis now is that our target was also brought up in Launceston, and knew of both Hellyer and Heath, or Whittey as she was called then, at that time. I've made up a long list of names of male players from half a decade of tournaments. There are a few that might be good bets.' He replaced the newspaper on a desk. 'The other slightly redundant piece of print is the phone book. I won't bore you with the genesis of this one, but suffice to say, I've established there is no Gerard Ogden in the current time. DC Dunstan has discovered more. Andrew.'

Dunstan remained in his swivel chair at the side of the room; his large frame meant everyone could clearly see his face. 'Righto. Gerard Ogden is an unusual name. I did a search of the electoral roll and it turns out there's only been one of them alive in Tassie in the past fifty years. As the boss found out at the weekend, that chap has been dead for five years last September. He was formerly a clerk at DPIPWE.

Somebody has grabbed the name for this scheme, knowing there's almost zero chance of tracing him. That's it, Sir.'

'Well not quite. Andrew has also gone through the Public Service Gazettes for the past decade. Can you tell us about that?'

'Oh yeah, sure. All public service positions vacant, promotions and resignations are gazetted each fortnight, and I've got a longish list of people who have retired or taken redundancy from DPIPWE in the last five years. Being a public servant fits with the Cortese profiling.'

'Indeed it does. This is all much ado for one little thing, but if we get a real name we can work with, it's gold. If a Venn diagram of sorts can whittle these long lists down to a couple of names, then we're on to something.' Mahoney paused briefly to scan the incident board. 'Any questions?'

Geason surprised everybody—including possibly himself—by asking, 'How are we for photofit images of our guy?'

After a nod from Mahoney, Kendall answered. 'As of Friday we think he may have dyed his head hair a shade of auburn. Our last known sighting of him is the health retreat at Longley. We showed the images we have to the proprietors and they felt certain the one based on the Vroom Motors purchase was the closet in terms of facial structure. But they noted three differences: eye colour, hair colour and clean-shaven. All easy enough to alter with tinted cosmetic contact lenses, hair dye and a shave. Forensics from the bathroom in the chalet reveal plenty of dye rinsed down the drains. The owners remembered brown eyes, darkish hair but not black, and a neatly shaved face. That is from when he checked in on the Saturday using Hellyer's card as a security deposit. They didn't see him at all after that. It's the sort of place where you're left to your own devices if that's what you want. The husband saw what he thinks was the Mazda come back early on Thursday afternoon. He didn't see the driver but assumed it was the guy. That location tallies with the speeding infringement that put us in that area in the first place. Presumably, upon his return, he did the dye job on his thatch. He used "Autumnal Hue" so his hair would have gone a reddish-brown.' She cupped her hair and smiled. 'I went to an unorthodox source on Saturday myself. The salon was quiet, so the owner sat with me while my foils were on and gave me a mini tutorial on applying colour from the bottle. Essentially, the message was this: somebody is doing damage to his hair and, more importantly for us, could be doing a scrappy job. Self-administered is never quite the same as professional, and a swift succession of changes makes it look more amateurish each time.'

She nodded to Gibson who generated a fresh image on the smartboard. 'Thanks, David. Mike Eather, our police artist guy … sorry, I forget his title, but you know who I mean. Anyway, he's taken our best ID and created a series of digital images showing our suspect in various guises.' She paused to allow Gibson to run through a dozen photos, finishing with the face below a shaved skull.

'Now he's got alopecia.' Geason was on fire; somebody had a good break.

Kendall ignored him. 'All of these are available for download on your smartphones. Are they going further afield, Sir?'

'Yes, to all members of the force. And if there are no big breaks today, we'll release the images to the media for evening news bulletins and tomorrow's papers. Right, thanks Kate.' Mahoney rubbed a hand across his brow; today had a feeling of progress, and it was time to convince the troops it was genuine. 'We are more than good enough for this. The leads we've got through luck and proper detection are sound. We do our job and the result will come. Matt, keep your buoyant mood and get the database thoroughly up-to-date. You need to process the grunt work of cross-checking purchases of hair product, contact lenses, tennis balls, chloroform, tasers … and anything else you can think of based on the physical evidence. David, you're co-ordinating the dissemination of those images and getting back to witnesses to confirm we have a decent image of our guy. Grab whoever you need to help you. Dicky Dobosz is pursuing the LinkedIn angle?'

'Yep, hoping to hear from him soon.'

'Okay, that's social media and ID photos sorted. DS Kendall and I will be talking to the DPIPWE people and I'll get our Launceston branch to follow up the tennis angle. I think that's it. Anything else?'

No hands or comments. 'Right, get to it. We've done the sleuthing. Now we do the detecting.'

CHAPTER TWENTY-SEVEN

Oh my, they must be busy at Police HQ. Beavering away with their computers. Running ideas past each other. In the office I never came close to managing a section. The hierarchy gave up on encouraging me to take on more responsibility. I was good at my job, but they saw I was happier as a drone. I was left to my corner as I worked my way through a few decades of checking titles, administering policy and, basically, being quietly efficient.

I wasn't the spooky anti-social type who freaked people out. I went to the Friday happy hours in the social club and got on well with everybody. I played the role of the nice guy who didn't seem to have any ambition for the higher levels. In fact, I did have ambition but it was the hotshots who went to university or the good blokes that played football who got a free ride. The deck is always stacked.

I didn't hate the work. It suited me. I never experienced Mondayitis. I took my leave when it was due. I let people believe I wasn't the marrying kind. All up, three and a half decades of steady service. When the brass came knocking with offers of voluntary redundancies a few years back, I didn't sit on my hands. The death of the Oyman, way too early, had got me thinking. Why hang about? Pension fund was good. Out the door, thank you very much.

The funny thing is, retirement isn't all it's cracked up to be. It would be alright if you're married with offspring, I suppose. Then you become the designated carer for the grandkids while your children work double-time to pay the mortgage, school fees and credit card debts. Me, I found myself with a lot of time hanging heavy and got to thinking about life. My life. My less than wonderful life.

Don't assume it was shit. I was fed, clothed, and educated by my folks. Just not with the same enthusiasm granted to Adrian. He was two years younger and light years ahead in terms of parental affection. Early on he was picked out as a promising cricketer. Didn't that give the old man a hard on. Adie obviously needed the top of the range Gray Nichols bat, spanking pads and gloves ... the whole box and dice. He was sent to all the coaching camps, and driven to training on the other side of town from our suburb of Prospect.

Prospect, that's a laugh. Our house had the Bass Highway over the rear fence. Not a view to fire the imagination. Pater worked as a groundsman for the council and the old dear part-time at the local doctors' surgery. No ambition to further themselves as far as I could tell, so they pinned their hopes on Adrian making the grade. It wasn't that outlandish to be honest. Two of the country's best ever batsmen of my generation hail from Launceston, so it wasn't pie in the sky. And Adrian was good. He had that confidence that stops just short of outright arrogance. Could concentrate for long periods and didn't flinch when fast bowlers gave him some chin music.

At seventeen he was skipper of the under nineteen state team. The old man had a real spring in his step the day that was announced. By then I'd given competitive sport away. The booming serve that had won matches in my early teens became less effective as the other kids grew taller and got better at returning balls. After I turned fourteen

I couldn't make a semi-final. I kept playing the northern tournaments for a while but I was never going anywhere in real terms.

At the end of school I scored a job in the Lands Department and moved to Hobart. Stayed with rellies in Melville Street for a year or so. Spoke to the folks by phone on Sunday nights to get the old off-peak rates. Most of the time it was to be told about Adrian's progress. Then I got my own flat in New Town. Bedroom, kitchenette-cum-living room and bathroom-cum-laundry. The day it settled, I rang home. My mother was in bits. She couldn't talk to me at all. She left the old man to tell me. At cricket training Adrian had been felled by a cricket ball. Some clown tinkered with the bowling machine. Instead of getting a full length medium pace stock ball, a bouncer had reared up at pace and clocked him in the temple. Out for the count and never revived. On his third day as an adult.

It was as if I wasn't even at the funeral. I sat in the front row with my parents but wasn't given any part to play. Barely a word passed between us. The cricket coach did the eulogy and teammates read the prayers. And that set a pattern for the coming years. In my family home, Christmas was cancelled. Mum and Dad said they were taking their caravan to Ulverstone for the break and 'just wanted some quiet time.' No invitation so I let it slide. I'd ring from time to time but it was clear their lives were closing down. Post-Adrian was one long era of atrophy.

When the old man died of heart failure a decade ago, Mum gave up. She didn't want any visits. When we spoke—infrequently—all she talked about was stuff she'd heard on the radio: shock jock crap from the mainland. She went to the shops and that was about it. There was some cat she'd acquired. Lights on but no-one home.

Last year a lawyer called to inform me of her death, and to tell me the bulk of the estate was going elsewhere. So I got the tin-pot car. Such is life ... and death.

The next night I was watching some Pommy TV show and this woman started going on about what life's all about. She said, 'You commit to all this activity and in the end it probably counts for bugger all.' Right then, I thought, she's onto something. It really got me thinking. What about all those poor buggers who slave away for stuff and never get recognition, while the high-flyers soar onwards and upwards? Who's going to do something for those who could only look up?

CHAPTER TWENTY-EIGHT

Kendall and Mahoney were sitting in his office. 'Right. As you heard, Launceston CIB are going to do their best. DI Briggs said they're in a peaceful spell. Bit of rough stuff after hours in the shopping mall, but not a great deal on their plate. Briggsy reckons he can get most of it done for us.'

'That's still a fair chunk, delving that far back with three names.'

'I thought so too. He says it's doable so I'm not going to argue the toss with a man who's doing us a big favour.'

'Agreed. Let's hope this chap coming in can be as amenable.'

Mahoney held up a set of crossed fingers. There was a knock on the door and Geason stuck his head in. 'Visitor for you, Sir.'

'Let him in, Matt.' Geason stood aside for Paul Henderson, the retired cruise enthusiast Mahoney had met at the pub.

The two officers stood and Mahoney extended a hand. 'Paul, thanks for agreeing to this. This is DS Kate Kendall.'

'No problem. A friend of Munro's and all that.' He took the proffered chair. 'Your man who collected me from reception is full of beans.'

'I'll say, although he's usually quite taciturn. You got any idea, Kate?'

'He sold his house on the weekend. Three bedroom brick cottage in West Hobart he's had for fifteen years. Jackpot in our current market.'

'Little wonder then.' Mahoney turned to Henderson. 'Paul, our chat on Saturday afternoon may be very fortuitous.'

'What, the Ogden stuff?'

'Exactly. I don't need to bore you with all the background but, suffice to say, the name Gerard Ogden has loomed large in our current investigation.'

Henderson looked taken aback. 'But he's ...'

'Dead. I know. He went out on sick leave six or so years back, was granted early retirement on health grounds and succumbed to terminal cancer just under five years ago.'

'That's about right. How can poor old Oyman concern you?'

Kendall chipped in. 'Oyman?'

'Oggy, Oggy, Oggy, Oy, Oy, Oy. A bit of a chant we used to perform when he got his round in at the Social Club. Juvenile, but that's the atmosphere at Friday drinks, isn't it. The name Oyman just stuck.'

'Sounds like a good guy.'

'He was. It's a cliché but he was salt of the earth. He barely put a step out of line as far as I could tell.'

'I don't doubt it. What we should have made clearer is that it's not the man but the name that's become a lightning conductor. His was quite a rare name in Hobart.'

'That it was.' A smile spread across Henderson's face. 'His folks were ten pound Poms. He was born here but there was a big streak of Lancashire right through him. We'd do the chant and he'd come right back with "There's only one Gerry Ogden, one Gerry Ogden." You get the drift. Anyway, there really was. He was the only one in the phone book.'

'As I discovered,' said Mahoney. 'What Kate and I think has occurred is that somebody is utilising that fact to cause trouble. I'll be more specific. It's highly possible our chief suspect stole Gerard Ogden's identity.'

'How? Oyman didn't do much online. Apart from banking stuff, I think.'

Kendall leaned forward. 'If you know the particulars of a person's life, it's not overly difficult. The hundred point check which various institutions put you through can be massaged. For example, a driver's licence. When a person dies, letting Service Tasmania know isn't a top priority for the family or estate lawyer. A conniving individual could go into a branch a year or so later, claim they've lost their plastic card and organise a replacement that has a fresh photo of the new person on it.'

Henderson frowned. 'But wouldn't you need supporting stuff?'

'Other documents to make it up to a hundred points of course, but not all the verification documents have photo ID. Birth certificate, for instance. You could cobble together the points without a photo. One thing we do, a lot, is call out for information. The lawyer who dealt with Mr Ogden's affairs did all the right things. She settled the estate, probate was granted and the inheritance instructions were dealt with.'

Mahoney tapped some sheets on his desk. 'All proceeds from his estate were directed to charity. He had no living relatives and his wife pre-deceased him. No kids. Staff from the firm saw to the asset sale, including the house, and all was above board. We spoke to the clerk who was responsible for sorting out the house and contents. He remembered it well because he found it a bit odd at the time. A few things you'd expect to find weren't there, like a desk drawer or an expanding file of the sort most of us keep vital documents in.'

'Some bugger lifted it, then.'

'Precisely. Hence the possibility of identity theft. We're hoping you might have some idea of who did that.'

There was agitation in Henderson's voice. 'Not me for a start. Do you think I could …'

'No, no, no. You're about the last person we'd consider. If you were a suspect, we'd be talking downstairs. I'm sorry, I put that query badly. Let's go back. Was there anybody at DPIPWE or in Ogden's circle of acquaintances who could have had that sort of access. Someone who knew his address, for instance.'

The red in Henderson's cheeks faded and he breathed more slowly. He gazed out of the office window and a soft chorus of song came from his lips. 'Brother Michael, Brother Michael, Brother Michael, we love you. You got the beers in, you got the beers in and we're drinking now till two.' Sadness and resignation drained some colour from his face as he turned slowly back to the Detective Inspector. 'I'm assuming you have a list of employees?'

'Not quite. But we do have a series of names that need some work.'

'Does Michael Fowler appear on it?'

It certainly does, thought Mahoney, remaining deadpan; not only was it on the catalogue of redundancies taken in the past five years, but it was also one of the three names he'd emailed north to Briggs. 'I'll check when we're done.' He made a show of writing it down. 'Why him in particular?'

'After Oyman's wife died ten years ago they became very close. Michael helped him through a stiff patch. They joined a walking club together and went to the local soccer to see some club or other most weekends—Metro Claremont I think it was.' He rubbed his hand across the stubble on his jaw . 'Anyway, they were pretty tight. Confirmed bachelors without the innuendo. Gerard would sing "Brother Michael" at the Sundowners and, when he got poorly, it was Michael who sorted stuff out for him. After Oyman passed away, Fowler lost interest in the social side of things and pretty soon in turning up to work. A round of redundancies came at a good time for him. He got out and nobody I know has seen him since.' Henderson looked Mahoney in the eye. 'Do you think he could be this maniac?'

'We're looking at lots of options. This Michael Fowler is probably just someone we need to talk to.'

Like hell. Inside Mahoney felt the heat rising. 'I would ask you to keep this chat confidential. Never good to frighten the horses.'

'Don't fret. I wouldn't know where to find him.'

Neither would we, thought Mahoney, but now at least we are tackling a real name. 'There's just one more thing you can do for us if you have time.'

'Sure.'

'Sergeant Kendall is going to show you a series of identikit pictures. If you do recognise anybody, that will help us.'

'And if I do, I'll keep that under my hat?'

'Yes, absolutely. Thanks again.'

□

Mahoney had decided a decent cup of coffee wouldn't go astray, so he took himself out of the building and across the intersection to Artisan Coffee. He had already arranged to meet Signor Cortese and as he entered the café he spied him sitting at a table abutting the red brick wall.

'Bonjourno, Inspector. What a lovely space.' He held up a miniature white cup. 'Expresso par excellence. Good choice.'

'I hoped you'd appreciate it. Not quite Brunswick Street, but kind of close.'

'Mmm, Melbourne. I never imagined I'd contemplate this, but a move here is beginning to seem possible.'

'It's going well with Doctor Pitney then?'

Cortese was taken aback, then his features relaxed into a smile. 'But of course. You are the detective. I shall have to admit there is a connection. Madeleine is certainly a compelling attraction, and her adopted city has much to offer. Aside from working on the report, I have been playing the tourist. A cottage in North Hobart puts most of my favourite things within walking distance.' He asked for a water as Mahoney's drink was delivered to their table.

Stirring in a half-teaspoon of sugar, Mahoney asked, 'So a move may be on the cards?'

'Yes, I think so. I have been much amused by complaints in your paper about city traffic, which is very small beer compared to

Melbourne. People spend hours in their cars for what used to be a straightforward commute. Still, we are not here to plan my future. I'm assuming from your demeanour that there is progress.'

'There certainly is. Well, we think so. Your modelling indicated the perpetrator to be middle-aged, reasonably well-educated and outwardly calm. Correct?'

'Succinct but a sound precis.'

'It's the first characteristic that interests me. The person we now have as our prime suspect is recently retired, so he has the requisite time to plan and enact this scheme. We think he has committed some form of identity theft to cover himself as he goes about his preparation. And his particular way of doing this is slightly old school.'

'Not a disciple of cyberspace?'

'I don't think so, which helps us.'

'How so?'

'Well if he purloined the documents and ID cards in that manner, he would be much harder to trace for a start. It could be anyone, anywhere, doing it. One of my colleagues ran me through the process and it's mind-boggling. Passports, medical insurance cards, licences ... all at your fingertips if you've purchased the software.'

'I understand. It is a different world. But you believe your suspect is more traditional in approach. Therefore, it needs to be someone with particular access to material.'

'Got it in one. Of course we have plenty of other clues guiding us here. The guts of it is that we've identified a man who has the right birthplace, background, age and working capacity to be our guy. DS Kendall is drawing together a dossier of bullet points as we speak. Would you be able to pop into the office to run your eye over it?'

'Of course. I'm at your disposal.'

'Good, thank you. We don't want to be premature. Even when we've surer, I don't want to release this on the public stage.'

'You prefer to quietly ensnare him?'

'Absolutely. This guy is adept at hiding. My fear is that if he knows we're right on his tail, he may move quickly.'

'And perhaps kill again.'

'Well, yeah. I can't help feeling that the quick break we got on the van wasn't something he'd anticipated. Perhaps it forced his hand to accelerate and murder Patricia Heath.'

Cortese's hands spread palm down in a dismissive gesture. 'No. I did say to you at Opossum Bay that he would kill again—that he did so six days later is not your doing. The window of opportunity for the second murder was in line with his meticulous preparation, with her family being away and the strong likelihood she would be alone in her house that morning. The second homicide was not an acceleration but simply a planned step in his campaign.'

'Okay, fair call. I don't suppose you can predict the pattern. Do you think there's another shock coming our way? Say, on Wednesday?'

Cortese smiled ruefully. 'The number of the beast: six, six, six. And the perfect tennis score of a straight sets win.'

Mahoney leaned back. 'You're right. It's too much of a stretch. But a third victim is on the cards?'

'Three is the magic number. That is less fanciful.' Out came Cortese's e-cigarette; he briefly considered it then replaced it in a jacket pocket as if thinking better of the idea. 'Have you considered opening a dialogue with this man?'

Seriously? thought Mahoney. If I could call him, I'd nab him. He reigned his incredulity back in. 'And how might we do that? Via the media?'

'Yes, and very carefully. You could aim to flatter without seeming to. Do it in a way that hints that the forces of law and order are not coping.' Cortese signalled for another coffee. 'Or make a public statement claiming you are reassessing the one-perpetrator theory.'

Mahoney had an edge to his voice. 'Yeah right. A public about-face that undermines our reputation.'

'What is your main goal? To enhance your reputation, or to make an arrest as soon as possible, before number three?'

'All right. But how can we do it while still looking like professionals? This guy is smart. Won't he see through feigned ignorance?'

'It needs to be done subtly, in a way that suggests to him you are chasing your tails. The general public will assume you are making a call-out for information.' The e-cig came out again and Cortese manipulated it through his fingers, becoming almost trancelike. Mahoney took the opportunity to visit the toilet.

Back at the table, Cortese had returned to the land of the living. 'Forget the multiple perpetrator idea. Too much has been released on the lone wolf theory, and he'll see through the ruse. But do muddy the waters, in a manner that shows you are still searching for meaning in his methods. For example, you could suggest—by your demeanour or the statement—that you are focusing on the violent methodology rather than the psychology.'

'How will that help?'

'This man wants—sorry *demands*—to be understood as a redeemer. He is repairing the world, correcting history. He is a righteous figure … in his mind anyway. Deliberately overlooking this will perhaps lead him to an attempt at guidance.'

'By writing his mission statement on the wall with his next victim's blood?'

'Touché, but no. He will endeavour to communicate with you because he wants you to acknowledge him.'

'Would a public appeal from a relative or family member assist?'

Cortese pursed his lips. 'Again, no. This figure does not care for the opinion of those he regards as privileged. His mode of behaviour indicates a desire to bring his victims down from a height. He is proclaiming "See how the mighty have fallen". Despair in the hearts of those affected would not move him. What could catch him is this skewed admission that we are flummoxed by the motivation.'

Mahoney felt the trip down the odd blind alley could be worth it; this tangent appeared plausible. It wouldn't rock the boat of public confidence, nor would it alert anyone how much closer they were to a factual identity. It was time for a move. 'That makes sense. Any chance you could draft something once you've read over the new material?'

'Of course. And I won't charge by the word. Regard it as a complimentary extra. I am as concerned as you about this man. Who would have thought such intrigue would manifest itself in this appealing locale?'

'You just never know, do you? I doubt the good people on the Shetland Islands ever realised how turbulent their private lives could be.'

'Quite so. Anywhere two or more are gathered, chaos is a distinct possibility.' He rose from his seat. 'Are you going back across?'

'Yep. I've got just one call to make first. I'll be hearing from you?'

'Certainly.'

CHAPTER TWENTY-NINE

The first thing Mahoney noticed as he entered the incident room was Gibson securing an image to the caseboard. As Mahoney traversed the floor, the young blood nut turned around as Kendall slapped Dunstan's shoulder.

'Let me guess. Another window's opened.'

Kendall swivelled in her chair. 'No, a few have. Show him, Andrew.' Her voice brimmed with enthusiasm.

Dunstan nodded, clicked the mouse, and a full head shot filled the screen. 'There you go.'

Mahoney stared at the portrait: a nondescript male with dark hair greying at the temples. If tasked, he was unsure he could discern anything unusual about the face. Clean-shaven, regular sized nose, blue eyes … ordinary looking, bland even. This is a man who could walk the streets and be seen but never really *noticed* by anybody.

'I'm assuming we think this is a photo of Michael Fowler?'

Dunstan's reply was to move the image up the screen, revealing the name next to the words 'Tasmanian Government'. Next to the name was the Tasmanian tiger logo of all government documents. Mahoney had always thought that using an extinct carnivore for this purpose was slightly defeatist—mind you, the chances were the other endemic mammal of the state, the Tasmanian Devil, wasn't far off the same status.

'Where is this from?' Mahoney asked.

'The personnel department at DPIPWE,' Kendall replied. 'Since the start of the millennium employees have had to wear ID tags. Part security measure, part administrative measure. Each worker has a photo taken then that image is transferred to a plastic card with relevant work data including their name. All the photos are on file and Andrew was given access, after explaining the gravity of our request.' Before Mahoney could interrupt, she continued. 'Naturally, we asked for all the pictures so no alarm bells went off at their end. I kept the reason for the request as general as possible. Andrew scrolled through all the images of employees who've departed in the past few years. No-one else leaped out, and we do now have the ID photo of this Fowler guy.'

If I go, thought Mahoney, she's ready. Had he specifically taught her to cover all bases? She'd worked it out anyway. 'Good. Has Paul Henderson seen this?'

Kendall shook her head. 'I thought it best for objectivity if Eather takes him through a photofit construction. Am I crossing the t's too emphatically?'

It was Mahoney's turn to shake his head. 'It's consistent with what we've done with the other witnesses, so that closes any loophole that could materialise in court. Once they're done, we can show him the earlier images and this one. He should confirm that this is the Michael Fowler he's referred to.' Mahoney peered closely again at the face. 'Everyone else with recent sightings mentioned the man they dealt with was quite gaunt around the face, but this fella looks a bit more jowly.'

Gibson flexed his upper torso in a pose. 'He's been training, hasn't he? Both murders, particularly the first, required a fair bit of hefting. Hellyer was a fair weight to manoeuvre, and at the Heath house there were no signs of drag marks on the carpet. He lifted both bodies to their final positions. So, he's been doing strength training and his fat percentage has dropped right off.'

'Of course, that's right.' Mahoney gave his constable a mental tick. 'That would account for it. Right, next step. Upload these images and get them to all our officers. What else have you got here?'

Dunstan clicked again and an image of a small vehicle came up. The friendly giant spoke. 'I couldn't find any useful contact information for this Fowler guy. His last known address was the one he gave to Vroom Motors and that, as we know, is a dwelling that no longer exists. The money from that sale and the lump sum he took from his superannuation account both went to his ANZ bank account.'

'Now terminated?'

'Yes, Sir. About twelve months ago he visited the Liverpool Street branch and withdrew the whole lot as a bank cheque. I spoke to the business manager about it. They thought it odd and, from their viewpoint, imprudent.'

Kendall chipped in. 'They would rather have their hands on the dosh.'

Dunstan smiled. 'For sure. Anyway, as they admitted, it was his money after all. He closed the savings account and credit card facility that day. So, he would have walked out with a thumping great wad of money on a slip of embossed paper.'

'And then dematerialised,' said Mahoney.

'Pretty much.' Dunstan held up his wallet. 'If you think about it, you can travel through life pretty lightly if you decline all the offers made to join things and you own no property. The driver's licence in Fowler's name expired six months ago. No bank cards. There is a Medicare card in his name, but that's fairly anonymous and no help in tracking him. He has no identifiable online presence. All the accounts a household would usually have are defunct. He's transformed himself into a cleanskin.'

'I sense a "but" Andrew?' Mahoney knew there had to be a kicker.

'Two as it turns out. First, the money. He walked out of ANZ with a cheque for thousands of dollars, a couple of hundred thousand actually. He couldn't do much with that unless he cashed it somewhere, which was unlikely given the questions that would be asked, or opened another account. David helped with a ring-round. The week after closing at ANZ, Michael Fowler opened an account at the Bank of Queensland branch in Murray Street. A chap called Don Cook confirmed it all. He was glad of a new customer but thought it a bit odd.'

'Money laundering?' asked Gibson.

'Sort of. More the amount and why Fowler was changing accounts. Fowler said he wanted better service from a boutique enterprise. Cook thought that was fair enough as that's what they advertise. He offered him all the bells and whistles, but all Fowler wanted was a savings account with easy access and a linked debit card.'

Mahoney nodded. 'How soon can we get hold of a transactions record?'

'Not immediately. That requires a warrant processed to their Internal Criminal Division who then send it back through to the branch. I've set that in motion and we should get it all by the end of the day.'

'Perfect. Mind you, all we'll probably see is a series of ATM cash withdrawals that he then used for purchases. Why did he use his own name and not an alibi?'

'Cook inadvertently answered that. They'd had an instance where a young woman had tried to open an account with a cheque for a million bucks. Alarm bells rang a bit and, after a few discreet checks, they discovered it was fraudulently obtained.'

'Fowler would have needed to be very discreet, so he used the same identity he had with ANZ,' said Kendall. 'Besides, he didn't fabricate the Ogden licence until weeks later.' She looked at Mahoney. 'Sorry, I forgot to tell you that we've made progress there too.'

'No problem. We'll get to that. So, the money has been followed. What's the second thing you mentioned?'

Dunstan tapped the computer glass. 'A car similar in appearance to this was previously registered in the name of a Mrs Maureen Fowler of Launceston. She passed away a decade or so ago and, according to the Perpetual Trustees office in Launceston, the car was inherited by her son, Michael Fowler.'

Dunstan looked chuffed and he had every right to be. The momentum of the contest was swinging their way. 'Superb. I presume one of DI Briggs's people got through to you?'

'As soon as we had that name, I called them. David made the call to the trustees, and the link's done.'

Mahoney felt a team hug was in order, but held off—and not just because he wouldn't get his arm around Dunstan's shoulders. A favourite saying of his former Superintendent in the London Met chimed: 'Careful John. A bit previous.' Meaning always beware of getting ahead of yourself. Don't be the hare; the tortoise wins.

'And the licence?'

Kendall replied. 'Transport Tasmania have a record of a driver's licence being reissued to a Mr Gerard Ogden in July last year. It looks like Fowler did exactly what we thought: accumulated the necessary docs and fudged it.'

Mahoney pulled up a chair and motioned for Gibson to follow suit. The quartet made for a tight huddle.

'Let's establish a chronology. I'll jot a few words down for my benefit. Andrew, be secretary.'

'Sure.' Dunstan clicked a blank page open on his screen.

'Michael Fowler grew up in Launceston, which is also the birthplace of Scott Hellyer and Patricia Whittey. He played tennis in his early teens but dropped away by sixteen or so.' He looked up from his jottings to Gibson. 'Ever heard of him up there?'

A shake of the head. 'No, Sir. Whittey, yes. She was big news, swimming for Australia and that. Not him.'

'Okay, that makes sense. Well, Hellyer certainly knew of him.' Mahoney paused as the others took that in. 'Going back through those newspaper clippings was pretty interesting. Backstories emerge. In junior high school, Fowler was beating Hellyer. Not by much but he was getting over the line. A few years later and Hellyer was wiping the court with him. By the under sixteens Hellyer was kingpin for his age group. In one match, which looks like Fowler's last tournament, Hellyer handed him the doughnuts.'

'Wow,' said Gibson. '6-0, 6-0. That stings.'

'I bet it did. I'm not arguing that this was his sole long-term motivation for revenge, but it clearly establishes a link. After that, nothing. As Andrew has found there's no other archival material for Fowler. While you've been beavering away to great effect, I've been chatting to Cortese. Anyway, I'll get back to his ideas later.' Mahoney turned to Dunstan. 'Did you find anything about his family, another Fowler?'

Dunstan nodded. 'Yeah, I did. Adrian Fowler was a gun cricketer. He could have been the next David Boon, but died prematurely in a tragic accident.'

'Michael Fowler's brother,' Mahoney confirmed. 'I also got that from Briggs. Very helpful crew up there. We owe them. Anyway, the Fowler family lived in Prospect. Two sons: one the golden child, the other not so much. No prizes for guessing which one Michael was. All he inherited after his mother's death was a pink Nissan Pulsar. Correct?'

'Yes, Sir,' Dunstan confirmed.

'We'll get back to Transport Tasmania and establish that for sure.' Mahoney gestured to Kendall. 'Michael Fowler moved to Hobart as a young adult, landed a job in the public service and lived a quiet unblemished life. A solid employee who got on pretty well with his colleagues. Was a stout ally of Ogden, especially when his mate became grievously ill. Then he took a redundancy package.' He paused to invite any contribution.

Gibson leaned in. 'Ogden's death made him think about life and start the mother of all retributions. He must have been really hurting over that match.'

Mahoney went on. 'It is darkly funny, but I believe the grudge did start building there. Hellyer had all the gear, weekly coaching and parental support. Fowler had zip. He started to see that some folk have a smoothly crafted path to success, while others have to crawl through a muddy bog to get anywhere. I'm sure the following decades will supply countless examples of how successful individuals become more successful.'

'It's easier to make a great first impression if your reputation precedes you.'

'Yes, Kate. It does seem so. And his world view fits with the profile Cortese has been assembling. Very early on he said family is at the heart of this. Fowler appears to have long believed that his family let him down. The slings and arrows of his lack of fortune perennially underscore his philosophical contention that, for some people, life truly is a bag of horseshit. To put it bluntly.'

The crew seemed to be pondering their own fortunes, but Mahoney pressed on. 'Fowler has succumbed to that age old flaw. He assesses the quality of his life in comparison to others, which is not always a good way to evaluate your worth. Perhaps this is now his time to make his mark. Regardless of the motivation, his magnum opus is reprehensible. Simple as that. We now have really good leads. It's been a bit arse about, but we've assembled a lot of circumstantial proof as to identity. But we also have the trace evidence in waiting.' Mahoney banged his fists together. 'Now we couple them.' He pointed to Dunstan's screen. 'Put out an alert with the images of Fowler to all officers. Kate, come with me. We need to see the Commissioner.'

□

The Commissioner's first query of the two detectives was mildly surprising. 'How are you both sleeping?'

Kendall replied to the effect that all was fine, and Mahoney proffered a similar answer. 'The exhaustion of last week has gone.

The renewed momentum of the past few days has pepped me up if anything.'

A subtle nod from Baker. 'Good. No-one minds you being tired at day's end. Stressed ... well, that's another thing altogether.' There was no mention of her supply of pills to Mahoney as she gestured to her computer screen. 'I see significant steps have been taken. Am I correct to assume we now have a prime suspect?'

Mahoney looked sideways to Kendall, who acknowledged the signal to be the messenger. 'Yes, we do. The team has identified an individual by the name of Michael Fowler as the probable perpetrator. He seems to have had the means and motivation to commit the two murders.'

Baker cut in. 'Sergeant Kendall, "seems" and "probable" are not terms I wish to hear. You've come here, I presume, with a specific request. If I require an update of your suppositions, I can view the progress log.'

She's testing her, thought Mahoney; she wants to see the steel beneath the skin. Kendall blinked once, then continued in a barely altered tone. 'Of course. Michael Fowler is definitely our chief suspect. He had the opportunity to commit the two murders, and the case that's been built conclusively establishes his motivation.'

Both senior officers appeared to wait for more. Mahoney appreciated that Kendall was employing the dictum 'less is more'. She had given the Commissioner what had been asked for: certainty. It was the Commissioner's turn.

'Better. What do you require of me?'

'A significant diversion of resources to this case, particularly manpower. Inspector Mahoney and I believe Fowler intends to keep striking until he is caught. He knows we will eventually apprehend him so he wants to make as grand a statement as he can. Public concerns should be put aside and we should institute a manhunt.'

Baker's eyes were fixed on Kendall as seconds crawled by. 'I agree. In fact, a degree of public apprehension may cause people to be more wary of lone strangers. It won't reach fever pitch and it could flush out this man. You'll be going to the media again.'

Mahoney sensed his sergeant had passed the test, so he leaned slightly forward in his chair. 'Yes. Print, television, radio and our social media alerts. We have a very good likeness to put out. It could send him underground, but balanced against that is the likelihood of recent sightings emerging. It could stall his scheme.'

'Granted. If he does bunker down somewhere, this is the state for it. An island of nooks and crannies.' Baker swivelled in her chair to view the computer screen. 'You're fortunate. It's a quiet week so I can give you the extra troops. I'll call the Academy. The cadets will also be at your disposal. The latter come free of charge. Try not to send the overtime requisition to kingdom come.'

'It shouldn't be necessary. Extra bodies on regular shifts will help immensely. That's us done, Commissioner. Thank you.'

Baker stood. Neither tall nor physically intimidating, she still managed to appear imposing. Perhaps it was her uniform. 'I know you'll get this done. If it's accomplished very soon, so much the better.'

CHAPTER THIRTY

When Mahoney and Kendall departed to meet with the Commissioner, Gibson shuffled back to his desk. Dunstan didn't need him to create the alert. He could review the collation of physical evidence: purchases of tennis balls, rope, and all the sundry items, but with Geason, Mr Methodical, on top of all that, there was little point of duplication. Dobosz was trawling through the online histories of the victims so best leave him to it.

Just as Gibson began to feel like a shag on a rock, Herrick appeared at the edge of his desk. 'Hey, Gibbo. Need anything done?'

'Not sure, Hezza. Everything and nothing. It just feels like there's too much on, know what I mean?'

'Yeah sure, but you do what you can.' Herrick turned to go and then stopped. 'Where did this guy train? He could do weights at home but where did he practise that serve?'

'You're right. Did he join a club? Unlikely. So where can he practise?'

'A hitting wall.' Herrick's tone suggested it was blindingly obvious. 'There's a few about the 'burbs, big walls where you go and belt a ball. There's a good one near where I live.'

'Where's that?'

'The oval at Lenah Valley near the RSL. Think it's called John Turnbull Park nowadays.'

Gibson bit his lip then shook his head. 'I don't know that area.'

'Nah, you wouldn't unless you lived out that way. It shoots off from New Town into the foothills of the mountain. One of the few suburbs in Hobart without its own pub.'

'Full of Methodists?'

'Don't get you. Anyway, at the top of Creek Road is this huge park. It's got a fitness trail, doggie section, footy oval, hall, kids' playground, all that sort of stuff.'

'And a tennis hitting wall.'

'Yeah. Bakers Milk did a factory extension years ago and up went a massive brick wall on the boundary of the park. I guess part of the deal for permission was to lay out a concrete space on the ground for people to use. The wall's one big mural. Quite a few people use it to whack a ball about.'

'There might be loads of places like that around town.'

'Not really. Me and Kristy play a bit during summer, AYC twilight pennant. Been to most of the clubs down here and not many have hit-up walls. Taroona, Lindisfarne, that's about it. Even if you had the space to practise in a backyard, someone would kick up a stink. Reckon this is how he did it.'

Given that it beat sitting at a desk, Gibson stood. 'Let's you and me go out for a look. Can't hurt.'

'Sure. I'll get a vehicle.'

They drove haltingly through the traffic works dotted along Elizabeth Street. At a T-junction, with the Polish Club on one corner and a grocer on the other, Herrick turned the car left onto a large boulevard. A row of handsome dwellings lined the road for a kilometre until they passed an imposing red-brick hospital on their right.

'I was born there. Good old Calvary.' They went down a dip and over the crest of a hill before arriving at a small shopping strip. 'You're now in Lenah Valley. Aboriginal word for Kangaroo.'

'You know it well?'

'I grew up here. Live here now. Go for another couple of k's and you're right in the bush. Tracks up the mountain. Gem of a spot.'

Gibson had to acknowledge it seemed pretty nice. They headed down through another basin and up a slight rise to an intersection where Herrick turned right. 'Turnbull Park. Not bad, eh?'

'Yeah, bloody good.'

Herrick pulled into a parking bay opposite a primary school and pointed back up the hill. 'We've got a unit up in Ruth Drive. Loads of sun and a view of the Organ Pipes.'

Mount Wellington appeared over the foothills, looming behind the city. They traversed the football oval and came to the milk factory wall. Now they were here, Gibson wondered what he'd hoped would happen. Was he expecting Fowler to saunter up and start belting balls in front of them?

'Well this is kind of useful, but ...'

'But why are we here?'

'Umm, yeah.'

Herrick let out a low growl and started walking down a grassed slope to a metal fence. Gibson followed. They went through a child safety gate and in front of them was a substantial area of scrubby turf. Straight off the DC counted seven dogs with their owners.

'Regular as clockwork most of them,' said his uniformed offsider. 'Someone must have seen him if he came here.'

'If.'

'Yeah, but it's worth a try.' Herrick bent down to pet a Labrador that had galumphed its way over to them. 'Hello, boy. You good?'

'He certainly is.' A tall woman was marching towards them, holding a plastic sling with a tennis ball balanced in the spoon. 'Are you checking licences?' Her posture and voice was not a million miles from Penelope Keith on the old TV shows.

Gibson showed his ID. 'Not exactly our remit. We're out here on an associated matter.'

'Dennis the tennis menace, perhaps?'

They both did a double-take; Herrick gathered his wits first. 'Sorry, what was that?'

'I complained, most vehemently, to the council. Nothing happened, of course.'

'What was the problem exactly?' asked Gibson.

'A most truculent individual threatened my Marmaduke.' She pointed at the large bundle of fur sniffing Herrick's ankles. 'No sense of propriety at all. Disgraceful.'

Gibson endeavoured to adopt Mahoney's calming manner. 'Could you explain the particulars of the incident, Mrs ...?'

The woman lifted her chin. 'Ms. Ms Lynnette Fraser. Do they train that awful monotone into you, Constable, or is it natural?'

Gibson pressed on. 'An affectation, Ms Fraser. Now, what happened and when?'

'Ah, that's more like it. I prefer directness. It was January long weekend, the Monday morning, when Marmaduke and I were visiting the doggie enclosure. We passed a middle-aged man serving ball after ball at the mural. Just one of a number who practise there. Mind you, he was particularly vigorous. And accurate. I have excellent eyesight. I was something of an ace shot in the old country.'

'Not many pheasants down here, I'd imagine.'

'Those days are long gone. I followed my daughter to the Antipodes. She fell in love with the place on a student exchange and felt this was her dream come true.'

'Is it yours?'

'Not overly, Detective Constable. But family is important. My husband passed and London had become something of a nightmare. Gangs, rubbish, people everywhere. Here it is altogether more pleasant. And, of course, my only daughter is here. With her local husband.'

The last sentence hinted at a son-in-law who wasn't quite the ticket. Gibson steered them back. 'So, the man was serving vigorously, as you said. And then?'

'We skirted the edge of the pavement and approached the gate. I unclipped Marmaduke before fiddling with the child lock, but in an instant he was back off to the tennis man. Naughty dog. He raced over to one of the balls and picked it up in his mouth. A natural reaction. What this man did next was most certainly not.'

'He whacked another ball at your dog?' guessed Herrick.

'A correct assumption, young man. An underhand swipe drove a ball into poor Marmy. It was dreadful. I got over there quick-smart and protested the cruelty, but he totally ignored me. He spent a couple of minutes collecting balls from the ground and then strode off with his bag and racket.'

'Did he speak to you at all?'

'No. No acknowledgement at all. He simply strode right off unconscionably.'

'In which direction?' asked Herrick.

'Up towards the traffic lights on the corner. But by the time he was halfway, I'd given up on him and gone into the enclosure.'

Gibson hoped her memory was as sharp as her sight. 'Would you be able to describe his appearance?'

'Most certainly and with great relish.'

Herrick was dispatched to the vehicle to collect the iPad so their witness could view the images of Fowler. Gibson did not disabuse Lynette Fraser of the notion that animal cruelty was the focus, but she was no fool.

'I assume you are not here merely to investigate my complaint, Detective?'

'A fortunate coincidence is closer to the truth. This man you encountered may be a person of interest in an important case we're investigating.'

Her hand went to her mouth. 'Oh my Lord. That brutal murderer lives here.'

Gibson was completely taken aback. How did those dots get jointed up? 'I'm sorry, I'm not sure how ...'

'You disappoint me, young man. Two officers, one a homicide detective, asking questions about a dog attack. Please credit this member of the public with some common sense. The brute I challenged is a suspect in the current murder enquiry, is he not?'

'He could be. I'm not stonewalling. He could be a man we're keen to see.' He glanced up at the main road then back at their witness. 'When you said he lived around here, was that because he left on foot?'

'I doubt he drove here. Otherwise he would have parked his vehicle, as you did, on the other side of the Community Hall.'

'That's a reasonable assumption. Bus maybe?'

'Somewhat unusual.' She leaned forward to pat Gibson's forearm. 'Thank you, Detective.'

'For?'

'Granting me honorary Miss Marple status.'

Gibson smiled. 'I was thinking aloud, but you're right. A local inhabitant is probably more likely.'

'So, following my perusal of some photos and a positive identification, I can expect an influx of the constabulary going door-to-door.'

Another wide smile. 'That is pretty much guaranteed.'

□

Lynette Fraser's response to the identikit photos of Fowler was a confident 'Indeed it is he.' With that under his belt, Gibson got straight onto Mahoney and ran his boss through the latest development. He was instructed to coordinate a doorknock enquiry of the immediate vicinity. Four uniformed officers would be immediately dispatched to assist the operation.

Ms Fraser agreed now was as good a time as any to make a formal statement at the station. So, with Marmaduke in tow, she was first driven home by Herrick to drop off her bundle of enthusiasm and be taken into the city. This left Gibson to nut out the most effective way to deploy the manpower. He waved to his colleagues as the police car drove up Creek Road to the intersection and walked across the lawn to the corner. He did a slow turn to assess the geography. Fowler had walked off on the long diagonal towards this spot. The park boundary at this point ran back down Creek Road on one side and on the other along Augusta Road to the Athleen Avenue turn-off.

Gibson made the assumption that if Fowler had wanted to go towards Athleen Avenue, he would not have taken the diagonal path Lynnette Fraser was certain he'd taken. Also, he was unlikely to have come this way if he was returning to a dwelling on Creek Road or Wellwood Street which ran next to the primary school. That meant Gibson could focus the uniforms on the stretch of Augusta Road leading back to the city and the start of Pottery Road stretching up the hill from the traffic lights.

The promised quartet arrived; they had walked up the pavement from the small car park to join him. The only one he recognised was Alan Wagin who did the introductions. It transpired the other three were mature-age cadets who had been only too happy to sacrifice a lecture on traffic regulations to assist this investigation. With the Google map screen open on his phone, Gibson delineated the search area and they set off. He allocated two hours with the promise of coffees at the end— or a few rounds of beers if they turned up anything really useful.

Gibson gave himself the short strip of Augusta Road between the intersection and the RSL Club one hundred metres along to his right; he decided to start at the club and work back. Having signed himself in at the foyer, Gibson approached the bar. A man giving a tray of glasses the once-over with a towel looked up. 'You look official. Licensing?'

Gibson showed his ID. 'Not at all. Just wondering if you can help me locate a chap we're looking for. Any chance a Michael Fowler is a member?'

The rangey man put down the towel. 'The name doesn't ring a bell, but I know all our regulars by sight. Got a picture?'

Gibson showed him the iPad but the man's concentrated perusal proved futile. 'Nah. No-one like him's been in here. Sorry. What's he done?'

'Routine. He might be able to help us with a case we're on.'

'Yeah, right. And my name's Barack Obama. That's the snoozer you reckon done those murders.'

'At the moment he's simply a good lead. So you haven't seen him about?'

'Nah. Fancy a drink?'

'Yes, but it'll have to be another day.'

'Come on a Friday. It's meat tray night. Gets a few in.'

'Will do. Thanks anyway.'

The childcare centre next door and the remaining two houses before the Pottery Road corner proved fruitless. At the traffic lights he looked up the hill and saw one of the cadets shutting a front gate behind her; the other must be inside a house somewhere. The Augusta Road pair were now out of sight down the hill. No-one had called him, so no joy thus far.

He crossed to the adjacent corner and entered a hair salon. A strictly suburban affair, its décor had seen better days. In the far corner an elderly lady was under a dryer flicking through a glossy magazine as her perm set. At the counter the lone hairdresser put the phone back in its cradle. 'Hi, I'm Robyn. Looking for an appointment?'

She sounded so hopeful that Gibson felt sorry to disappoint. He flashed his badge and stated his business. 'It's a bit of a long shot, but you haven't seen this fella by any chance?'

'Not for a bit.'

'I beg your pardon.'

'Not for a couple of weeks.' She gestured behind her. 'There's a unit out the back attached to this. You enter off Pottery Road. I'm pretty sure it was him there over Christmas for a while.'

'And you're certain it was this man?'

'Close enough. Not real friendly like. I never actually spoke to him, but I'd see him off and on. You right there, Mrs Evans?' After receiving no response from her customer, she turned back to Gibson and cocked her head to one side. 'I reckon it was him in there from around Show Day till about a fortnight ago.'

'So more like a few months then?'

'Yeah, 'spose so. Time flies, eh.'

'Is the dwelling you're referring to completely separate from the salon? No shared entrance?'

'Nope. Same landlord but.'

'And who's that?'

'Fella that has the shop across the road too. He doesn't run it, just owns the building. Nick Hatzi. Not a bad person really. Not very keen on funding improvements to the outside of this place, but the rent's affordable so I'm not too fussed.'

'Any idea how I can get hold of him?'

'I've his number here somewhere. But if you want a key, nip across the road.'

'Really?'

'Yeah. His son, Mani, runs the takeaway. He should be able to help you.'

Gibson was straight out the door.

Ten minutes later Gibson was at the entrance to the brick flat with a ring of keys. Mani Hatzi had been very accommodating and confirmed the photo as belonging to the tenant—a tenant who had skipped off about two weeks before without notice so wasn't going to be seeing his bond money in a hurry. As to a name, Hatzi stated the man had showed ID material for a Gerard Ogden. And, no, Hatzi hadn't been into the unit yet; he'd been too busy.

Gibson practically skipped out of the shop. He quickly called Mahoney who said he'd head straight there. The DC slipped on evidence gloves and put the Yale key in the lock. After a slight struggle, the mechanism gave a grudging turn. He crossed the threshold into a musty smelling reception area and stepped lightly into the kitchen. What he saw next set his eyes out on stalks. It was an easy decision to retrace his steps to the front stoop.

CHAPTER THIRTY-ONE

On the drive out to Lenah Valley Mahoney tempered his expectations. From what his favourite blood nut had told him they had stumbled on a massive break. All the checking thus far had moved them forward, but this could be the giant leap every case needed.

At the intersection he turned left into Pottery Road and parked several car lengths up from the corner. A utilitarian mesh fence marked the edge of a scrubby block which contained a weather-beaten weatherboard shed. Far beyond shabby chic, it looked as if a strong gust could dismantle it.

Gibson was standing expectantly by the side gate. 'Well done, David. Wise move not blundering in.' Mahoney slapped his constable on the shoulder blade. 'Where are the doorknockers?'

Gibson hoiked a thumb behind him. 'Wags has taken them over to the corner shop for a brew. They're awaiting instructions.'

'Righto. We'll leave them there for a bit. Kitchener and his forensics team should be here very soon.' Mahoney glanced back towards the shed. 'Actually, no. We'll get them out again with the van images. That old shed could be a ripper place to park a vehicle without garnering too much scrutiny.'

He put on booties and gloves and pushed open the gate with his index finger. It gave easily despite a creaking or two. 'If you could stand guard, I'll take a shufti.'

Gibson nodded. 'It's worth it.'

Mahoney entered and was struck by the sheer dowdiness of it all; not a great deal of time or money had been spent on this residence. The wallpaper was faded, although it was probably a blessing given the lurid brown and orange pattern. In the kitchen, he walked across torn linoleum to the formica table. Smack in the middle of it was a green plastic baby bath containing, submerged in approximately a foot of water, a Barbie doll. In the corner under the window was a tennis racquet balanced against a blue bucket of used tennis balls. The DI could now appreciate the excited gabbling that had been Gibson's call.

The remainder of the kitchen held no surprises, save for the fact it was something of a time warp; it must have been kitted out sometime in the 1960s. At the end of a row of head-high cabinets was a mesh-doored receptacle for condiments. Both pockmarked with age, the kettle had a fraying roped cord and the toaster two side-opening panels. The whole room was too cruddy to be deemed retro. A low hum from the Kelvinator fridge indicated the power was still on. Perhaps their man intended to return, although it was doubtful.

Mahoney passed through the door frame into a dingy hall. On his right was a stand-alone toilet adjacent to a small bathroom. Neither looked to have been used for a while, nor cleaned for that matter. Next in line was a snug double bedroom. With the curtains drawn, it was gloomy. He flicked the light on. Nothing stood out aside from the hideous décor. Neatly spread across the bed was a blue crimplene cover; everything had been left tidy.

The final area was the lounge room. As the unit wrapped around the hair salon, this room had some east-facing windows and was a touch brighter, although it still didn't warm one's heart to step in. Not only were the carpet and the couch dated, but they looked as if they'd been bought second-hand years ago. He wondered how much rent was charged; it was a convenient location but hardly a luxury pied-à-terre.

Back at the front gate Gibson was tapping on his mobile.

'Property history?'

'Got it in one, boss, but there ain't much to see. No sale or rental data to speak of. Probably been part of the Hatzi portfolio for years. I wonder how Fowler found out about it.'

'Sure our chap across the road can help. I'll go over when SOCO arrive.' Right then two vans pulled up at the kerb. 'Which looks like right about now. Let them control the scene. You go into the house on the city side, 176 I reckon, and get as much detail as possible on what they observed over their side fence.'

'No problem. I'll take one of the cadets with me and let Wags sort the rest out. Sightings of the man and/or the van?'

'Spot on.' As his constable took off, a door slammed and Kitchener stepped towards him. 'Mike and company. Welcome.'

Kitchener's arms were loaded with protective suits. He looked up and down the path. 'I'm guessing we do our stuff right here?'

'I'd say so. Can you mark off this section of pavement?'

'We might have to. Entry is almost right on the street.' He called over his shoulder. 'Donna, grab some witches' hats and tape. Seal off that top end of the fence around the vans and tie off back down here where the post butts up against the salon.'

Givens waved acknowledgement and Kitchener turned back to the DI. 'So, this is our guy's bolthole?'

'It must be. At least up till the Hellyer death. There'll be traces of him everywhere, so this is a chain of evidence exercise, but it would really make my week if you uncover anything that will help us trace his current whereabouts.'

'Or his intentions.'

'That would make my year.'

□

Gibson and Cadet Moira Flaherty were sitting comfortably at a large oak table in the kitchen of number 176 with Dolcie Evans, the owner of the property. On the first sweep nobody had been home; they were about to give up when Mrs Evans appeared from next-door where she had been getting her hair done. All three had pale blue china mugs of steaming hot coffee in front of them. Next to Flaherty was a notebook with her pen hand poised above it.

The kitchen-diner was toasty. 'I hope you're not too warm, Constable. In my dotage any cold is unwelcome.'

He assured her they were fine. 'This is a lovely house. Traffic not a bugbear?'

'Oh yes, it's very busy these days but my son installed double-glazing on the front windows so I get the northern sun without the din.'

'How long have you lived here, Mrs Evans?'

'Fifty-five years, next month.' She waved at a small urn next to the coffee and sugar canisters on the kitchen bench. 'Geoff and I were very fortunate. This was our first home. We brought up two children here and now there's just me.'

Gibson determinedly avoided glancing at his drink; that would make for an interesting beverage if you spooned from the wrong jar. 'A few changes over time, I reckon.'

'Oh yes, indeed. One of our sons is a glazier and the other's a master builder. Richie took out quite a few walls to open the house up and now it's much brighter.'

'Much brighter, and more comfortable, than next-door.'

'Well, that's been a rental property for many years now. The salon used to be a pie shop, and the Higgins family who were the owners lived there. That would be, let me think, up until Whitlam's election in 1972. Then the lovely Hatzi family moved in. They took over the corner shop next to the butcher's. It's not there now, of course, the butcher's that is. They changed the pie shop into a salon and various people have run that since.'

'And the dwelling?'

'When Mr and Mrs Hatzi started a family they moved up the hill into a new brick house in Bealey Avenue. That would have been 1977, the Queen's jubilee. It's always been tenants since then. Some lovely, others not quite so much.'

Gibson could have foregone the social history, but he'd learned from the boss not to rush. All in good time, son. As long as you've got the witness talking, you're on the right track. 'We're pretty interested in the most recent tenant.'

'Well I'm afraid I'm not going to be much help there, Constable. I never met him. He wasn't what you'd call sociable. In the four months he was there, I barely got a word out of him. It's not that he was rude just … withdrawn.'

'Four months, you say?'

'Yes. I remember it was Show Day because that's when I plant the tomatoes. I don't have a hothouse you see. I was in the yard and I noticed a faded pink car in the yard. The new chap was unloading a suitcase and some boxes so I called hello. All I got was a tiny tilt of his head, so I thought to myself no tea and scones for you.'

'Did he look something like this?' Gibson slid the iPad across the table.

'Yes, he did. At the start certainly.'

'Changes?'

'My word. He lost quite a bit of weight. He became, as my Richie says, rather buff.' She smiled cheekily as if something risqué had passed her lips. 'When he wasn't off to the park with his racquet, he was traipsing up and down the hills in his walking gear. By the end of the summer his appearance had changed considerably. He was quite gaunt, but strong, if you know what I mean.'

So this had been Fowler's base for a summer training camp. First Ms Fraser and now Mrs Evans—the Stasi could hardly have been as efficient at monitoring behaviour. 'Did you speak to him again after that first encounter?'

'Just the once, about a fortnight ago. By then the pink car had gone and he had a white transit van. He parked that in the shed behind the old door.' She turned to Flaherty. 'Now, where was I?'

'The last time you spoke to this man.'

'Yes, thank you. He was burning material in an old forty-four gallon drum and the smoke was quite acrid. A breeze was up and I wanted to put some washing out, you see. I asked him how long he would be. Without even turning around he said "a short while" and that was that. The very next day he was gone.'

'And that was?'

'The Friday before last. It was my birthday.'

Gibson nodded to his offsider; he doubted she had any questions, but it never hurt to afford respect. She gave a small shake of her head, signalling that they could go. That drum was going to be vital.

□

As Mani Hatzi drew a mesh tray of fat-cut chips out of the deep fat fryer, Mahoney tried to calculate how many calories he would ingest from a large serve. Hatzi shook the tray then tipped it into a large metal basin and applied large doses of seasoning, before the Heart Council's least favourite food was transferred to the bain-marie.

'You look tempted, Inspector.'

'I am. How do you resist?'

'By thinking back a year or two. When I first took over from Dad, I'd be picking away all day and the pounds went on. Long hours and a poor diet are a bad mix for any café owner. I might have got away with it when I was still playing soccer, but not trapped in here.'

'You look fine now.'

'Thank you. I have Mediterranean Greek salad for lunch, I stopped the nibbling and each morning I use the fitness circuit in the park. I feel good, sleep better and I can run around with the kids. Result.' He gave a theatrical thumbs up.

Mahoney looked around the store. There were a few wooden tables with chairs, soft drink fridges and a full-scale coffee machine. 'Good business?'

'Would a Greek be here otherwise?' The smile revealed bright teeth beneath the bushy moustache.

'Probably not. Good point.' Mahoney gestured behind him. 'Can I ask you about your property across the road?'

'Shoot.'

'I'm very interested in your most recent tenant in the domestic accommodation.'

A frown replaced the smile. 'Dodgy fucker. Took off about a week or two ago. No notice. No thank you. Nothing.'

'That's certainly what it looks like. What was the arrangement?'

'Month to month. He paid in advance. No lease. Handshake agreement. Suited us.'

'How so?'

'As you've probably seen, it's hardly upper-end stuff. Starting at Easter it's going to be done up. We're going to do an extension out the back. So that bloke was a bit of a stopgap till we got started.'

'No great loss then?'

'Nah, probably not. When I get a chance, I'll go in and get it going. Still, it'd be nice to get some word from him.'

'That's unlikely I'd say. How did he get onto you?'

Mani pointed to the entrance. 'Handwritten sign in the front window. It had only been up a day or so and in he walked. Chatted to me about it and then said it suited him while his own place got the plumbing fixed.'

'References?'

'Not much point. He looked pretty respectable and it was only short-term as I said.'

'Cash?'

The smile returned. 'We are businessmen, after all. But don't worry. I have a cousin in the tax office, so it'll get declared.'

How much of it would be declared is another matter, Mahoney thought. 'What name did your tenant give?'

'Gerard Ogden. To be honest, I barely saw him after the first day or so. Straight after that first chat I gave him a quick look over the place and he coughed up three months' worth of cash in exchange for the key. That was pretty much it. He never shopped here and we didn't need to check in on him. He kept himself to himself. Perfect, really.'

'Apart from shipping off early.'

'Mmm, but that's not such a tragedy. He did pay for this month.'

'So, strictly speaking, he's still the tenant.'

'Yeah. Do you reckon he'll be back?'

'Only if he's monumentally stupid. Certainly not now with our bods all over the place. Thanks for that by the way. Allowing quick access to my constable really helped us.'

'No worries. They can take it apart if they want. I don't need to go in just yet.'

Mahoney nodded. 'I'll see what I can organise. If we can keep it as a no-access crime zone for a few more days, that would be good.'

'Sure.' A thought occurred to Hatzi. 'What's he done in there? I haven't even asked. Was there a body?'

'No. But this guy is an important part of an investigation. For now I'd appreciate if you kept that to yourself, okay?'

'No worries. All co-operation from this end. Take all the time you need.'

Mahoney leaned across the counter and shook the proprietor's hand. 'Thanks, Mani. I reckon you'll at least get a bit of business out of it.'

□

Mahoney paused to allow a cyclist to keep his momentum through the intersection before crossing Augusta Road to the hair salon.

Around the corner the crime scene tape was stretched out from the wire fence; he ducked under and walked into the yard. Through a window he spied Kitchener and Givens inching through the kitchen, but his attention was drawn to the two figures by the paling fence looking over a rusty container. Gibson stood a few feet away from a fully-suited female officer who was inspecting the bottom of the metal drum. As Mahoney approached, she lifted her head. 'Hey, Sir. We might have something here.'

Mahoney hadn't seen Jane Manning for a while now. She had been one of his own prior to a transfer to Forensics, but her methodical approach suited the branch. 'I hope so, Jane. It would justify Constable Gibson dragging you outside.'

Gibson, to give him his due, didn't apologise. 'Acting on a hunch picked up next-door. Mrs Evans pretty much confirmed our guy was here. The tennis stuff, fitness schedule, the vehicles, all that.'

'Righto, good work. Now why this?'

'Apparently he was burning a heap of stuff in this makeshift furnace just before he shot through.'

'Which we now think is around the time of the Hellyer slaying. How reliable is she next-door?'

'Mind like a steel trap.' Gibson shook his head in amazement. 'Mrs Memory I'll call her. She's sure it was a Friday, her washing day, that Ogden was out here turfing stuff into the blaze. He created a fair bit of smoke.'

Mahoney considered the drum; it was a typical makeshift construction. An upright forty-four gallon steel cylinder with the top end cut out and half a dozen ventilation holes drilled near the base. 'And we're hoping haste left some waste.'

'Yep. Mike Kitchener's team are working away inside. Those were obvious mementoes which we were meant to find. Perhaps out here is some gear he didn't want discovered.'

A chance encounter outside Royal Hobart Hospital a couple of years before had led to Gibson coming into the homicide squad. Now he was here practically calling the shots. With Kendall hitting her straps, Mahoney might even contemplate moving up to the executive. He may no longer be needed on the ground. 'What can you see in there, Jane?'

'Plenty of ash, but there are also lots of scraps of paper. It looks slightly glossy so it wouldn't have burned quite so well as ordinary pages. Beneath the topmost surface it's hard to tell, but it certainly hasn't disintegrated into white ash. There could be good material to sift through.'

'Presumably you'll shift the whole thing back you to your lab.'

'Yes, Sir. We're quite open to the elements here. I'll seal it off and get it sifted.'

'Good stuff. Thank you. We'll leave you to it. David, come with me.' They turned and walked back to the unit.

Stopping by the rickety shed, Mahoney scanned the interior while Gibson stood by silently. Mahoney puffed his cheeks and let out a breath. 'He knew we'd find this lair. Why else would he lay out the baby bath and tennis gear? Is he telling us anything else?'

It took a few moments before Gibson replied. 'You don't need to be Cortese to decipher those signs. Maybe it's what isn't there.'

'How so?'

'Only two ritual murders and there's nothing to suggest a third. Was that the grand scheme? Hellyer and Heath were all he planned.'

'You'd hope so, but three is the magic number. Three points to prove a straight line.'

'We keep chasing then. He no longer has a solid hidey-hole like this one, so he's on the move. It makes a thoroughly planned third attack less likely, you'd think.'

'Unless there is something in the drum or inside to indicate otherwise.'

Before Gibson could reply, there was a sharp rap on the kitchen window. They turned to see Kitchener waving them in. They went through the ritual of booties and gloves—irritating but necessary—

and, once inside the entrance, they could see Kitchener standing by the old stove. His hand was hovering by the handle of the solid oven door.

'Old school, John. You ready for it?'

Mahoney nodded and took a few paces towards the stove where he crouched down for a better view. Kitchener pulled down the handle and opened the door. Perched on the bottom rail was a cloth doll: a bearded figure in a chef's uniform. With its back facing the rear of the oven, it was seated with a box of matches tucked between its legs.

Gibson peered over his superior's shoulder. 'Looks like you're right. There'll be a third.'

□

'So what do you think of the photos I sent through?' Mahoney had his mobile on speaker mode so Gibson could hear as well.

Cortese's voice was calm. 'Your suspect is relishing the playing out of his quest. From what you've told me of the scene, and from the content of the photo attachments, that much appears obvious. One's first reaction might be that he's endeavouring to taunt those on the chase, with the tennis equipment and the baby tub, but the stuffed toy indicates something more.'

'He wants to be caught?' asked Gibson.

'Ah, I thought I was on speaker. Yes, Constable. Indeed he does. The power of three. But he has the knowledge that, in a place this size, it will be increasingly difficult to evade capture. His self-determined bounds for the quest are quite contained.'

'He knows there'll be an end point.'

'Certainly, Inspector. That is without doubt.' The pause was extended. 'Sorry. I'm pacing the lounge room and encountered a dead spot. Regardless, we can assume there is a third victim in the equation, but obviously you'll be hoping the task is incomplete. From what I've read of the investigation, the next steps will be operational rather than theoretical. So, godspeed. I'll further analyse the findings regarding the suspect and keep myself available.'

'Alright, thank you. We're definitely on the trail so we'll crack on.' The call disconnected and Mahoney turned to his offsider. 'You heard the man. Let's get on it.'

□

The first stop had to be the squad room where Kendall was updating the incident board. As they entered, she turned to them. 'Jane Manning just called. Said you'd really want to know this. At the core of the ash pile was a cardboard fold-out map of new eateries in Hobart. It was charred but mostly intact. Five of them were highlighted with a green marker. She's sending through images to us.'

Their quarry was moving into reach. They must act now and act quickly. Mahoney called across the room. 'Andrew, has a message from Forensics made it through to you?'

He gave a thumbs up, so Mahoney strode over. 'Good. Open the attachments.'

Dunstan obliged and magnified the page. 'Here you go. Important?'

'God, yes. Don't know what you've heard, but getting this list has really opened things up. Flick that page to everyone in the squad, then bring up whatever material you can on the five places. Particularly the people in front and behind them, okay?'

'Of course.' His chunky fingers started tapping.

As Dunstan brought up Google Maps on his screen, Gibson's mobile rang.

'DC Gibson.'

'Very formal, aren't we? It's Sergeant Manson at the front desk.' As if the rasping tones could be anyone else.

'Yes, Sarge?'

'Just had a call come in from outside that should interest you. Fella with a pizza restaurant in Battery Point. Reckons he could be the target of a potential arson.'

How Manson knew this would be relevant now wasn't worth pursuing, but the lead was. Gibson got Mahoney's attention by waving his mobile.

'Fuzzy downstairs knows something.'

'Put him on speaker.' Mahoney spoke. 'Sarge, what's up?'

'That blood nut's got his head up his arse. If he's Mr Detective Constable, I'm Senior Sergeant. You got that, David? Plods at the front desk do keep across what the Sweeney are up to, you know. The alert from Manning came through to me as well. Anyways, practically right as that happened, this Duncan Edmunds rings in with a concern that something dodgy is going on at his pizzeria in Hampden Road.'

'As in?'

'Very iffy smell in the kitchen, John. Gas, he thinks.'

'Have you dispatched anyone?'

'Nope. I called young Morse first.'

'Good. Don't dispatch anyone. We'll deal with it. Text me the details please.'

'Sure. Good luck.'

Mahoney took his own phone out. 'Silver Ball, 94 Hampden. Is that one of the five?'

Dunstan hovered over a red flag on the screen image. 'Yep, it is.'

'Call this Edmunds guy and tell him we're on the way. Call the firies as well. Advise Edmunds not to touch anything and to wait for us out the rear of the building.'

'Righto.'

'Kate, you and Andrew find out what you can about Edmunds, okay?'

'Of course.' She smiled. 'And you're off with Endeavour to follow up?'

'Correct. David, let's go.'

CHAPTER THIRTY-TWO

The lights were with them so, even allowing for the construction outside the hospital refurbishment site, they made the trip in just over ten minutes. Some aggressive lane-changing helped. Amazingly, a kerb space was open for Mahoney's car behind a fire truck.

They crossed the street and walked up the pathway in front of the stucco brick restaurant premises. A tall figure was waiting for them; he was dressed in a white shirt and chinos, and had designer stubble with a hipster haircut.

'Hi guys. Thanks for coming so quickly. Mind you, I was expecting uniforms.'

'These are ours,' said Mahoney. 'You're Duncan Edmunds? I'm Inspector Mahoney and this is DC Gibson. This your place?'

'Yeah. Eight months in and we're going gangbusters. It helps being up the street from D'Angelo's.'

'I'd reckon it would.' Mahoney peered around the corner to the open back door. 'What alerted you?'

Edmunds led them to the space outside the rear entrance. 'I turned up as usual to receive deliveries and prep for tonight. As soon as I opened the door, the waft hit me.' He tapped his nose. 'A good sense of smell is the main part of a job in the kitchen.'

'Did you do anything else right then?'

'No fear. I wasn't going to flick a switch. I like charred meat, just not mine.'

'You didn't even check the ovens?' interjected Gibson.

'Oh yeah, I did that obviously. I could see from the door that the dials on the main cooker were all full on, so I ducked back out and shut off the main tap. It's dissipated now but you can still sense the smell.'

'No chance it was staff error?'

Edmunds laughed. 'No chance. Errors do happen, but all the dials ramped up? No.'

'Made sense to call it in then.'

'Hope you don't mind me asking, but this level of police interest is more than I expected.'

Candour seemed the right option. 'You're right. We're actually homicide detectives.'

Edmunds's eyes widened. 'So, this was like a real threat? To me? Not arson then?'

'It could be arson but, in the strictest confidence, it could also be personal. We'll need to talk. But first, so we can best sort this out, you'll need to be shut for tonight.'

'Fair enough. The bookings are light for once. I guess you guys want to give it the once over. I'll need to grab the bookings sheet, call a few customers and staff, and make a sign.'

'Constable Gibson will grab the book for you. At the front desk?'

'Yep. What about the firemen inside?'

'Of course. Hang on a tic, David.' Mahoney peered around the corner to witness a pair of fire officers emerging through the rear door. 'Everything okay guys?'

'All clear. It needs airing out, but there's no ongoing threat.'

Mahoney thanked them and gestured to Gibson who went straight in. There was enough light for him to see a way through to the tables.

Mahoney took out his phone. 'Kate, it's John. We're here and it looks very iffy. The firemen attending have cleared it, but get someone from Arson over here straightaway. The restaurant will be closed for the evening. David and I will be interviewing Mr Edmunds. He's right here with me now. Text through anything you've found, okay?'

The young owner was sending text messages. 'Just letting the crew know.' He paused. 'Oh shit. Couldn't be one of them, could it?'

If it was, they'd be surprised to receive a text from their boss. 'I doubt it, to be honest. We'll need their details to touch base, but it's not my first thought.'

Gibson stepped back out with a register in one hand. 'I can call round if you like. I used to work in my dad's pub so I know how to rearrange times and stuff.'

'Sure, I suppose. I get the impression your boss is itching to chat.'

'I am. David, do the ring round from the car while Mr Edmunds and I hang here for a bit.'

Gibson nodded and took himself off around the corner.

'So, how long have you been in hospitality?'

'A couple of years. I started with a no-frills pizza outlet in Claremont. Only two attempted hold-ups, but about a thousand Hawaiians.'

'Oh yes, the lure of ham and charred pineapple.'

'No point reinventing the wheel, Inspector. Eighteen months in, the lease for this place came up and I went for a slightly classier operation. More pasta dishes and salads.'

'And the name Silver Ball?'

'I scored a mirrored disco ball from a nightclub that was being refurbished. It hangs in the main dining space. It's a gimmick but it seems to work. Want to see it?'

'Better wait. Our tech guy will be here pretty soon.' Mahoney gazed down the roof line of old properties. 'The great location must help, not that I doubt the food is any good. From memory, the tenants here before you were rubbish.'

'Yeah, nothing was fresh and they bailed after a year. That helped me get a super deal with the rent. I hope this doesn't stuff up our good run.'

'As I said, it should be just this evening. Fortunately, there's no damage.'

'Or a body.'

'Are you still wondering why plain clothes detectives are attending?'

'Well, yeah. Not that I don't appreciate the response.'

Mahoney shuffled his feet. 'I am interested in why you could be a target.'

He shrugged his shoulders. 'No idea really. Ange Farracio at D'Angelo's and I get along well. Actually, it was him who told me about the vacancy here. He's always chock-a-block, so I'm hardly competition. The immediate neighbours are fine. God knows.'

'Right. And before the Claremont place, what were you doing?'

'Pulling beers at the Prince of Wales while I did a Bachelor of Business at UTAS. I might seem overqualified, but the most important part of this business is marketing and accounts.'

'I imagine so. Where's home?'

'Down here, a flat in Dynnyrne. Originally, up north.'

'Launceston?'

'Yeah. My folks still live in Trevallyn. I went to Saint Pat's. Some learning and plenty of sport and hellfire.'

'I know what you mean. I had the southern version.' Mahoney narrowed his eyes for the crucial query. 'Which sports?'

'Usual stuff. Soccer in winter and tennis through summer.'

'Any good?'

'Oh, you know. State underage rep in both but I was never going to go much further. It instilled good habits and all that though. I still have a hit of tennis on Monday nights.' Edmunds broke off. 'Is there a background thing in all this?'

There was no other way to put it. 'Yes. I'm here because you may be a potential target for a suspect we're after. Ever heard of a Michael Fowler?'

His brow furrowed. 'Nope. But is that the psycho who got Trish and Scotty? Really?'

'We've established a link between that suspect and your premises. And, in the strange schema of our suspect's head, there's also a tangible connection to the two victims you mentioned.'

'You think he did this?'

'Quite possibly. As you noted, the police response is more urgent than you might expect.'

'Fuck. What now?'

'Stick with me. Literally. I'll get a team around to look over your flat. We've got an arrangement with Accord Hotel to put people up if needs be. You'll have round-the-clock cover.'

'Like witness protection in some US drama? You're kidding me. All because there's a gas leak? Piss off.'

The anger was understandable but had to be quelled. 'You're right. It feels a bit over-the-top but the danger is real. This is substantially more than a leak from a dodgy stove top. Believe me, it's very specific and you have to be protected. The hotel is secure. Officers on rotation will keep an eye on you. One of us will escort you home to get some gear. Tomorrow the business can run as normal. This way is by far the best option.' Mahoney didn't say it was the only option; hopefully, Edmunds would recognise that.

His shoulders dropped. 'I guess so. If I can avoid what happened to Scott and Trish, I should be grateful.'

'How did you know them?'

'Oh, you know, this is not the biggest city in the world. They were well ahead of me at school in Launceston. I'd heard of Trish, national rep and all that, when I was younger, but then I met her at a fundraiser last year. She used to come in here every so often with her family. Scott and I met through the business. He was a good sales guy. Gave us a great deal on their beers. I'd see him at tennis on those Monday nights too.'

Before Mahoney could inquire further, a gaunt man in blue overalls appeared around the corner carrying a large plastic clip-box of gear.

He had clipped russet-grey hair, a sharp nose and aqua blue eyes. A bony hand shout out. 'Inspector, I'm Sergeant Adams. Arson Squad.'

Mahoney laid out the basic facts. 'Anything you can pick up would be appreciated.'

The reply was as spare as the physique. 'Sure.'

'Not the chatty type,' observed Edmunds.

'Job to do. As have we. Let's get you sorted first. Anything you need from here?'

'Nah, it can wait till tomorrow.'

Mahoney led the way down the path to the kerb where Gibson was finishing a call.

'All good. I've contacted everyone who was down for tonight. I had to leave a few voicemails but those I spoke to have mostly rebooked for later in the week.'

'If you're up for any moonlighting, let me know,' said Edmunds. 'You've done a better job than most of my staff.'

Gibson smiled unabashedly. 'Cheers. Just helping out. I'll stay here and check the skeleton doesn't eat all the food then.'

Edmunds laughed.

'If you stay and liaise with Sergeant Adams that would be appreciated,' said Mahoney. 'Call Kate and ask her to send Geason down to Mr Edmunds's apartment.'

'He's there already.'

'You've already called?'

'Yep. I'll text him to let him know you're on your way.'

Mahoney was quietly impressed. Had he indicated his intentions somehow? Dammed if his offsider wasn't running the show. 'Perfect. Do that. And the Accord is sorted and ready?'

'Yep, all done.' Gibson was deadpan. Surely he hadn't instructed that too? Initiative from colleagues was what Mahoney wanted; he just didn't want to be made redundant—not quite yet.

'Sign for the front door?'

'I'll do it now.'

'Righto.' Mahoney leaned down to open the passenger door for Edmunds. At least he was good for something.

□

Much later in the incident room, the inner circle gathered. Mahoney was standing in front of the case boards with Kendall and Gibson seated a few feet away. He tapped the fresh photo. 'Duncan Edmunds is tucked away at the safe hotel. He collected some clothes and toiletries from his flat in Star Street, nice place with a view down to the Casino. Geason was there and gave it a once over. Nothing untoward, and Edmunds confirmed nothing out of place, so all good on that front.'

'Under surveillance?'

'Yes, Kate. Geason is there till midnight and then Sergeant Wagin will step in. Our perp may try there. It fits his home invasion pattern. Heaven help him if Wags collars him.' Mahoney turned to Gibson. 'Did Adams find anything?'

'He sure did. The wiring from the main light switch had been diverted to a detonator sitting in the oven grill. One flick of the switch and it would have been kapow! The mother of all explosions. Without his chef's nose, Edmunds would be toast.'

'Prints, traces, anything?'

'Not so far. Mike Kitchener arrived after you left and had a good look, but the place was clean as a whistle.'

Kendall spoke up. 'For the other two murders he's been hands on. We've pushed him into fast forward.'

'I'd say that's correct. When David and I arrived at the restaurant there didn't look to be anyone lurking around, although that doesn't mean there wasn't. In the morning we need to do a reccy of properties nearby in Hampden Road. Maybe Ogden settled for watching his handiwork this time.'

Kendall pointed to the photo of Edmunds. 'Does this guy truly fit the silver spoon scenario?'

Before her boss could answer, Gibson chipped in. 'As much as anybody could if you ask me. While I was waiting for Adams to finish his site inspection, I made a few calls home. Edmunds is from Launceston, tick. He's running a successful business, tick. He showed plenty of sporting promise in his teens, tick.'

'And Trevallyn's one of the more affluent suburbs, isn't it?'

'It is. It's right up there. But the Edmunds family weren't. Don't get me wrong, they didn't struggle, but very little was served on a platter. Can I jot what I found on the board?'

'Sure.' Mahoney handed over the fluorescent marker as they swapped places.

The constable started by underlining the name, twice. 'Duncan. It's not some toffy affectation. His old man was from Scotland. He came out from Glasgow in the sixties as a ten pound Pom, hardly a prosperous economic migrant. He met his wife at a soccer function not long after he arrived in Tassie. They …'

'Sorry to butt in, David, but how do you know all this?' asked Kendall.

'My folks were hoteliers. There isn't much a publican's wife doesn't pick up on the grapevine. So, Duncan is the good Scottish king in Macbeth. Just straight heritage. They literally set up shop in Trevallyn. They rented premises and ran a grocery for years, living above the business. Now this is before Hill Street Grocer type operations became trendy. Back then all these suburban outlets were being outmuscled by supermarket chains. The family made a living, but it certainly wasn't beach house in the summer stuff. They worked really hard apparently. The dad is a life member of Riverside Soccer Club and Mrs Edmunds the same for the local tennis club. Real doers my mum reckoned.'

'And the lad?' Mahoney asked.

'Sporty, yes. Privileged, not at all. Saint Pat's is Catholic. Much, much lower fees than the two private colleges where Hellyer and Heath went. My take is that anything this guy has got, he's earned the hard way.'

Mahoney scratched his head and frowned. 'I suppose there can only be so many who precisely fit the pattern we think is at play here. It's close enough to what we think is the killer's motivation.'

'And we can't ignore the link material that was found at Lenah Valley,' Kendall prompted.

There was silence as they waited for the boss to respond. His stare was fixed on the board. He stood abruptly as if thrusting up from a weightlifter's squat.

'This is all the work of our guy. None of them deserved it. We gather again bright and early tomorrow. We've been lucky today and we're getting closer. Much closer. Much of Fowler's focus now has to be eluding us, and that detracts from enacting his obsession. Get whatever rest you can tonight and I'll see you at eight o'clock. Good work, David. Thank you, Kate.'

As they departed, Mahoney remained staring at the board. Where to next?

□

It only took Gibson ten minutes to drive home. His place in South Hobart was just off Macquarie Street near the sprawling retirement home complex. He lived in a one bedroom flat in a 1920's block of four. The curved edges on the façade and the original leadlight windows gave the block a hint of art-deco.

He parked his Mazda in the street and trotted up the stairwell to his front door. He couldn't be bothered checking the mailbox; it had been another long day and he was bushed. Once through the front door he dropped his keys on the hall sideboard table and padded out to the kitchen. Tiredness was overriding hunger so he decided a mouthful of milk was all he needed. He leaned down to open the fridge door and pull out the milk carton—just a quick slug and he could collapse.

CHAPTER THIRTY-THREE

By eight o'clock Mahoney and Kendall were in his office. An early call from Alan Wagin had confirmed that nothing untoward had occurred during the night at Edmunds's Dynnyrne apartment. That afforded some relief, although neither detective had truly expected there would be trouble.

'I'll call the Accord Hotel and check on Edmunds, but I doubt there'll be much to report there either.'

Kendall nodded. It would be a turn-up for the books if the hideaway was breached. Mahoney's call was transferred through to the hotel room.

'Hello?' a hesitant voice answered.

'Mr Edmunds, it's DI Mahoney here. How are you?'

'Oh right, it's you. I didn't want to identify myself, just in case … you know.'

'Of course. Good thinking. The early report from our constable at your flat confirmed nothing went wrong in the night. Just checking how you slept and if you mind popping in to make a statement.'

'Yeah, sure. I can come round with my minder pretty soon, okay?'

'That would work. How do you feel?'

'Bit washed out. It sort of hit me late on how lucky I'd been. I got a bit stressed and didn't sleep too well.'

'That's understandable.'

'How's your fella?'

'The suspect?'

'No, your guy. David. He was a huge help sorting the bookings out and stuff. Funny how he's from back home and everything. It's a small world.'

It was as if a jolt of electricity shot through Mahoney, but he kept his voice as level as he could. 'Right, I'm pleased you're all good. We'll arrange for you to be escorted to HQ and then another plain clothes officer will tag along with your movements during the day.'

'If you think so, okay. I'm right to go into the restaurant later, I assume.'

'Yes, no problem. We're done with the site.'

'Will you be there when I come in?'

'Perhaps not. I'll get a good person here to take everything down.'

'Alrighty. Thanks again for yesterday.'

'Least we could do. Have a good day.'

Mahoney hung up and turned to Kendall.

'Where's David from?'

'Launceston.'

'Good at sport?'

'Sure. Was very good as Herrick tells it.'

'Loving parents?'

'As far as I know … oh, shit.'

'Yes, a whole bucketful.'

□

The first thing Gibson noticed was the stiffness in his knees. As he came round, he shook his head—it was a bit wooly but not too bad. He blinked his eyes open and worked out where he was; he was parked square in the middle of his lounge room floor, strapped in his favourite comfy chair. His wrists and elbows were secured with plastic ties to the cushioned armrests. Not a smidgeon of give. The same with his ankles which were tethered to the front legs of the chair. This did not bode well.

Gibson kept his breathing slow and steady. The whole place reeked like a mechanic's bay at a petrol station. He felt dry, but the carpet looked stained. He had been meaning for some time to ask the agent if it would be alright to lift the carpet and expose the floorboards. The odour was acrid in his nostrils. He kept his breaths shallow to minimise the burn and lessen any hallucinogenic effect. What felt like gaffer tape covered his mouth and chin and there was almost no give as he tried to waggle his jaw. He dropped his eyeballs as low as he could and glimpsed a flash of blue beneath his nose—how appropriate. Bluey: the vernacular moniker for a redheaded bloke. Someone had a sense of humour, and Gibson had a good idea of who that someone was.

A sound to his left caught his attention; the balcony door was clicking shut. A tallish stranger with a shaved skull stood several feet to his side—except he was hardly a stranger at all.

'Surprise,' Fowler said in an enthusiastic Sesame Street voice. 'Can you believe your eyes?'

Gibson rolled his eyes. Attitude would be everything. He knew that giving any sign of how shit-scared he was wouldn't help.

The lithe figure advanced on him, leaned into his ear and whispered, 'Cocky little bugger, aren't ya? Well if you're so smart, how come you're the one trussed up like a chicken ready for the roasting tray?' Fowler flicked Gibson's ear. 'Now, I'm going to take this face tape off you, but if there's any noise I'll join your ear canals up with a skewer. Nod for yes.'

Gibson nodded as instructed and there was a flash of movement as the tape was torn away from his lips—quick and painless. The intruder stepped round and stood straight in front of his captive.

'You look just like a fella all strapped in for some stag night shenanigans. Afraid the stripper won't be able to make it though.'

The constable looked as nonchalant as he could; it was a facial expression he had learned to adopt over time when facing a mouthy bloke. Appear as if you couldn't care less and the bluster usually blew away. Gibson jutted his chin towards the kitchenette. 'White and one sugar if you're making any.'

His visitor laughed, a deep cackle. He pulled over a free chair and sat himself down a couple of feet from Gibson. 'I like your style, but how about we have a little conversation?'

'Sure. Chinese foreign policy?'

'I don't think you're taking this seriously. By now you must know who I am.' He pulled a tarnished zippo lighter out of his pocket and flicked a flame alive. 'And what I can do.'

'Yeah, all right. You're Mike Fowler and this is the next episode in the series.'

'That's better.' He ignited the zippo again and reached the bluish flame towards Gibson's crotch. He smiled briefly and retracted his arm. 'No need. Reckon you'll talk. You look like a chatty guy. And if you're talking, you're still alive.' Fowler gave Gibson a quick wink.

'I can't argue with that. Guess you'd like to find out what we know?'

'Spot on, my boy.'

Calling him out as a sick, twisted fucker was probably not the way to go. 'Well, I'm pretty new to this game but those with more experience reckon this case has been a tough nut to crack.'

'By those you mean Mahoney?'

'Yeah. You've been agitating his thought processes, with the *how* and very much the *why.*'

Fowler sat back in the chair. 'Good. It's taken some planning, I can tell you. Between you and me, I'm a bit pissed off that you're onto me this quickly. I thought there'd be more time.'

'Bit of luck. Hell of a lot of work.' Gibson shimmied his backside. 'Maybe a lot of luck.'

'Yeah, how so?'

'The speed camera at Longley.'

Fowler's eyes narrowed and then he nodded. 'You'd already traced that old bomb to me?'

'Yep. That was the hard work bit.'

'You've got the van I take it?'

'The boss appreciated that part. Clever move ditching it at Salamanca so it was all taken care of for you. Trawling through the car dealerships joined a few dots.'

He flicked the lighter almost absent-mindedly. 'So, you were on my tail from then. But how'd you hit on Lenah Valley?'

'How do you know we did?'

'I get around. Don't suppose you noticed a lycra-clad cyclist riding past the other day?'

Gibson shook his head. They couldn't be expected to take everything in. 'Finding that hidey-hole was a long shot. We were simply looking for a tennis hitting wall and we ended up out there. You'd been noticed and we ploughed on from that. A bit more luck.'

'Well, it saved one bloke's life. The clock started ticking faster then, otherwise I would've done Edmunds hands-on. Doing the MasterChef wannabe was always in the plan, but once you guys turned up at the restaurant, I couldn't finish the job personally. Pity, but there you go.' This time the flick of the lighter was very deliberate. 'And here we are.'

For the first time Gibson became aware of his bladder. Fear was working his insides. This had all the makings of a finale. Fresh tape was stretched across his jaw.

'Don't panic, boy. The fat lady's not even warming up yet. It's your boss I really want to meet.'

□

Dunstan switched his focus from the screen as Mahoney approached.

'No Gabster?'

'Not as yet. Kate called him but it went to voicemail.'

'Not like him. Usually up and at it.'

'I know.' Mahoney dropped his voice a touch. 'That's why I'm worried. Can you trace his phone?'

'Assuming it's on, yep. If not, I can give you a pretty accurate location from where it was last active.'

'Right, do it now.' He swivelled in the chair and called out in what he hoped was his everyday voice. 'Kate, got his home address yet?'

Kendall came across with a laptop. 'Gore Street in South Hobart. Looks, according to Google Maps, like one of a couple of buildings yet to be part of the Vaucluse Retirement complex.'

'Yeah, that's it,' said Dunstan. 'He told me the landlord is holding on to the block until Vaucluse make the sort of offer you can't refuse. From what Dave's said before it's a double-story house divided into four flats, right by the rivulet that runs down from the mountain. He goes hiking from his place up past the Cascade Brewery every few days.'

Mahoney turned his gaze from Kendall's laptop to the desk computer. 'We'll assume he's not doing that now. Any pings yet?'

Dunstan magnified the grid map on his screen. 'Here we go. His phone is on and it's at his flat. Shall I call him again?'

'No,' Mahoney blurted. 'We don't want to frighten the horses.'

Dunstan had a puzzled look on his face. 'What's up?'

'I think David's in danger. I've realised too late that he too fits the victim profile.'

'The bastard's after one of us. You're kidding?'

'No, Andrew. It's very real. You'd hardly label Gibson as privileged but he is making a good go of life. His upbringing is not unlike the others. He was good at sport, brought up well, from up north. Unfortunately, he ticks all the boxes for our man.'

Kendall cut in. 'How has he traced David?'

'Well, I'm not being funny here but he's hard to miss. If Fowler was anywhere near the Silver Ball yesterday, and he probably was to witness his handiwork, he could have tailed David. We assumed he'd get out of the vicinity but his motivation is to witness the destruction he causes. This is random thinking, but maybe the Silver Ball was set up as a prelim to trapping David. Edmunds was supposed to sniff the gas and get us in. We defuse the threat and then relax having saved a potential victim.'

'And now he goes for the jugular,' said Kendall. 'Either that or Gibson woke up late and he's in the shower.'

'No, he'd be here by now, or at least have replied to your voicemail. Andrew, set yourself up as Intel co-ordinator here. Let us know if there's any movement on David's mobile. Kate and I need to get cracking.'

'What's your next move, Sir?'

'We'll be briefing the Armed Response Unit. Dennis Newton should be available.'

□

The administrative hub for the Armed Response Unit was located two blocks from headquarters. Cheek by jowl with the Metropolitan Fire Brigade Centre was a double-storey warehouse: vehicles and equipment at ground level with some office space upstairs. In an open space that served as a tactical planning area, Mahoney and Kendall sat with two officers of the ARU.

Sergeant Newton had included Communications Officer Angie Briant in the initial briefing. Fit, lithe and brown as a berry she didn't look like an office type. When being introduced, an apology was offered for any whiff of chlorine lingering from an earlier swim session at Hobart Aquatic.

Newton launched straight in. He had buzz cut hair and a firm jaw— no messing about in any respect. 'Situation, at present, is one officer absent. Deemed irregular. Assumed position is own residence in Gore Street. Correct?' Mahoney nodded. 'Nil phone response to earlier call. Threat level is high because you fear it's a hostage scenario.'

'Or worse. I'm assuming our killer is there.'

'Same, same. Absolutely right to involve us. Arrest is preferable, if possible?'

'Yes, but Gibson's safety is paramount.'

'I agree, John. If someone's to be taken out, it won't be Gibson.' Newton turned to his left. 'Angie.'

Briant held an iPad in her hands. She tapped a button and a live feed appeared on the screen. Front and centre was a rugged male face underneath a weathered green cap.

'Tommo, it's Angie. What's it look like?'

'No sign of a red-head, but I sighted a white male with a shaved head, on the balcony ten minutes ago. He opened a glass door and propped it open. There are curtains across the rear-facing window.'

Mahoney tensed in his chair. 'Can you send a picture?'

'Already done. The bugger was half in, half out the door frame, puffing on a cigar. Like that Joe Hockey guy.'

Newton cut in. 'Evans and Gulline in position?'

'Yep. Perfect line of sight. Tapp, Colegrave and Wright are here and ready. All set.'

'Roger that. Sit tight until I arrive with the homicide detectives.'

Briant tapped the screen and a photo materialised of the balcony. She zoomed in on a full profile of a muscular male staring at the cigar in his right hand.

'This your suspect?'

Mahoney narrowed his vision. They'd been chasing a shadow, and now here he was. 'As far as I can tell, yes.'

Newton stood abruptly. 'Right, we're off. Angie, keep all channels open. Get the drone up. ETA for us is ten minutes.'

'Right, Sir.'

Newton started moving. 'Come on, John. Sergeant Kendall, best if you stay so we've got a good set of eyes here.'

Mahoney nodded to her. It was no longer solely his operation; Newton was the man.

□

Mahoney thought he could drive well, but Newton's ability to negotiate the crowded CBD streets had him awestruck. Lights flashing and siren on, they slalomed up Davey Street in no time at all, the old Army Barracks flashing by on their left. A bottleneck at Antill Street stymied progress temporarily, but Newton bullied the police vehicle through and they were into the grounds of Vaucluse. The siren had been killed a block back and now the lights went down as Newton eased into the kerb.

Before they got out of the car Newton spoke. 'Bottom line is Gibson's life comes first. Best case scenario we save him and capture the suspect. But if it escalates, the guy gets it. You have to be okay with that because that's the only way it's going to be.'

Mahoney nodded; there was no other way. He wanted the arrest, but he needed Gibson alive so much more. He imagined facing his parents if it went wrong and it could have been prevented.

The man from the video call approached the car. Newton quickly introduced Thomas Casey. 'Tom, any change?'

'No, Sir. Gulline and Evans have a clear view of the balcony. Both are perched on roofs with an eyeline view of the scene. Tapp and Colegrave are on the west side in Gore Street if we need to batter our way in through the front. Wrighty's this side watching through the fence. There's nothing to indicate the target is aware of us.'

Casey was one squared-away officer: clipped speech pattern, no panic, no emotion, here's the situation.

Newton spoke first. 'Gulline and Evans are to keep crosshairs on the balcony. If it looks anything like our officer Gibson is threatened, they take the shot. Right?'

'Yes, Sir. Are you going to initiate contact with the suspect?'

As Newton took a long breath, a buzzing sound started: Mahoney's mobile. He whipped it out from his pocket; the caller ID was Gibson. Newton nodded for him to answer and he affected a smile to help mask his voice. 'Gabster, did you sleep in, boy?'

There was a harsh chuckle in reply. 'No, he's wide awake.'

'Who is this?'

'Nice try, Inspector. You know exactly who this is. Either you're gaming me or you're an idiot. I doubt it's the latter, so I advise you to stop the former.'

'Fair play. Where are you?'

'We are both sitting in David's lounge room. If you waver at all from my instructions, the only way he'll leave here is in a little urn. Can you hear this?'

Mahoney heard the distinct scratch and hiss of a cigarette lighter. 'Yes, Montag.'

'I like it. Is that my assigned codename? Quite a literary touch.'

'The Masked Avenger was taken. What do you want?'

'Some quality face-to-face time, to brief you on what the authorities should be doing.'

'Is Gibson unharmed?'

'That's for me to know. You'll find out soon enough.'

'Alright. Where and when?'

'Here at his apartment. At your earliest convenience. I dare say that won't be long.'

'Give me ten minutes. What then?'

'Text me when you're in the street.'

The call went dead. 'Not much choice then.'

'It seems there's not, unless we take him out next time he ventures onto the balcony.' Newton rubbed his brow with vigour. 'I'll walk with you round to Gore Street. We can't be seen from Gibson's flat and we can assess the playbook.'

For the first few hundred metres, Newton briefed his officers on the situation. The summative directive was to the marksman; any opportunity for a clear shot was to be taken. The ground level personnel were to storm in immediately. It wasn't Mahoney's first choice, but it wasn't his call. The ARU were trained for precisely this scenario, and the bottom line was to save Gibson.

The pair turned into Gore Street and started down the slope. Ten metres short of the street entrance to the apartment block, Newton held a stiff arm sideways to halt his colleague. 'Are you armed?'

Mahoney's mind went blank. Was he? He felt his jacket pockets: nothing. 'No, just my phone. Shit, sorry.'

'Don't worry. This is not your everyday moment.' Newton passed over a Glock pistol holstered in a Velcro strap. He lifted Mahoney's shirt and fastened it just above the belt line where the weapon sat flush against the detective's lower vertebra.

'Leave your shirt loose at the back and it's almost impossible to see. Walk as normally as you can. The safety is off so it's pull and shoot.' Newton smiled. 'The barrel's facing down, so any accidental discharge will be through the floor. Got it?'

A slow nod. 'What if he checks?'

'He has to get close to do that, so he won't. Now, place a call to my mobile.'

Mahoney did as he was told, although it felt idiotic calling a man six inches away.

'Put yours on speaker too and set it to full volume. I'll be able to hear what's happening. Okay?'

'Yep, I think so.' .

'You know so.' There was an edge to his voice. 'Breathe, be calm. You're fine with this, believe me. Now, text him from the front gate. I'll be here with a clear line to the front door.'

Mahoney took the few steps to the gate and texted 'I'm here.'

He received a reply quickly: 'Front door is ajar. Walk down the passage. No stuffing about.'

Mahoney breathed deep; he was about to glance back to Newton but stopped himself. If he was being observed, that would be a giveaway. He went up the steps to the front porch. He gave the wooden door a tentative push; it gave easily and swung into the hallway wall with a slight thud. He edged his head forward, half expecting a projectile. At the far end of the carpet runner was a man clad in athletic gear: blue

Nike singlet, grey shorts and runners on his feet. He was leering at Mahoney and flicking the lighter in his hand on and off.

'Welcome, Inspector. Do you like the Johnnys? Great band from the past.'

Mahoney stepped inside and started down the hallway; he had not expected a round of music trivia.

'Something about about the greenback dollar?'

'Nice work.' Fowler's left hand waved Mahoney forward. 'Don't be shy.'

The detective entered a large open kitchen-diner and lounge space. Fowler was still several metres away, leaning back against the door frame at the rear wall. To his left, Mahoney saw his constable strapped in a lounge chair with his mouth gaffer taped. Gibson raised his eyebrows and flicked his eyes down to the floor where a long strip of soaked cloth lay across a carpet stained dark with what smelled like petrol.

In the time that Mahoney's appraising glance took, a small pistol materialised in Fowler's left hand. He pointed it across his midriff and straight at the captive.

'Don't step forward, Johnny. You don't mind me calling you that, do you?'

'Not fussed. Least of my concerns at present.'

'Quite right. Well, you know your eighties bands. My favourite song is very, ah, pertinent. There's gonna be a showdown right here. Quite apt in the circumstances.'

'If you go for gallows humour, yeah.'

'Oh, I do. And there'll be a winner. If you even lean forward, I'll plug the kid. He's gone the moment you lunge. Going to risk it?'

'No. I don't really want to lose him.'

'The future, eh? Very good.' The gun arced around a quarter turn. 'Perhaps you then. Nobody's indispensable.'

'Quite right. Mind you, I have come at your bequest so that could be construed as bad manners.'

Fowler let out a throaty laugh. 'You two are ballsy buggers. I'll give you that.' Another flick of the lighter. 'Here's the deal. I'll be exiting through this door. This gun dictates that there'll be no heroics from you. Actually, strike that from the record. There might be. As you can sense from the atmosphere, this room is one big petrol bomb. If I ignite it, your blood nut is very rapidly going to be toast. I exit stage left, not pursued by a bear. You get to save yourselves as best you can from horrendous burns. You get to live, I guess, but what sort of life, really?'

'Shitty like yours.'

'Bravo, Johnny. Attitude with a capital A. You're a judge now.'

'Just a bloke trying to figure what the grand scheme is.'

'The grand scheme is fucked. The rich get richer, the poor get the picture. Good start in life and you're cruising the highway. Bad start and you're stuck in the alleys. It's simple really.'

'Rubbish. You've done alright. Solid career. Friends from there who miss you. If nothing else, the run-around you've given us proves you're a smart guy.'

'Flattery will get you everywhere.'

'Just to the point where I can understand your motivation.'

Fowler exhaled slowly. 'My own chaos theory. At the heart of all we do is futility. We live, we die. Why play favourites? Why reward the lucky ones? Why not just put all the money and resources into giving everyone a fair go?'

'Proper socialism.'

'Yeah, I reckon so.'

'But this is a rather extreme method of enacting your manifesto.'

'The ballot box doesn't work. It's all a charade. History shows that winners are grinners and the rest get butt-fucked. End of story.'

'But the winners you've selected are mostly helping others.' Mahoney gestured towards Gibson. 'This guy, for instance. Sure, he sort of fits your scheme, but he is the last person I'd envisage as part of the privileged elite. He doesn't have to go.'

'Which is why you'll get a chance to save him.' Another flick of the lighter. 'And he's not such a prick after all. We had a quick chat while you were getting here. I whipped the tape off so the boy could provide a neat precis of the investigation. You got lucky with the van, you'd have to agree.'

'I think so. I was hoping we'd wind things up a tad differently, but them's the breaks.'

'Yes, they are.' A frown creased Fowler's brow. 'I'm just thinking you're a bit too cool, Johnny, so I'm going to curtail our discussion in case the A-team suddenly appear.'

Fowler twisted his foot to swing the rear door open. He crabbed sideways and crouched down on his haunches. His eyes and weapon were on Mahoney the whole time.

'Come on, Montag. Surely there's another way?'

Fowler lifted his cold eyes to Mahoney and waggled his head as if weighing the options.

'Nah. We've reached the …'

Whatever word was coming next was obliterated by Fowler's skull exploding. A second bullet whistled into his back pitching him forward.

Mahoney froze. They heard rapid footfall up the corridor before Newton brushed past with his pistol drawn. He halted a few feet short of the downed man then spoke tersely into his walkie-talkie.

'Target down. Hold fire. Ground crew approach with caution.'

A series of voices acknowledged him. The cavalry was coming on site. Newton stepped forward and bent to feel for a pulse in the neck. He eased himself up and turned to Mahoney.

'You can breathe now, cobber. Untether your guy. I'll check this balcony.'

Mahoney had to will his legs to move the six steps to Gibson. He drew the tape off his constable's face and Gibson sucked greedily on the air.

'Thanks, boss. I guess this is where I thank God you're here.'

'Just think it for the moment.' Mahoney nodded to the kitchenette. 'Scissors?'

'Top drawer. Wiltshire Staysharp knife in there as well.' He winced. 'Quickly if you can. My hammy's cramping.'

Mahoney was back in a flash. He sheared the tape around the ankles first and bobbed sideways as Gibson extended his left leg. After a quick cut to the wrist restraints, he bent forward to lift his constable upright, propping Gibson's right arm around his own shoulder to hold him steady. Newton was back inside while two of his men waited on the deck.

'All clear. I'll contact SOCO, and I reckon we'll go with an ambulance for your man.'

'Don't worry about me.' Gibson made to step forward and stumbled.

'At the very least you'll need to be assessed for shock. And a lie-down in fresh pyjamas could be just the ticket.' Newton stared purposefully at the stain on Gibson's crotch.

Bending his head, Gibson registered the darker patch at his groin and smiled gingerly. 'Least I didn't crap myself. That's something.'

CHAPTER THIRTY-FOUR

Mahoney leaned on the fence at the front of Gibson's apartment block and stared up towards the cliff face of Mount Wellington—kunyani as it was known to the original dwellers of the island. The aborigines had lived here for thousands of years and the mountain had existed for aeons, silently witnessing the evolution of organic life. This is what we've come to, thought Mahoney: a society in which any individual at odds with whatever social contract we've cobbled together will try to dismantle it. Mahoney had read a bit about Hobbes and Locke without fully comprehending their ideas—something or other about the legitimacy of government—but what now chimed clearly in his head was a line from a school drama text: 'civil blood makes civil hands unclean'. The Bard? Probably. That guy understood a thing or two about the operation of power and the lengths a wrecker would go to wield it. Was this what Fowler represented? A dissident hellbent on usurping authority, or merely a dangerous nutter who didn't like the rules? That would surely play out in the media in the coming days.

'Inspector, you look philosophical.' Rex Chambers interrupted Mahoney's thoughts, his attire fit for a job interview: charcoal grey three-piece suit, clubland tie and a parade ground shine to his shoes.

'Sergeant Chambers, I thought …'

'… I was venturing to sunnier climes? I may be, but at present I'm still part of Professional Standards as we are now titled. An initiative of the new Commissioner. PS, I like to call it. The extra bit that needs including at the end.'

'Nicely put. And you've been landed with this? Good luck. It's multi-layered.'

'No doubt. From what I can gather it's the Armed Response Unit side of the operation that will be the most scrutinised. I'm sure you appreciate that any weapon discharge by an officer must be reviewed very carefully.'

'Of course. Just as with Dunalley a few years back.'

'Precisely.' Chambers reached into his jacket pocket. 'Smoke?'

Mahoney grimaced. 'In the circumstances, I might pass thanks. Anything to do with a lighter will give me the shakes.'

The cigarettes were repocketed. 'Understood. My bad. Is Gibson okay?'

'He seems to be. The ambulance took him down to the hospital half an hour ago. The initial relief will possibly morph into delayed shock. I doubt you'll be able to speak to him real soon.'

'It'll be a tale worth hearing, but it can wait. Initially it's Newton and his team who are the focus.'

'They were brilliant. They saved our lives.'

Chambers stepped back and held up a palm. 'Yes, they did. But I have to shine a light on the facts and be clinical.'

Chambers would draw the ire of the squad, but that was his unenviable task. 'Sorry, you're right. When would you like to get my version?'

'Tomorrow morning, but not first thing. Go home tonight. Sleep. You're alive and that's the bottom line.'

'Yes, I suppose it is.' As Mahoney moved to walk off, a thought struck him. 'How will you deal with Kate?'

Chambers shrugged. 'Apologise first off, then explain what I was really trying to say.'

Mahoney looked confused. 'Please explain.'

'Oh, right. You were referring to the official conduct interview. I got the wrong end of the stick.'

'Looks like it, yeah. I don't want to pry into your private life.'

Chambers decided to light up a cigarette anyway. 'When I was talking about the "other side" to Kate, she got completely the wrong idea. I only found that out later. I was talking about work.' He took another measured draw. 'My role can be the absolute pits. The crims may hate you, but your colleagues, probably to a man, respect you. Pretty much everyone loathes me. I wear this suit, but there's no armour to shield the sneers and the backlash.'

'It's that bad?'

'Trust me, it's worse. Whenever I turn up, it's like I've laid out a smorgasbord of shit sandwiches, but someone's got to do it. I believe it's necessary. I know you, and a few others, do as well. But it wears you down, grinds you into the dirt. Lately, I've come to see it's not a holiday I need but a proper change.

'But Sydney?'

'Oh, that? I was simply floating a thought bubble. Winter's coming and I've decided I'm definitely leaving this department. I thought a few months up there could be a possibility. The "other side" stuff was about being a civilian for a while. I was thinking of doing a semester of study, maybe drama.' A double-puff to re-invigorate the dying cigarette. If Kate doesn't know I'm a confident and committed heterosexual by now, she's not the whizz-bang detective we all think she is.'

Mahoney had to laugh at the theatrical delivery. 'You should tell her.'

'John, once this is concluded I'm going to damned well show her.'

'Too much information.'

'By the way, you might want to think about getting some mixed doubles on with your good lady.'

'How do you ...'

'... know that? One thing I will miss about this job is reading between the lines of a report.'

□

'And you did everything you could to diffuse the situation?'

'For God's sake, Rex. You've got the bloody recording.' It was a clear attempt by Claire Midson, the Police Federation representative, to draw proceedings to a close, but Chambers sat stony-faced.

'Sergeant Chambers, I appreciate your aim for transparency. We both do. But that tone does sound a touch judgemental,' she continued.

Mahoney didn't want her here, but he knew it was the smoothest way through the hoops. A union official on hand was a designated part of the rigmarole, and it was best to sit quietly and let the process take its due course.

Chambers tapped his pen on the desk. 'Point taken. I'm merely double-checking the facts of the incident. Detective Inspector Mahoney was a significant participant in the operation. Transcripts and recordings are all well and good, but my report will ring hollow if I don't get across the nuances.'

Mahoney was about to let him know that a high velocity bullet exploding a man's skull was hardly nuanced, but he decided to let it ride.

They spent the next half an hour dissecting the events of the day before. Mahoney gave background to the raid and his observations of the Response Unit's actions. Without being obstructive, he kept it objective. It was not his place to judge the operational strategy of that unit—at least, not officially; privately, he remained in awe of the way they'd dealt with the crisis.

Chambers, for his part, proceeded methodically through the timeline. 'Now, the decision to fire on the suspect. Who took that?'

'Newton had the final say, but I gave the signal.'

'A pre-arranged signal?'

'Yes. Just before I went in, Newton gave me a code word to use if the situation went tits-up.'

Chambers took notes and adopted a formal tone. 'DI Mahoney and Inspector Newton agreed upon a specific signal to employ in the event the situation became irredeemably critical.'

Mahoney allowed himself to smile. 'Yes, that covers it.'

'The code word was Montag?'

'Yes. I'd called the suspect that in an earlier phone conversation. Newton deemed it sufficiently clear and distinguishable. If I called that out, it was time for the cavalry.'

'And they arrived.' Chambers narrowed his gaze to his notepad. 'Just to check, Fowler was right on the verge of lighting the room up?'

'Yep, Gibson was strapped in and Fowler had a pistol trained on me so I couldn't jump him. As the recording should make clear, I'd tried to talk him round.'

'And he was having none of it?'

'Correct. No matter what I tried, his intention was to exit in an inferno.'

'Could you possibly have incited him?'

Mahoney pictured the moment. 'No, I'm certain. What triggered him was the realisation that it was unlikely to be just little old me on the scene.'

'He heard something, sensed something?'

'I'm not sure, but perhaps in my voice. The situation was precarious but I felt, deep down, that Newton and the others had my back.' Mahoney pointed to his phone. 'You can't see it, obviously, but you can hear in Fowler's last words that he's twigged something is going on.'

'You believe there was no viable alternative to calling the crucial alert?'

'Absolutely. It wasn't because Fowler was trying to escape, but because he was about to ignite the room. It would have gone up with me and Gibson in it. David would have been toast.'

'That sounds fair.' Chambers sat back in his chair and rolled his shoulders. 'The rest I know. The eagle-eyed boys did what they're trained for. It sounds like storming the flat was too risky, so the ultimate order was executed. Messy, but it had to be done. Is there anything you wish to add?'

'No, not really. I wish we'd apprehended Fowler, but he determined it was not to be.'

Chambers swivelled his gaze. 'Claire, anything for the record?'

She declined and Chambers jabbed the red button on the recording device.

'So, what's your next move, Rex?' Claire Midson asked.

'I can't release the determination of a PS investigation that is not yet completed.'

'Not that. I'm confident this matter has been dealt with judiciously. I meant what's your future? You'd be an asset to the Federation.'

'Gamekeeper turned poacher?' All three smiled. 'Thanks, but no thanks. Once this report is submitted, I'm out of here.'

'Away?'

'A few weeks in Bali and then, when I get back, it'll be over to the "other side".'

'Drugs Squad?'

'No, John. The Academy. When the mid-year intake of recruits fronts up in July, it will be yours truly instructing them on ethics and culture in the modern policing environment.'

'And I hope you'll be giving them some tips on standards of uniform?'

Chambers winked. 'I might have some advice to share about that too.'

□

ACKNOWLEDGEMENTS

Writing fiction is never easy: especially so, when the narrative takes you some dark places.

My eternal gratitude is owing to Rhonda McLaughlin for her ongoing support.

Thank you to my editors, Nicole Hayes and Georgina Gregory, for their assiduous work on the various versions of the manuscript.

I am grateful to Lucinda Sharp and the whole team at Forty South Publishing for their expert guidance and technical expertise in the production of this novel.

A special thank you to all the booksellers and readers who have supported the DI Mahoney series: I sincerely hope this instalment exceeds your expectations.

Finally, a nod to our dog Winston, who is always seemingly ecstatic to see me whatever my mood.

ALSO BY sj brown

Available as an
Amazon eBook or
from all good bookstores

Something is very rotten in the state of Tasmania.

Brad Finch, the marquee player of the Tassie Devils Football Club, is the victim at the heart of a new murder mystery. Intense media scrutiny, interfering superior officers, and corrupt business interests all threaten to derail the homicide investigation conducted by the Serious Crimes Squad.

Forensic analysis, dogged detective work, and inspiration may prove insufficient in the search for the true perpetrators. The team must face unpalatable truths about the nature of professional sport and the exercise of power in modern Australian society.

Detective Inspector John Mahoney, the hero of this international crime series of police procedurals, is an outsider in his hometown of Hobart. Disillusioned by his private life and shocked by the corruption he unearths, he queries his capacity to continue in the job.

He must decide if he has the courage to 'speak truth to power'.

ALSO BY sj brown

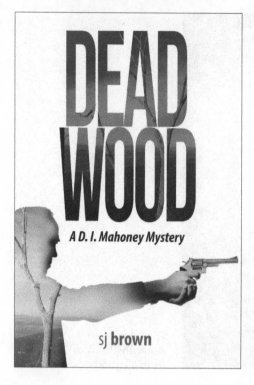

Available as an
Amazon eBook or
from all good bookstores

Tasmania is in trouble.

While mainland Australia surges through the backwash of the GFC the island state is struggling. Political infighting, bureaucratic ineptitude and a lack of investment have curtailed progress. Too many people are lodging on 'Struggle Street'.

DI John Mahoney knows this as well as anyone. Of more immediate concern to him is the brutal murder of a prominent business leader. The scale of public interest is high and the Serious Crimes Squad must make headway fast. As the investigation proceeds it becomes clear that whoever is behind the barbarity is sending a message to the whole community.

Another homicide quickly follows and pressure mounts as they seek to unravel the trail of clues. As Mahoney deals with fissures in his personal life and generational change in the police force he must call on his full array of investigative skills to get a result.

ALSO BY **sj brown**

sj brown
A D.I. Mahoney Mystery

Available as an
Amazon eBook or
from all good bookstores

Life's a gamble.

It certainly is for former jockey Roy Gilbert as he takes the wrong line to the finishing post. His premature death comes to the attention of DI John Mahoney and the Serious Crimes Squad. The subsequent investigation very soon becomes intertwined with the gruesome slaying of a retired bookmaker.

As Mahoney and his team attempt to make headway they encounter unexpected opposition from their Federal counterparts. Suspects are thin on the ground but the investigators doggedly press on in their quest to make sense of the forensic evidence. Turmoil in the personal sphere does little to help Mahoney track down the killers.

The third instalment in this series turns the spotlight on the damage inflicted by the prevalence of gambling in modern Australia. Mahoney and his colleagues soon realise that the glamour is cursory and the stakes are all too high.